KEEPER OF THE
SACRED
SHAWL

MARI DREAMWALKER

FLOWER *of* LIFE PRESS

FLOWER *of* LIFE PRESS

Published by Flower of Life Press
www.floweroflifepress.com
Jane Ashley, *Publisher*

Flower of Life Press books may be ordered through booksellers or by contacting:
support@floweroflifepress.com

Cover Art by Mari Dreamwalker
Cover and interior design by Jane Ashley

Library of Congress Control Number: Available upon request.
ISBN: 979-8-9987870-5-8

DEDICATION

To the wise and magical child within you who lives just behind the veil of your tears. Seek her and you will find the luminous threads of your sacred shawl. Thank you for surviving.

May this book be healing for my family and serve to reveal the bones that have been buried for so long. You are loved.

To my brother Ricardo and my sister Lynda for protecting me.

"Keeper of the Sacred Shawl *not only recounts the ancient cautionary tale of the risks of misbehavior told to Mexican children for generations, but it also narrates women's continuous struggle for validation and honor. The book's mythical scenes shift to modern-day conflicts between the traditional Catholic hierarchy and a humanitarian priest in San Francisco who works to aid migrants seeking help. La Llorona follows because she lives timelessly in the consciousness of those who attempt to awaken and evolve. We are also witness to the difficult relationship between a guilty mother and a haunted daughter who, with much perseverance, finally transcend the effects of generational abuse through La Llorona's healing. Mari Dreamwalker's impressive knowledge of traditional mystical arts and rituals educates and fascinates. Her willingness to share comes through in her honest portrayal of people searching for the truth. Her tales are relevant, whether narrated through the mystery of immortal spirit or the practical struggles of contemporary life. I value the feminine power to be gained from* Keeper of the Sacred Shawl *and encourage other seekers to read Mari Dreamwalker's book.*"

—Loretta Carpio Carr, Contributing writer to Sonoma Valley Sun newspaper; Great Valley Stories, San Joaquin Valley Writers anthology, 2023; Somos Xicanas, Somos en Escrito, Literary Foundation Press, 2024

"*In* Keeper of the Sacred Shawl, *Mari Dreamwalker proves herself to be a major new talent, conjuring a love story that spans 500 years, two continents, spiritual magic, personal trauma, and historical drama. Aurora, who has survived unthinkable child abuse—though her spirit is unbreakable—is caught in a maelstrom of confusion and inner pain as she begins her own adult healing journey. La Llorona reveals herself through Aurora's art, painted in altered states, that illuminates deep personal secrets. Her lover, Nico, is also an artist...yet can their relationship survive Aurora's distrust and tumult?* Keeper of the Sacred Shawl *is richly imbued with herbal folk medicine, sacred ritual, sumptuous Mexican food, wisdom, love stories, and magical art. It is a book I will revisit again and again...a balm...both for me, and a world deeply in need of its medicine. The ending leaves the reader thrilled that the story continues. This is only the first book in a series! I can't wait to see what happens with Aurora, Nico, and her inner children. Kudos to Mari Dreamwalker on her magnificent storytelling debut!*"

—Caryl Anne Engel, Author of the forthcoming book, Girl Remembered

Note from the Author

Trigger Warning

Beloved Reader, if you have experienced childhood sexual abuse, I invite you to be gentle with yourself and seek support if you find yourself triggered by any of the material in this book. Please be advised that this book contains explicit depictions of childhood sexual abuse and trafficking, alcoholism, self-harm, and violence against women. Although this material may be difficult for some readers, I feel it is important to depict these issues honestly to promote awareness and support of these ongoing global issues. It is crucial as a society that we continue to strive to provide emotional, spiritual, legal, and financial resources for survivors and perpetrators, so that those who have suffered similar abuse will know that they are not alone and that there is hope of healing.

As a survivor of childhood sexual abuse, severe dissociation, and trafficking, I wanted to share my experience through a fictionalized story that allows me to encapsulate the journey of decades that it has taken me to be healed enough to find a certain amount of wisdom through my journey. I was able to do this with the help of Tonantzin-Guadalupe and La Divina, AKA La Llorona, the goddess of lost souls, healing, and transformation. The healing medicine within these pages is based on actual sacred rituals and medicine I received from La Divina. I hope to share "The Way of the Sacred Shawl" with survivors through future workshops. I created characters, whom I have come to love dearly, to tell the story. They hold and express parts of myself, and I hope you will see your own reflection of strength, hope, wisdom, and courage in them.

Sadly, my story is not unique. In the healing work I have facilitated for survivors over the last 30 years, I have witnessed similar patterns of abuse repeating from generation to generation. My prayer for writing

Keeper of the Sacred Shawl is that you will see that no matter how abused, neglected, or unloved you have been, healing is possible. It is part of my soul work to de-colonize the myth of La Llorona, which relegates her to a nightmarish figure of colonialism and seeks to enforce a misogynistic morality. This version of La Llorona minimizes her ancient and powerful status as a healing goddess of the Americas.

I also wanted to honor the beautiful community of the Mission District of San Francisco, where I grew up. I was surrounded by wise, fierce, and creative women who mentored me and sheltered me during my most vulnerable times. I also chose to include the genocide of Guatemala in my story because it was impactful to me while growing up during the 1970s–1980s. While this genocide was still occurring, many families received political asylum through the Liberation Theology Movement of the Catholic Church, of which my parish of St. Peter participated. I personally met many women who generously shared their stories with me. One in particular was Maria Flor, who fought with the rebels. I met her through a mutual friend. She told me the story of how she was captured, raped, and tortured to near death. I have never forgotten her and wanted to honor her story within the character of Luz. Sadly, Maria Flor's story is not an isolated one. History reveals that this was common practice among the military during the civil war in Central America. Today, all over the world, rape is still used as a weapon of war. We will continue to move forward and heal, one soul at a time. I thank you from my deepest heart for joining me on this journey, and may you find your sacred medicine.

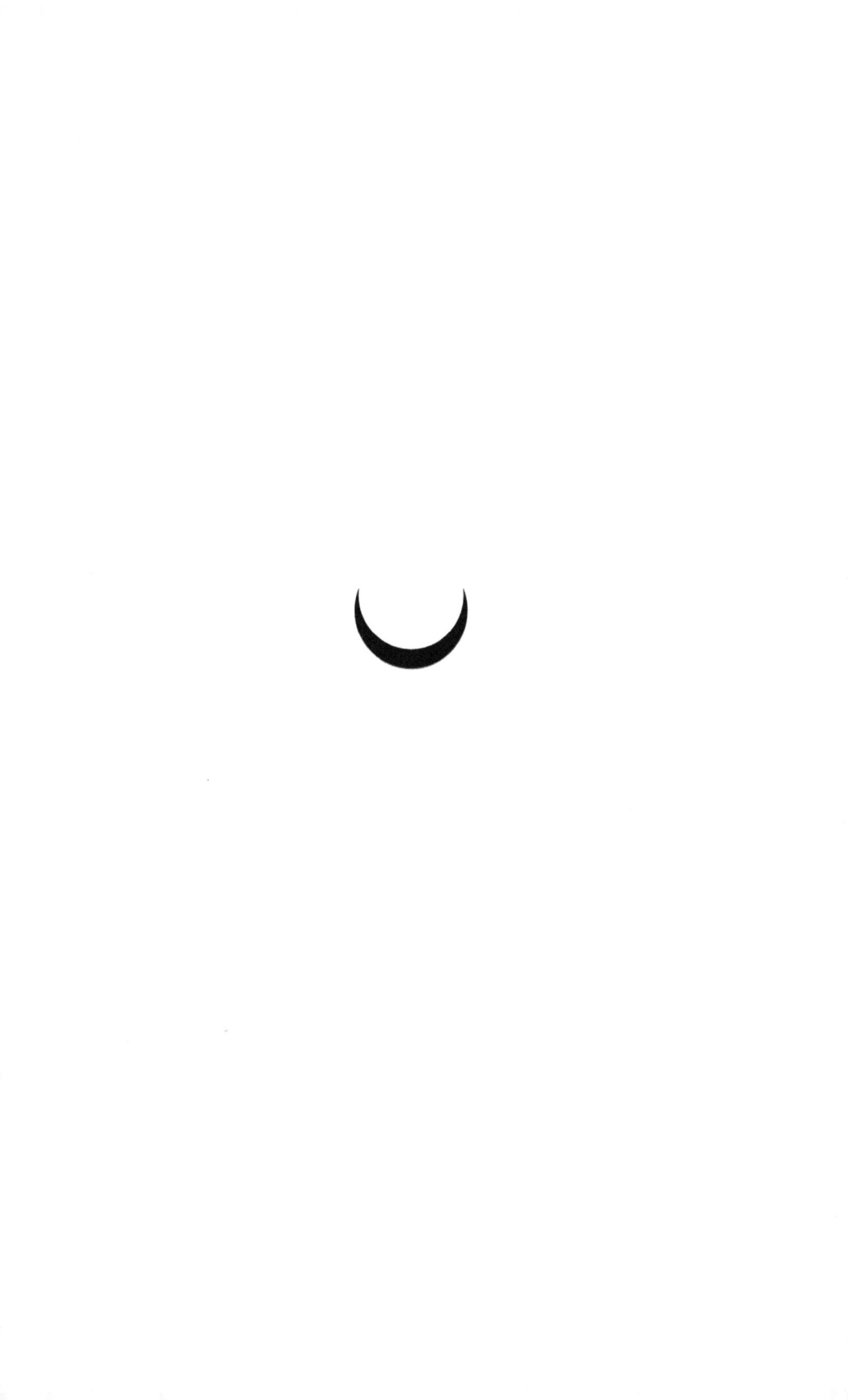

PART 1

The Creation

You might know me as La Llorona. There are hundreds of stories about who I am and how I came to be. None of these stories are my story. Sit with me, and I will tell you the story told to me by my sisters, Las Cihauteteo, the Divine Women, goddesses of the Americas. So, please make yourself comfortable, and I will begin.

It was the time of the 7th moon, in the year of 1520 by your sun calendar. The Spaniards called this night La Noche Triste, the night of sorrow. It was the night the Mexica warriors had gained a temporary victory over the Spaniards. When they first arrived, the Mexica warriors and their priests did not fully understand our ways; they demanded that the original people worship their warrior-sun gods. They called themselves the people of the sun. They were highly intelligent, inventive, and creative people. They lived among us and studied our traditions and rituals. Eventually, they adapted our traditions, synthesizing them with their own. The Mexica appropriated the land by dissecting the wisdom and beauty of our earth medicine, infusing it with fear to force our people to pay tribute to their gods. The Spanish were no different. They brought their own strange rituals and demanded that we worship their one God, whose body they carried around on a cross of death. Many pretended to convert to their religion but continued to practice their traditions in their homes.

For hundreds of years before the Mexica and the Spaniard arrived, the original people of the lands thrived in small villages. They were farmers, craftsmen, healers, and midwives who traded their goods, herbs, and medicines. Of course, they too had conflicts over land and resources, but never on such a devastating scale. The Mexica stood in awe of the great city that the Tolteca left behind. They called it Teotihucán, the place where men become gods. They dreamed of building a city such as this. For nearly 200 years, they realized their dream in the city of Tenochtitlan. The city you know today is Mexico City.

Our sacred women remained devoted to us. They retained the knowledge of how to connect to the earth and listen with the heart-mind. These women revered us and called us Las Cihuateteo, the Divine Women. After the first humans were created, we imparted knowledge of weaving, ritual, birthing, and healing medicines. We also taught them the importance of honoring the cycles of life, death, and renewal. We are guardians of the mysteries of the West, the dwelling place of the Divine Feminine, and the womb of the Earth mother, where all elements collide. Here dwells the medicine of dreaming, visions, and the place where the Sacred Bowl of Light is ignited.

Our sacred women have always been devoted to us. They expressed their love by creating our likeness in clay, which they kept on their hearth. We loved these clay figures that had hair made of red threads. They attached the red threads to the heads of the figures with bits of resin and finished the figures with breasts for nurturing and clawed feet to connect to the earth. They made daily ofrendas filled with love and gratitude for all they have received. On nights when the moon was full, the women carried the clay figures to a small temple they had built in our honor, which stood at the crossroad. They placed the goddess figures on the mesa along with flowers, a bowl of water, tamales, toasted corn, and cakes baked in the shape of butterflies and bolts of lightning. Then, they went outside to sing and dance beneath the moon and stars. It was their love cast with ecstasy upon the luminous threads of their sacred shawls that created a lasting connection between us. They opened their heart-minds to us, and we imbued them with our essence.

During this communion, we showered ancient codes of light into their sacred shawls; remedios to assist them in their evolution of remembrance. The women wove the story of the codes into their textiles and painted them on their bowls. We imparted all medicine that was necessary for them to grow in wisdom, allowing them to pass on their knowledge to the next generations.

So, on this day of the seventh moon, when I had not yet been created, my sisters stood in a half-circle on the hill of Tepeyac and watched as the Spanish and Mexicas spilled more blood, and innocent women and children were murdered out of consequence. The men battled until they could fight no more, and the Spaniards, realizing they had lost the battle, retreated.

My sisters could no longer bear to watch the devastation of our people. The sickness of violence overcame them, and they began to wail, causing their sorrow and rage to rise in a blaze of fury. They screamed their rage in black curls of smoke that went out to the four directions. Their screams and screeching shook the Earth and turned the moon red. Black clouds filled the sky, and the day became dark. The Spaniards called upon their priests to pray to their god, for they feared it was the end of the world. The Mexica saw it as a sign that their gods were pleased and continued to fight.

Las Cihuateteo watched as the disembodied souls of the dead wandered towards them, faces full of sorrow and confusion that moved like a cold wind through the goddess women. The souls of the dead waited at the foot of the hill, unsure of where to go. Then, one by one, the ghosts walked up the hill and stood before Las Cihuateteo, who felt the shadow of their confusion move through them. They breathed light into the crowns of their heads and transmuted their fear into the remembrance of peace. Hours went by when finally, the last soul was purified, the sky opened up, and rain poured from the heavens. The goddess Ix Chel swept her hands across the sky and an arched prism of light appeared, allowing the dead to pass into the land of the ancestors.

Las Cihuateteo were still filled with much rage and sorrow. They lay down on the ground—angry tears flowing on the earth. Then one by one, they fell into a dream. In their dream, they traveled to the heart of the galaxy, where they stood in the presence of the Ancient Ones who stood in a circle around them. Eagle Woman called each of the goddesses to her and placed a white feather on each of their tongues. The goddesses held the feather on their tongues and waited for them to dissolve. As the feathers dissolved, they were filled with a cornflower blue light that emanated two feet around them.

⌣

When they awoke, Las Cihuateteo felt movement in their wombs; it pulsated and throbbed. The sensation was arousing and uncomfortable at the same time. They stood up slowly and noticed a thick layer of white feathers scattered on the ground, along with a small pile of iridescent kernels of corn. They knew collectively that they should eat the corn.

They sat on the ground and waited for what would happen next. Tonantzin was the first to sense a quickening in her being. She placed her hands on her womb and felt a cutting pain. She grabbed at her belly. "Ohhh. Ahhh," she moaned. "What is happening? How can this be? There is life in me."

Abruptly, the other goddesses felt the same sensation. They sat on the ground with their hands on their wombs, moaning in agony. "Ohhhh. Ahhh." They watched in confusion and amazement as their bellies quickly grew full and heavy.

"How can this be?" They shouted.

They moaned and cried out in unison as they labored.

"Ohhh. Ahhhh. How can this be?"

After a time, their wailing settled into a soft keening, and the keening initiated a praying song.

"*Oh na na hey, oh na na hey, shhh, shhh, shhh, hey ya na hey, na na na ho, shhh, shhh, shhh.*" When their song was complete, another wave of stabbing pain filled them, and they gave an immense push.

I was born into the center of the circle.

I was an etheric being. I was made of sweet hues of every kind of blue. There were long threads of luminous light that extended from my body and wafted through the air, searching for connection. As my sisters gazed upon me, they were filled with boundless love. They circled around me and each of them gently pulled one of my threads. They passed my threads around and around, from hand to hand, weaving the threads of light into a sacred shawl that would contain my soul. They sang the frequencies of ruby, violet, turquoise, topaz, carnelian, garnet, gold, and diamonds into my sacred shawl. Their song reverberated into the cells of my being, and I feel myself becoming. At last, when my sacred shawl was complete, they sealed the edge with a golden thread of light.

Next, they marched in a circle around me, stomping their feet hard on the ground, entraining me to the heartbeat of the Earth Mother.

"*Bom bom. Bom bom. Hey na na, hey na na, bom bom ho waaay, yaaaaa. Hey na na, hey na na, ho waaay yaaa, bom bom, bom bom, bom bom.*" Their song thundered through me, awakening me with life force from the Earth.

My sisters continued their circling movement, singing and stomping. They sang me bones and muscle, and sinew to connect my bones. They sang me a beating heart, blood and veins, and lungs to breathe. They sang me muscles and tissue, organs, nerves, a brain, and eyes that could see, and a mouth to speak, and all the things I needed to be almost human.

I felt the heat of oxygen and blood rushing through my veins—I could breathe. My sisters moved close around me, kneeling on the ground, as they dug up handfuls of clay. Each of them added spittle until the clay became moist and soft. They took turns rubbing the moist red clay over my blue etheric form. They massaged the clay over me until I was completely covered. They blew their breath over me to dry the moist clay, until the clay became beautiful, soft brown flesh, and my human likeness was complete.

I stood up slowly, encircled by love. I tried to make sense of all the sensations I was experiencing, sounds of creatures around me, the green scent of the earth, the sound of birds singing, but most of all, it was the tingling sensation moving through me that extended out of the palms of my hands and fingertips. I wanted to feel everything and experience the miracle of touch.

Each of my sisters welcomed me into my new life with a warm embrace and kisses on each of my cheeks. Their affection sent a river of heat through me that settled in the center of my chest. Then a rush of energy filled me, and water fell in droplets from my eyes. These were the first tears I cried. Little did I know that these tears were the quintessence of who I am.

I was alive.

Coyolxauhqui, the goddess of the moon, bent over in front of me and scraped white bone dust from the earth into her hands. She rubbed her hands together, then gently patted the dust on my face. Next, she took out an obsidian blade from a fold in her dress and carefully carved a black crescent moon in the center of my brow. I felt a sharp discomfort on my skin. I reached up to touch where she had made her mark. When I looked at my hand, it had drops of blood on it. I was filled with wonder at seeing my own blood. Then she placed her hands on my head.

"Mi Divina, my beloved, daughter, and sister of the Moon. I attune you to the healing power of water, and to the mysteries of the soul. I bless you with the medicine to feel the emotions of humans. Your divine heart will take their sorrow into your soul as if it is your own. I give you medicine to release their sorrow from your body and transmute it into light." She kissed the crescent on my brow and blew her breath into the top of my head. I bowed my head in respect, although I did not yet know what a soul was.

My sister Tonantzin, goddess of heaven and the earth, approached me next. "Mi Divina, you are my beloved daughter, sister of the Earth and the Stars. It is the dust of the stars and the blood of the earth that flows through your veins."

She reached into a small leather pouch hanging around her neck and took out several pinches of red powder, mixed it with spittle, then rubbed it between her hands until it became a deep red paste. She placed her hands at the bridge of my nose, then pulled her hands outwards in opposite directions, painting a red mask across my eyes. Then she placed her fingers beneath my eyes and drew the red paste in a trail of tears down my face.

Tonantzin kissed me softly on the mouth and gave me a long white cotton dress. She placed it over my head, and I placed my arms through the long sleeves. The gown cascaded around my ankles. It was soft and comforting against my new skin. My dress had bright orange Marigolds and Monarch butterflies embroidered around the neck, with a bright red thread that sealed the hem of the dress. Then she whispered a spell into my ear.

"Blood, eros, and fire. Blood, eros, and fire; a life, a human, a soul. A life, a human, a soul. A life filled with beauty, ecstasy, and joy. But as there can be no joy without sorrow, and no light without shadow, humans live dancing between the two. Humans are created from the same divine spark of consciousness that all creation is made from. They have forgotten this. They believe they are separate from creation. This causes a sense of deep loneliness in them. We are here to ignite the sacred fire within them so they will remember their true origin. This, too, will be your task. But as you are not fully human and not fully spirit, you will not feel these things in the same way we do. You will have your own unique expression of being in the world. You will understand this soon enough."

She gently kissed each of my breasts, and a deep red rose blossomed in the center of my chest. Then she kissed the space just below my navel and filled it with a bowl of light. Finally, she kissed the center of my brow and the palms of my hands, where roses of light also appeared. I closed my eyes and tried to take in all that I experienced. I felt a river of stardust pour into the top of my head and move through my body. Roses of light in the colors of the rainbow appeared along my spine. Tonantzin placed one of her hands on my brow and the other on the center of my chest.

"These roses of light are centers of knowing, healing, and wisdom. They open and close with your breath and intention, and will draw to you the medicine you need." Tonantzin stepped back into the circle and bowed to her sister, Tlazoltéotl, the dark goddess of death, forgiveness, and transmutation.

She stepped forward and stretched out her arms to me, taking my hands in hers. Out of nowhere, two large serpents with fangs and tails that rattled slithered down her arms, across to mine. They moved down my torso and belted themselves around my waist.

"My beloved sister. This is a great task you have been given. I honor you." She kissed me on each cheek. Then she placed one black key and one gold key in each of my hands and continued.

"I give to you the keys to death, forgiveness, and transmutation. Forgiveness is yours to offer to humans, as it is very difficult for humans to claim it for themselves, and without it, they will not be able to experience their connection to their divinity and all the blessings it holds. This is your medicine now."

Then Tlazoltéotl moved closer to me, running her hands down my long black hair. She parted it into two sections and braided into them small golden bells, red cotton thread, golden owl feathers, and small shards of obsidian that caused lightning to spark from my hair. Then she removed the obsidian mirror from in front of her torso and placed it in front of mine. Instinctively, the serpents around my waist stretched and shifted themselves, gripping their fangs on either side of the mirror, securing it to my body.

"This obsidian shield will reflect truth that hides within the shadow. It will illuminate the parts of themselves that humans reject. The new religion the strangers brought with them teaches that humans must reject their human form and strive to be divine. They have forgotten that they are divine and chose to have a human experience in order to evolve, thus assisting the universe in its evolution. This is the part of their evolution that many of them have forgotten. Your task is to find the humans who wish to awaken, remember, and evolve, and then help them to do so. In doing so, they will be able to integrate more of their essence. This is the medicine of alchemy I give you."

Then Tlazoltéotl raised her arms and looked up to the sky. She screeched a high-pitched cry to four winds, and thirteen Great Horned owls swiftly flew through the sky, then circled above me. The beating of their wings and piercing cries shook the air around me, binding a part of me to the wind, the night, and the underworld.

"These owls are your companions. They will help you to navigate the various dimensions you will travel to and give you the ability to see through evil and darkness for what they truly are: fear and pain. You will transmute the darkness into light and restore humans to balance. But they must be willing."

Tlazoltéotl kissed my mouth softly, infusing my heart with infinite love for humans. A love full of fire that would become my eternal quest to activate their remembrance and ease the suffering of their souls. Tlazoltéotl stepped back, and each of the other goddesses welcomed me and imparted their gifts to me. Tlazoltéotl stepped forward again. She took my hand in hers.

"You shall be known as La Divina, for you are a divine gift and beloved to us."

I was complete.

⌣

I turned and looked out across the vast valley as the men continued their fighting, and women and children ran to escape the sword, the spear, or worse. I saw bodies slain everywhere. I closed my eyes and listened to the screams of these humans who were now my people. The scent of death was thick in the air. The spirits of my people wandered the streets, eyes hollow, confused by their violent death. Their lives had been taken before their destined time. I felt their pain that filled my being with a liquid blackness. Their suffering clawed at my insides, like a wild creature seeking escape from captivity.

Then I remembered the words my sister Tonantzin had spoken to me about how deeply I would feel the suffering of humans. I breathed deeply and shifted my sight to the center of my brow. Then I saw the luminous threads of their sacred shawls, now frayed and disconnected, the light of their threads drained from fear.

My heart welled up with an immeasurable love for them, stabbing and tender all at once. I was desperate to alleviate their torment. My chest tightened, and suddenly, my lungs could barely find air. I began to gasp and cough, while water poured from my eyes, nose, and mouth. My sisters watched and waited in silence.

Then I could no longer contain the pain that tore through me. I wept. I screamed and howled. I was inebriated with the sorrow of my people. I screeched and wailed until I fell to the ground, my body shaking with sobs. I lay there until I was depleted of emotion. Then suddenly, a fire ignited and rose up from my core. It flared in the base of my spine, blazing up into my stomach; anger and rage engulfed me.

At that moment, I knew my destiny.

I set off for the streets of Tenochtitlan, accompanied by the fierce wind and screeches of thirteen owls flying ahead of me, announcing my arrival. I howled and screeched into the air. At first, the soldiers thought they heard a woman weeping in the distance, but as I grew closer, the piercing screeches and the thunder of wings assaulted their minds. The Mexica and the Spaniards froze when they encountered my specter. I walked through the crowds of soldiers and warriors. My rage announced my presence, and the soldiers suddenly halted their battle and moved to either side of the street. I stomped my feet and shook the earth beneath them. I made my way through the crowds of soldiers and warriors, who were now immobilized with fear. My eyes painted red, tears streaming down my white face, I screamed, crazed with rage. As I passed in front of them, I raised my obsidian shield to their faces. They rubbed their eyes, but it was no use. They saw their reflection covered with putrid, bloody sores. Their eyes yellow and hollow, bones protruding from their flesh.

"This is witchcraft," the Spaniards screamed, falling on their knees. The soldiers prayed and made the sign of the cross, but their prayers and crosses offered no protection from my rage. The soldiers and warriors covered their ears, running in circles, like men gone mad. Some of them fell over dead from fear.

The story of the weeping, screaming witch-woman spread throughout the city and beyond. The soldiers warned each other not to look at the witch's face, for they would fall impotent or worse, even though they could not imagine what could be worse. The Mexica warriors called upon their bloody priests to make sacrifices for protection. The Spaniards warned their families to guard their children against the weeping witch who would steal them and eat them as a sacrifice to the devil. They called me witch, they called me puta del diablo, but it was the name La Llorona they chose for me. They did not understand who I was.

After my rage had finally sated, I turned to walk back to the hill of Tepeyac, where my sisters waited for my return. I saw the streets littered with bodies of wise women, midwives, healers, and seers. Their bodies were desecrated and left to rot in the hot sun without proper ceremony to release their spirit back to the Ancient Ones. I knelt beside them, placing my hand on their chest to see if there was still breath in them. When I felt no breath, I sang a medicine song to release their souls, as my sisters had taught me to do. I watched pale blue swirls of light from the top of their heads ascend to the sky. The frequency of my song created a path of light back to the Heart of the Universe. Then, I sat down among the bodies, unable to comprehend how humans who were created from an infinite love were capable of such cruelty. I wondered how they became disconnected from the light of their souls. They had forgotten the truth of their origin: divinity and humanity. This is something I would come to better understand much later.

As I arrived at the edge of the city, I came upon a woman who I could see from the design on her huipil was a healer. She lay surrounded by a pool of blood, a spear in her side. I placed my ear to her chest. Her breath was faint, but she was still alive. A fierce desire flared in my womb and my heart. I felt a desperate need to save her. I sat down and pulled her into my arms, gently rocking and singing to her. I could see her etheric form standing a few meters in front of me, watching me, confused and in shock. This woman, who was called Patli, was a holy woman who kept a loyal devotion to my sisters. Suddenly, I felt the wisdom of my sisters inside of me, and I understood what must be done. I could see images in Patli's sacred shawl. I saw images of her home and hearth where she kept flowers, herbs, an obsidian mirror, and a bowl of fresh water. She had made a clay likeness of Las Cihuateteo, which she kept on her hearth. I was overcome by her love. I felt the beauty of her love in contrast to the devastation around me. It filled me with awe and humility.

"Save our daughter," my sisters whispered. "She is precious to us. The love she feels for us sustains our presence on the earth. She is a keeper of knowledge and healing ways. Breathe into your womb, and we will guide you in what you must do to save her."

I breathed deep into my sacred bowl of light three times. It was as if the stars themselves filled my being; light exploded within me, connecting me to the luminous fibers of the web of creation. As this energy raced through my being, I saw how everything in the Universe is also contained within the human body, as we are all created from the dust of the stars and the breath of creation. I carried Patli up to

Tepeyac, but my sisters were no longer there. Instead, I found an ancient, Grandmother Cottonwood tree where they had stood. I laid Patli down on the large roots of the tree, then placed my hands on its trunk, unsure of what to ask for or what I expected to occur. The trunk of the tree began to expand and contract harmoniously with my breathing. I removed a shard of obsidian from my hair and made a small cut on my forearm, offering a few drops of blood on her roots. Then, to my amazement, her trunk opened to me. The opening was large enough for the two of us to pass through. I gathered Patli into my arms, and we stepped into the tree.

In an instant, we were on the ground, standing in a large cavern of some kind. Above me, the ceiling was covered with thousands of Amethyst quartz points. On the wall of the cave were shelves made of tree branches. They stretched from ground to ceiling and from one end of the cave to the other. The shelves were filled with countless small, corked clay pots. They were filled with various herbs, salves, and potions. In front of us flowed a sparkling turquoise river that emitted a healing frequency I could feel. The ceiling above the river was covered by tree roots that were woven into a lacey canopy above me. Hiding in the roots were all types of creeping and crawling beings, as well as dragonflies, butterflies, and hummingbirds. My Great Horned Owls perched themselves in roots. Their presence and hooting song were a comfort to me.

I looked to my right and saw a table made of opalized crystal quartz. I had only seconds to take this all in, as I needed to tend to Patli. I carried her into the river and set her down in the water, and pulled the blade from her side, and as I did, the wound did not bleed but healed completely. The cuts and bruises on the rest of her body faded quickly, as well. I washed the blood off her body. I carried her from the river and laid her upon the table. She opened her eyes, but could barely speak, so I moved my ear close to hear. Tears rolled down her cheeks as she spoke.

"I do not wish to live in this world. My children and husband are dead. Release me, La Divina, I beg you."

Her words pierced my heart. I placed one of my hands on her heart and the other on her womb. It was then that I saw images of the unspeakable violence she had barely survived, leaving her with an opaque shame that did not belong to her. I tried to convince her to stay with me, but I had nothing of value to offer her, except to release her. The world that she knew was gone. She had the right to be released from this world, and it was my duty to help her pass to the other side. I held her and wept. She was the first human I loved, and I did not want to say goodbye so soon.

"I will find you again, my daughter. I promise. No matter how many lifetimes pass."

"Yes. Thank you for your love and blessing, Mi Divina."

I held Patli in my arms, wept, and watched the luminous threads of her sacred shawl disconnect from her body, carrying her soul up to the Heart of the Universe.

And so began my path of easing the suffering of humans. I traveled across the Americas, but it seemed that no matter how much suffering I eased, most humans could not see me for who I am. The Catholic priests continued to perpetuate a fearful version of me. They portrayed me as a demon, a succubus, and a mad woman who drowned her children and herself. A woman who is damned for eternity to search for the lost souls of the children she murdered.

PART 2

SAN FRANCISCO ~ 1963

Father Tom

Father Tom O'Malley straightened his collar before knocking on the open door of Father Flynn's office. He had recently graduated from the University of San Francisco Seminary and was the youngest priest at St. Peter's Parish. He was tall and muscular, with blue eyes and the palest, unruly blonde hair. He had been a boxer before he felt his calling to become a priest and continued to spar at a local YMCA to keep in shape. He brushed away loose strands of hair with his fingers. No matter how much he combed his hair, they still fell across his face, so he developed a nervous habit of swiping at his hair. Father Flynn was the senior priest of St. Peter's Parish for over 20 years. He tried to be kind, but the lines on his face and around his eyes revealed his disdain for the new catechism of Vatican II. He thought it too permissive and that it made the younger priests and nuns lax in their devotion to God. But the final straw was when he learned that the nuns would no longer be required to wear their traditional habit, nor were the priests required to wear the full Jesuit robes. He planned to retire at the end of the following year, but before his retirement would be approved, he had some issues at St. Peter's that he needed to attend to.

He looked up from his desk, where he was preparing Sunday's sermon, to see Father Tom standing in the doorway, not wanting to interrupt.

"Father Tom, don't just stand there, come in and sit down." Father Tom walked into the office and sat down in the chair opposite the desk. Father Flynn reached into his desk drawer and pulled out a pint of whiskey and two glasses. He poured two fingers into each glass and placed one in front of Father Tom. He took a big swallow from his glass and looked over to Father Tom.

"Now, Tom, you know I don't usually give much heed to rumors in the parish, but I have heard several complaints from Mrs. López,

Mrs. Santos, and Mrs. Ortíz, who are all devout members of the parish. The complaints are about Mrs. Camacho, so I am inclined to believe there is some truth to them. I would like you to pay her a visit and find out what is really going on over there. I am hoping this could be an opportunity for you to bring her back into the church. I know she is a deeply troubled woman, but she only makes her problems worse by drinking, and honestly, Tom, I'm tired of hearing about her antics at the bar every weekend. She needs to repent and come back to God."

Father Tom nodded and cleared his throat to speak. "Father Flynn, you know Mrs. Camacho had a son who died mysteriously two years ago. The child died without being baptized. She was denied a funeral mass, and there was no priest or family members at the burial. Afterwards, many of those same women who complain about her now were the women who gossiped about how her baby would burn in hell because he died without baptism. I can understand why she might not feel welcome at mass."

"Are you condoning her ungodly behavior, Tom?"

"No, Father, I just believe that it is only for God to truly know why his children turn away. Perhaps Dolores needs our help more than those other women of the parish?"

Father Flynn slammed his glass on the desk.

"Don't you tell me about Mrs. Camacho. She is upsetting the women of my parish. Loyal and devout Catholics. Dolores pretends to be fragile, but she is calculating and seductive, and that is a dangerous combination for a woman. She is married, but her husband left her shortly after her second child. She has had children from several men, including a colored man whom she was also not married to. It is almost as if she sets out to break every rule of decency a woman is supposed to uphold. Did you think I was unaware of how she spends her weekends at O'Donnell's bar, carrying on with married men instead of staying home caring for her children? Do not let her deceive you, Tom. She has turned away from God and is paying the consequences for her choices. I am not surprised to hear she is being haunted by a dark presence. She could be haunted by the devil himself for all I know. Whatever it is, she has brought it upon herself. I expect you to attend to this situation and let me know when it is taken care of. Do I make myself clear?"

"Yes, Father. Perfectly clear." Tom took a deep breath before standing. He straightened his collar, walked out of the rectory doors, and headed down Alabama Street to O'Donnell's bar. He usually met up with the men of the parish as they stopped to have a beer or two before heading home after work. He checked his watch and noted it was just a little after 6:00. The bar would be empty and a perfect opportunity to have a relaxing drink with his old friend Bill. As he strolled through the streets, he thought about how most of the men who drank at the bar did not attend mass with their wives and children on Sunday, yet Father Flynn did not find issue with them.

Father Tom found Dolores Camacho to be an intelligent, articulate woman who was knowledgeable about history and politics. She was an activist like himself, and the two of them were always present to protest the war in Central America and support the boycotts with the farm workers. Father Tom had also witnessed a darker side of Dolores at times when she had drunk beyond her limit, which was often the case. She became angry and started arguments with men, as if to taunt them and show them she was smarter than they were. She took a certain pride in the freedom of not being married. No man could tell her what to do. She did what she wanted regardless of who disapproved. She loved to flirt with the men, even though she knew they were married. She was a complex woman, yet he could not help but like her.

⏝

Bill O'Donnell was the owner of the bar and Tom's oldest friend. They had met at the boxing gym when Tom entered Seminary. Bill was a stout, barrel-chested Irishman with gray hair and kind blue eyes who loved to laugh. The bar was empty, as the men who stopped by in the evenings had gone home to have dinner with their families.

"Evening, Bill," Father Tom said as he removed his coat, laid it across a bar stool, then placed his black leather bag on top of his coat, and his hat on top of his bag. He sat down on the stool in front of his friend. Bill poured two glasses of his best Irish whiskey.

"Oy, Tom. I hear you've got serious business to attend to tonight."

"Word travels fast around here. What do ya hear, old pal?"

"Oh, the fellas have all come and gone. I'll tell ya this. Folks on the block have been hearing strange noises. The sound of a woman crying at night. Mrs. López said she saw a specter of a woman in a white dress in her backyard. She was wailing like a woman in mourning. Everyone nearby heard it. It's a Banshee spirit, if you ask me."

"Really? That's strange because Father Flynn didn't mention that it was a ghost of a woman. He said it was a demon."

"Oh, believe you, me. Folks are smarter than to tell Flynn something like that. Well, they'd have you knocking on their door with bottles of holy water, waving your Rosary and such." Father Tom laughed and pointed to his black bag on the stool beside him.

"Well, that part is true, but seriously, how has Dolores seemed to you lately?"

"You know I am acquainted with Dolores a bit more than most of the men here. I really like her. Sometimes she hangs around here with me after the bar closes. We've gotten to know each other, if you know what I mean. She's had a hard time with it. She barely makes ends meet with five children to feed and lives on welfare and all. The boys are three, five, and six. There's an older boy who is about twelve, I think. But he spends most of his time in the streets with his friends, and I've heard he drinks and takes drugs. She has Aurora, who is as sweet as an angel. She's about four, I think. I fear for that child in a house full of boys.

"Anyway, Dolores has had social services snooping around more than once. They come to see if the house is clean and if the children look like they are properly cared for. I try to help her in any way I can. I send sweets home with her for the children, along with whatever food I have left after the dinner crowd. One night, the second-oldest boy wandered in here to take Dolores home. He said they were hungry and had no food. Ahh. That broke my heart. I tell you, it's a sad thing to see a woman struggling so hard. I don't charge her to drink here, and I'm not sure whether that's helping or not. It's enough to make a person want to drink to forget their problems, isn't it, Tom?"

"I can only imagine." Tom winked.

"I think Dolores reminds me a bit of my Ma. My Ma found out that she was three months pregnant a week after my Da died. In those days, the church didn't allow women to keep their babies if they didn't have a husband, even though in the eyes of the church, she was still considered a married woman. The parish priest insisted that she would not be able to continue her job and care for me at the same time. They tried to shame her into giving me up for adoption. She had worked as a cook for a kind, wealthy English woman named Bitsy. When she told her she was pregnant and that the church wanted her to surrender her baby to the church, Bitsy wouldn't hear of it. She bought my Ma passage on a ship to the States. About six months later, when she arrived very pregnant, she met John Ryan, a kind man who owned Ryan's bar and restaurant on 24th Street."

"Yes, I know it. It's been closed for a long time now. I didn't know your family owned that place," Tom said.

"I'm getting to that. When my Ma explained that she was recently widowed and was looking for work, he offered her a room above the restaurant and hired her as a cook. My Ma helped him run the restaurant, and they got married a little after I was born. He was good to her and the only father I ever knew. A few years later, my brother Tim came along. We were very happy."

"You never told me that story, Bill. So why did the restaurant close?"

"It turns out that my Da loved the drink. He secretly drank a lot more than we knew about. After a while, he began to lose a lot of weight, so one day my Ma called the doctor to come for a visit. It turned out that my Da had Cirrhosis of the liver. The doctor told him he needed to quit drinking, and he promised again and again that he would, but he never did. He continued to deteriorate until one day, he just didn't wake up. It was a slow and ugly death. I was 17 when he died. Afterwards, my Ma fell into a depression. She was in and out of institutions, but nothing they did helped. I took over running the restaurant as best as I could. My brother Tim helped, but I just couldn't take care of my Ma and the restaurant, too. Tim couldn't bear watching what was happening to our Ma, so he left home and went to live with our Uncle Robert and his family. One day, I came home and found my Ma dead in the bathtub. She had cut her wrists. After that, I couldn't bear to work at the restaurant or to live in that building, so I just closed it all down. I travelled for a while, and when I returned, I found this place for sale. I took out a small loan and bought it. It felt good to have a place of my own."

"I'm so sorry, my friend. I can't believe you never told me about any of it."

"Yeah, well, you're my friend, not my confessor. It's not something I like to talk about. It's best to put it all behind me. I've moved on with my life and I'm happy for the most part, but as far as love goes, I think I'm doomed."

"Don't give up. You just never know when love will find you." Tom reached over the bar and gave Bill a pat on the shoulder. "So, how has Dolores seemed to you these days? I haven't talked to her in several weeks."

"Honestly, Tom, a part of me would like to have a bit more with Dolores, but she's still pining after the father of Aurora. I think some part of me wants to give her the happy ending my Ma never had, but she doesn't want me. Last I heard, her man went back to Mexico, where he has a wife and other children. She has strange ideas about freedom, that one, and she has a bit of a temper, if you know what I mean. I've seen bruises on the children. That's the part that I cannot have, and she has this dark, moody temperament come over her at times. Honestly, Tom, I'm surprised you became a priest at all with the way the church treats women."

"I had a call. God must have his own plans for how I can make a difference. But I know about Dolores. I have glimpsed her temper now and again. She certainly knows her own mind and is not afraid to say so. But I don't think wanting freedom is a bad thing. It's the world that is strange, if you ask me. It's the world and even more, the church that needs to change." Father Tom looked at his watch, then finished off his drink.

"Thanks for the drink and the talk, Bill. I best get over to see Dolores." He checked his watch to be sure he would not arrive in the middle of dinner, then put his long black coat and hat on. He shook Bill's hand and placed a five-dollar bill on the bar.

"Oy, Tom. I've told you time and time again, your money's no good here."

"And I've told you that I pay my own way in the world. Now wish me well."

"Alright then, grace be with you."

◡

Father Tom walked up the street, the short distance to Dolores' flat. He passed several three-story flats that were so common in San Francisco. He was halted in his steps by a sudden sense of deep sadness in the air. Then he felt a heavy darkness that seemed to float on the air. It brushed against his cheek. The sensation raised the hairs on the back of his neck, so he pulled up his coat collar. Then his eyes drifted to the stairway that led down to a basement. This was a common feature of all flats in the city. The garbage men used it to bring the garbage cans from the backyards out to the truck. He thought he saw a shadowy figure of a man move up the stairs and pass him by. When he arrived at 847 Alabama Street, he saw the shadowy figure pass in front of him and disappear into the basement door. He told himself that it was his mind trying to make sense of all the talk of spirits, ghosts, and whatever else the women of the parish were reporting. He removed his hat, ran his fingers through his hair, and knocked on the door. Dolores was expecting Father Tom to visit because she knew the women on her block were gossiping about how she was being haunted by a demon. She knew eventually one of them would mention it to Father Flynn, and soon, Father Tom would be knocking at her door.

She considered Tom her friend, more than a priest. He would stop by now and again. They would have coffee and discuss the current events happening in Guatemala, and their mutual disgust at how the U.S. supported and funded the genocide that was occurring there. Dolores smiled when she opened the door and saw it was Father Tom. She wore a dark blue dress with one large white rose on the front. She was a petite woman and stood barely five feet tall. She had short, wavy, raven-black hair, red lipstick, and painted nails.

"Hello, Tom. It's good to see you. Come in, but please excuse my home. It's a bit of a mess."

Dolores led the way through the small four-room flat into the kitchen, where a fresh pot of coffee was brewing. He tried not to stare at the piles of dirty laundry on the floor in the corners of the small rooms. There was an odor of mildew mixed with bleach that hung in the stale air. Father Tom sat down at the yellow Formica kitchen table. He placed his hat on the chair beside him, then opened his black leather bag and took out three jars of holy water, his rosary and Bible, and placed them on the table. Dolores poured Tom a cup of coffee and set it down in front of him. She saw the holy water.

"So, we're getting right down to business, are we? And three bottles? You must think there's a legion of demons in my house."

"Not at all. I was passing through the neighborhood blessing some of the houses tonight, I heard folks have been having some disturbances of a presence." Father Tom couldn't help smiling. Dolores looked at the back door.

"I know people are talking about me and the ghost that is haunting us. I know who the ghost is, Tom, and I want you to make her go away. She's after Aurora. I just know it, and I'm so frightened for my little girl."

"You've never told me about a ghost. I'd like to hear about it."

"I'm going to need a little something extra in my coffee to be able to tell that story." Dolores poured them both a cup of coffee and added a splash of tequila to her mug. She was going to pour some for Father Tom, but he politely placed his hand over his mug. Dolores sat down and took a long sip of her coffee.

⌣

"Well, you see, when Aurora was born, her face was blue. She wasn't breathing. Jesus, Tom, I thought she was going to die. Her soul was still somewhere in the spirit world. I remember screaming for the doctor to help her. Something they don't tell you is that nurses in labor and delivery don't like it when you scream in labor. If they hear you screaming, instead of coming to help you, they will ignore you until you quiet down. Anyway, I'll never forget that nurse's face. She had light brown hair, graying at the temples, with ice blue eyes and thin lips that looked like she never smiled. She moved her face close to mine and spoke in a firm, low voice so the doctor would not hear her.

"This would have never happened if you hadn't been drinking the whole time you were pregnant. You are a very stupid woman. Did you think you could drink alcohol night after night and have your baby come out healthy? You'll be lucky if she doesn't have brain damage. Now would be a good time to pray for God to save her, because right now her soul is floating between life and death, not sure which way to go. If that was my child, I'd be on my knees right now, begging for God's forgiveness and mercy."

"As soon as she said those words, I stopped screaming. She was right. Maybe I didn't deserve her. Maybe God had a right to take her from me. So, I prayed and promised God, if he gave my little girl back to me, I would never drink again." Dolores lowered her head and wiped her eyes.

"It was what was in your heart at that moment, Dolores. God has already forgiven you. We are imperfect beings, prone to breaking promises. It is why we have the grace of Christ's forgiveness. Please, go on." Father Tom sipped his coffee and waited.

"The doctor lowered Aurora's body between his legs and quickly swung her back and forth. I thought I would choke on the silence. Then, it was as if the air stabbed its way into her lungs, and Aurora let out an angry cry. It was the most beautiful sound I had ever heard. The doctor placed her on my belly long enough to see her pretty face. I tell you, Tom, she opened her eyes and looked right at me. She was so full of light. That's when I decided to name her Aurora. Then the mean nurse whisked her away. Aurora was jaundiced and still not breathing right. Then that nurse came back to punish me again with her words. She told me that Aurora had alcohol poisoning and was not breathing normally. Then the orderlies wheeled me up to the recovery ward. This was the first time the ghost made herself known to me. As I lay in my bed, the temperature in the ward dropped ten degrees. I began to shiver uncontrollably, and then I heard a woman weeping. It was a deep, mournful sorrow, so much so that I felt I was the one who was weeping. I asked one of the nurses if she heard the crying. The nurse turned from me and whispered something to the doctor, and he furrowed his brow. He told her to give Aurora fluids, and if I gave the nurse any trouble, they were to send me up to the Psych ward.

"At the mention of the word Psych, I was determined to block the sound of her weeping from my mind. As you know, Tom, I am no stranger to that maternity ward, and most of the orderlies who work there know me. It's a large rectangular room with two rows of ten beds on each side; twenty beds in all. It's filled with the constant chatter of doctors, nurses, and visitors talking loudly. But at night, only the nurses come in to take your vitals or bring your baby for feeding.

"The first evening, I was exhausted with worry, not knowing if Aurora would live or die. I half drifted in and out of sleep. My nerves were raw, and any little sound startled me awake. That was when I saw a woman, not human, but something else. I could see right through her. She paced back and up and down the aisle, as if she was waiting for something. She wore a long white dress that dragged on the floor like a wedding gown. Her almond-shaped green eyes seemed to glow against the pale skin of her face. I watched her pace back and forth, then she stopped and looked directly at me. She shook her head slowly from side to side as if confused, wringing her bony hands. She wept and wept. Suddenly, I felt my own sorrow well up inside me, but I choked back my tears. I didn't want the nurses to send me upstairs. The woman in the next bed pulled back the curtain that separated our beds. She introduced herself as Mavis."

"What's your name, honey, and why you crying?" she asked nervously.

"I'm Dolores, but it wasn't me who was crying."

Mavis got up from her bed and listened to see if any of the other mothers were crying. Mavis scanned the rows of beds up and down, but all the women were sound asleep.

"That sure is strange, cause I know I heard someone crying. I think you got yourself a haunt, honey. Whatever you do, don't tell no one, and don't look it in the face. Once you look 'em in the face, they can follow you home."

"Too late. I already looked at her."

"Oh, Lord. You're gonna have one powerful baby on your hands. It's a girl, ain't it?

"Yes. Aurora." Mavis stared at the foot of my bed.

"You can see it?"

"Yes. She's standing there."

"Sweet Jesus. Don't tell me no more. We best keep this to ourselves. If the nurses hear you talking about seeing or hearing things that ain't there, they gone take you upstairs with the crazies, and by the time you come out of there, you won't remember you even had a baby. So you just hush now, hear?"

"Yes. I hear you. I didn't hear anything."

"Good. Me neither. Now let's both get some sleep." Mavis closed the curtain and went to sleep.

"A week later, when I was finally able to bring Aurora home from the hospital, the ghost woman followed us home, and she's been here ever since. Quiet mostly, but I could always feel her presence watching us, and sometimes I would find Aurora talking to her. For some reason, I couldn't see her anymore, but Aurora could. Sometimes, I would find her talking to the ghost when she was alone outside. I punished Aurora when I caught her talking to her. After a while, we all just got used to having her around. Then last weekend, Aurora and I saw her in the backyard, hiding under the branches of the Willow tree, and she has been there every night since. Now the neighbors can hear her crying, and Betty, next door, saw her, and now everyone is talking about her. She's La Llorona, and she wants to take Aurora from me."

"You mean like the legend of the weeping woman? Why do you believe she is La Llorona?" Tom remembered hearing stories from the women who recently arrived from Mexico and Guatemala. They talked about a crying woman dressed in a long, white huipil standing on the corner of Balmy Alley and 24th Street. They left pennies on the curb of the sidewalk in the alley, along with prayers to her. He thought she was a manifestation of the deep grief they carried and were forbidden to express. A spirit woman who cried tears, the women could not cry for themselves, but they had never mentioned she was malevolent in any way. He was curious to find out more about her presence in this home.

"Please, Tom, just make her leave us alone. Make her go away." Dolores had tears in her eyes. Father Tom had never seen her so vulnerable or frightened. He stood up from the table and walked over to her, where she was standing in front of the stove, and put his arm around her shoulder.

"I'll do my best, Dolores. Now let's begin in the front room, shall we?" Father Tom picked up a jar of holy water in one hand, tucked his Bible under his arm, and laced his red crystal rosary through the fingers of the other hand. He and Dolores walked to the front room, which had a small couch, a coffee table, a small television, and a record player in the corner of the room. The floor was covered in light blue linoleum, with faded red roses on it; there were spots where the wood from the floor beneath showed through. Some nights, as he passed by on his way to O'Donnell's, he would hear Dolores playing the Beatles record loudly through the open window. It made him smile that she had this small joy for herself.

Dolores' children were outside playing tag with the other children on the block, but when Aurora caught a glimpse of Father Tom standing in the living room with her mother, she went to the open window in the living room and quietly watched. She wanted to see what he was going to do with the water in the jar and the red sparkling beads he held in his hands. She became entranced as she watched him dip two fingers in the jar of water, then sprinkle it in each of the corners of the room. She could see his lips moving, but she could not hear what he was saying. She went to the front door and opened it slowly to get a better view. He kissed the crucifix on his rosary, then proceeded to the next room, which was the small bedroom that Aurora and her mother shared.

Aurora snuck through the door and tiptoed quietly behind them. Father Tom repeated this ritual, stopping to listen before he moved to the next bedroom. It had one twin bed on each side of the room, and a small window that faced a wall of red bricks. The next room was also small and crowded. Father Tom sprinkled holy water over the beds and in the corners of the room, then he blessed the kitchen in the same way. He suddenly became acutely aware of the woeful condition of the flat. It was as if he had not truly seen it before, or perhaps he did not want to.

The lemon-yellow paint on the kitchen walls was streaked with nicotine stains that dripped down the walls. The last room was the back porch that had been converted into a makeshift room for Beto. The walls of the room were unfinished, with only a fold-away bed and a small dresser in front of a window beside the door. He looked to his right towards the bathroom and noticed the door was ajar. It was without a knob, but instead closed with an old hook-and-eye lock that had to be secured from the inside. The hook had been inserted and had fallen out more than once, so that the door was barely secured. The sight of it gave him an uneasy feeling in his stomach. The smell of urine and dirty laundry that wafted from the bathroom overcame him, so he quickly opened the back door to allow the evening breeze to move through the house. Aurora was happy that Beto was out with his friends, because she didn't think he would like Father Tom to sprinkle magic water or say prayers in his room. As Father Tom walked down the steps into the backyard, he suddenly felt lightheaded.

"Tom, be careful. She might be out there now. She usually comes at night." Dolores was standing just inside the doorway. Aurora sat quietly on her haunches behind her mother, watching to see what Father Tom would do next. Father Tom shivered as cold fingers crept under his collar, then he heard a woman crying. It drifted on the air from somewhere beneath the long branches of the Willow tree that dangled over the fence, long tendrils that scraped against the ground.

"Hello. Is someone there?" He stepped closer to the tree and, as his eyes adjusted to the dark, he saw luminous blue filaments of light swirling within the lace of the branches. He blinked his eyes, trying to clear his vision, but the apparition only sharpened. It was the profile of a woman in a white huipil dress, and except for the blue light around her, she looked completely human, and nothing like he imagined a ghost or a spirit would look if he ever saw one, which up until now, he had not. He felt a deep sadness, as well as kindness, emanating from her. As he moved closer, she turned to face him. There were tears flowing in her sea-green eyes.

⌣

"Dear Lady, who are you and what do you want with this family?"

La Llorona stretched out her arm and pointed towards the concrete stairs that led to the basement. The Ancient Ones are not allowed to interfere with the lives of humans, but they can give signs, speak through dreams, and offer guidance. She had been waiting for someone to pay attention to the signs she offered, in the hope that they would help this child.

"Is there something down there?"

Llorona covered her face and shook her head at the sins that took place in that basement. Betty, the woman who lived in the flat next door, came out to see what was happening.

"Is she here, Father? Are you going to get rid of her?" Father Tom ignored Betty and Dolores and walked down the stairs to the basement. It was dark, so he fished a lighter from his pocket. It gave off enough light for him to find the light bulb on the low ceiling. He pulled the string, and the light came on.

"Tom. You don't want to go down there," Dolores called after him, but it was too late. Just then, Aurora slipped past her mother and ran down the basement stairs to see what Father Tom was going to do next. She was so quiet; he didn't notice she was standing beside him. She startled him when she tugged on his shirt sleeve.

"You are gonna need a lot more magic water if you go in there." She pointed to an old wooden door on one side of the hall that was secured by a padlock. He thought it was probably used for storage.

"What do you think is inside that room, little one?"

"That's where the devil lives."

"Who told you the devil lives in there?

"My mommy. She calls him to come and get me when I'm bad." Aurora looked up at Father Tom with such deep shame in her eyes that it cracked his heart open.

"Once I saw him there. He has yellow eyes, and he says he's going to take me to hell to burn forever, because I am a bad little girl. I don't want to be bad. I try to be a good girl, but I guess I don't know how to be good." Father Tom picked up Aurora and gave her a gentle hug. She was precious, and he wanted her to know that she was good.

"Aurora, you are a precious angel of God. You are precious and good, and our Lord Jesus loves you so, so much." He kissed the top of her head. "Do you understand, Lass?"

She shook her head, no, and touched the rosary that was wrapped around his hand. "This is pretty." She ran her finger back and forth across the ruby beads. Father Tom put Aurora down, unwrapped the rosary from his hand, and gave it to her.

"This is for you, Aurora. It's a gift to protect you."

"What does protect mean?" She looked up at him, her eyes searching for something he knew he could not give her.

"It means to keep you safe. Out of harm's way."

"Then they won't work. I don't have safe. Except for the crying lady, so please don't send her away. She is my friend, and she loves me." He felt humbled in the presence of her innocence and light. He could not hold back his tears.

"I know, Lass. Don't you worry. I'm not going to send her away, although there are others I wish I could send far away from you. C'mon. Let's go back to the house."

She took his hand and held onto the rosary with her other hand, and they walked back into the house together.

⌣

When Father Tom and Aurora walked into the kitchen, Dolores was standing against the stove, smoking a cigarette, staring at the floor with her arms crossed.

"Did you send her away, Tom?" He didn't answer. He walked past her, still holding Aurora's hand. He walked her to her bed, turned his back so she could change into her pajamas, then tucked her into bed. She wrapped the rosary around her fingers, the way she had seen him do it.

"Can I really keep this? Cause you can have it back if you need it."

"No, they belong to you now, Lass; to keep, just for you." He kissed her on her forehead, then placed his hand on her head and asked for God, the Holy Mother, and La Llorona to watch over her. When he went back to the kitchen, Dolores was sitting at the table smoking a cigarette

31

and sipping a large tumbler full of red wine. He placed his hands in his pockets to stop them from shaking and took several deep breaths before he could speak calmly. He saw that Dolores' eyes were narrow with anger, and her jaw was clenched when she spoke.

"What did she tell you, Tom? She tells stories, you know. She's a liar. Don't let her fool you."

"I'm sorry to say that the evil I discovered tonight is not an evil I can send away with prayers and holy water, Dolores. Do you understand what I'm saying?" She took a drag of her cigarette and stared blankly past him.

"I want you to bring Aurora and your boys to my office at the Rectory tomorrow morning. I am going to register them for Catechism classes. I want to be sure they know that God loves them, and that Christ brings love and forgiveness, but most of all, I want Aurora to know that she is good and that God loves her. Do you understand my meaning, or do I need to make myself clearer, Dolores?"

"What if I don't want my children going to church? What are you going to do, Tom?"

He felt his own face flush with anger as he watched Dolores' temper flare with pride and stubbornness, just as Bill had warned. Being an Irishman, he had his own temper.

"You don't want me to answer that, Dolores. I don't think you want social services poking around here again, so I expect to see you at 9:30 a.m. with the children in tow. Goodnight." He placed the holy water into his bag, grabbed his hat and coat, and walked out the door. Dolores followed Tom to the door and watched him fade into the night. She had lost track of time, so she called her boys inside.

Aurora was not asleep. She had heard everything Father Tom had said to her mother. She didn't understand most of it, but she heard the angry sounds of their voices and feared that somehow, she was the cause of it. When her brothers had brushed their teeth and gone to bed, Dolores sat beside Aurora. Her gaze was sharp, and anger burned in her eyes. She pointed her long red nail close to Aurora's face. She knew what was going to happen next. Dolores spoke in a low growl, so the boys would not hear.

"What did you say to Father Tom, Yoya? You better tell me the truth, or you know what's going to happen. Do you understand me?" Aurora pulled the covers tight up to her chin.

"I was just trying to help Father Tom. He wanted to go into the brick room, and I told him not to, because the devil lives there and I didn't want the devil to hurt Father Tom."

"You stupid little girl. You did a very bad thing. Now we have to go to the church to see Father Tom in the morning. You know I don't like anyone knowing my personal business. Now get up from that bed." She yanked the covers off Aurora.

"No, mommy. I'm sorry. Please. I didn't mean to be bad."

"Yes, you did. You're always a bad girl, and you know what happens to bad little girls. Get out of that bed now!" Dolores yanked her by the arm and pulled her out of the bed, and dragged her through the kitchen, out into the backyard, and down the basement stairs. She pulled her keys from the pocket of her dress, unlocked the padlock, and pushed the door open. She flipped on the light and pulled Aurora inside the room. It was made of red bricks, and there were old, mildewed boxes stacked in one corner and a small window barely covered by old, yellow, torn curtains, where only a faint light came through. A window too high for a child to see out of. Aurora covered her nose against the smell of mold and urine. There was an old, dirty mattress on the floor, and a blanket full of holes thrown carelessly on it. Dolores pushed Aurora onto the mattress.

"When I close this door, you better start praying to God, so the devil doesn't come to get you." Without warning, a heavy numbness spread over Aurora. She was still holding the rosary Father Tom had given her. She kneeled on the mattress and started to pray.

"Hail Mary, full of grace…pray for us sinners, now at the hour of our death." She didn't know all the words, so she just repeated the few words of the prayer she remembered.

"If you're still here when I come back in the morning, then I'll know you are a good girl and God heard your prayers." Aurora did not open her eyes to look at her mother when she closed the door and put the lock in place. She nodded and continued praying. Then she heard

33

the padlock click and her mother's footsteps disappear up the basement stairs. Aurora continued her prayers.

⌣

"Dear God, please don't let the devil come and take me. I promise I'll try to be good, so he won't want me…" Suddenly, the room became filled with golden light, like the flame from a candle, and the sweet scent of roses permeated the room. Aurora was enveloped by a sweet calm. Her mind drifted into the silence between light and shadow. She became wisps of smoke, strands of silver, blue, and gray light. She felt herself being woven into a fabric made of light by gentle, unseen hands that held her with a love she had never felt before. Aurora's etheric self was lifted and guided by a cobalt thread that pulled her out through the small window and up into a blue-black sky.

She opened her eyes and saw that she was standing on a large precipice surrounded by the night sky. She heard the familiar sound of a woman crying, and she knew she was safe. The weeping dissolved into a rhythmic weaving of prayers and singing that etched themselves into her cells. Singing and tears, prayers and chanting spiraled inside of her. She turned to find out where the sounds were coming from, but she could not see anyone. Then out of the darkness emerged a woman dressed in red robes and a long turquoise veil. She was surrounded by a brilliant circle of red, full-bloomed roses. Her eyes contained the flame of sun, and her heart emanated pink light that enveloped Aurora and made her feel safe.

"Are you God?"

"I am your mother, my child. I am the same one who you saw under the Willow tree."

"Ohhh. I like the way you sing. It's pretty and it makes me feel good here." Aurora pointed to her chest. Then the Lady reached out and pulled one of the roses that surrounded her and placed it in the center of Aurora's chest.

"This rose is so that you will always know that you are my daughter and that you were created from love. You are perfect, beautiful, and you are good." Then she touched her hand to Aurora's heart.

"This is your sacred fire. This is your healing song. All you need to do is close your eyes, touch your hand to your heart to call me, and I will come to you. You are not alone, my beloved child. I am always with you. You are the light of my heart, soul of my soul; you are woven from the threads of my sacred shawl, and with these threads we are eternally connected, as I am to all my children."

Aurora understood safe. Then she woke abruptly back in the red brick room. She heard footsteps tapping down the basement stairs, and then the click of the padlock. When Dolores entered the room, she smelled the fragrance of fresh roses and feared that she was having another hallucination. She reached into her pocket for the bottles of pills that Aurora's pediatrician had given her. Dr. Hammish told her to take a white pill when she felt tired, or a blue pill if she needed to calm down. She popped one of each into her mouth, then went over to Aurora and gave her a big hug.

"I see you're still here, mija. That means that you prayed, and God heard your prayers. You are a good girl, and I am so proud of you. Now let's get you into the bath. It's time to get ready to go see Father Tom. Aurora picked her rosary up from the mattress and followed her mother out of the basement, up the stairs, and into the house, where a bath of warm water was waiting for her. As she sat in the tub, she thought of the beautiful lady. She remembered all she had said to her, even though she did not understand it all. She felt something was different, but she could not say how, exactly.

◡

Father Tom finished his coffee and waited. It was 9:30 a.m. and Catechism classes would be starting at 10:00 a.m. He hoped that Dolores would show up with the children. If she didn't, he would have no choice but to report her to social services, and that was the last thing he wanted to do, because he knew that they would remove the children from the home and separate them. This was seldom in the best interest of the children. Besides, Father Flynn preferred to hold such matters in prayer and allow God's divine will to be done. His thoughts were interrupted by a knock on the door from his secretary, who let him know that Dolores had arrived with the children. Father Tom went to open his door and invited Dolores and the children into his office. Aurora was the first one to run inside. She took the red rosary out of her pocket and lifted it up to show it to him.

"I took good care of it, Father, see? And the lady with the roses came to see me last night. She was so beautiful. I want to come to school here, so I can learn more about her. My mommy says there's a special prayer that goes with the beads. Can I learn it, please, Father?"

"Yes, of course, Aurora. That is why you are here today, isn't that right, Dolores?"

Dolores nodded, then pulled out a cigarette, lit it, and pulled Aurora back into her seat. "We're going to get all of you signed up for Catechism classes. That's where you will learn your prayers and learn about God's love for you. The prayer to Our Lady is called the Rosary." Father Tom handed Dolores enrollment forms to fill out. She grabbed them from him.

"I'll bring them back next week."

"Oh, no. You can fill them out right here, and the children can start right away. Classes start in about 30 minutes. That's why I wanted you to come in at 9:30."

"I really don't know who you are right now, Tom. I thought we were friends?"

"I am a priest and a friend who is trying to help you, Dolores." He smiled and handed her a pen. "I'll have Sister Ana María take the children to their classes. You can pick them up at 12:30."

"Memo's old enough to walk them home. He knows the way home. It's only four blocks. They'll be fine."

"Okay. Good. You can just leave the forms with my secretary when you're done. Now, if you will excuse me. I need to prepare for mass tomorrow." Dolores did not reply. She dismissed him with a wave of her hand, got up from the chair, and walked out without a word.

The next morning, before mass, Father Tom went to report to Father Flynn. He knocked on his office door and waited to be invited in, even though the door was open.

"Enter."

Father Flynn stood up and greeted Tom with a smile and a warm handshake, which was unusual for Father Flynn. "Tom, come sit down. I have some good news. Oh, but first, how did your meeting with Mrs. Camacho go?

"Well enough, I suppose. I was able to enroll the children in Catechism classes."

"Well, that's a start. Perhaps their mother will bring them to mass. And the entity that has been haunting Dolores?"

"It turned out that it was brought about by a combination of the overactive imaginations and gossip of the women on the block who resent Dolores for good reason, as you are aware, Father Flynn. I went ahead and conducted a house blessing for her," Father Tom lied. He could not bring himself to speak the truth of what he learned from Aurora. He held onto hope and prayers that La Llorona would find a way to help Aurora without having to call Child Protective Services.

"Well, that is good news, I suppose. I will pray that Christ will bring them back to the Church. Anyway, Tom, I wanted to tell you that I have chosen you for a very special assignment. The Archdiocese is sending you to Guatemala as the new priest for the Church of Saint Michael's in Guatemala City."

Tom was caught off guard. He rubbed his hand over his face, trying to take in what Father Flynn just told him. "I'm confused. I thought Father Esquivel was the priest there?"

"Yes, he was. Unfortunately, Father Esquivel was killed about a week ago. Soldiers discovered he was hiding parishioners in the church. The military believed them to be insurgents, or Communists, or whatever they are calling innocent God fearing people there. I learned that the soldiers locked everyone inside the church and burned it to the ground. Some of the people escaped through one of the side doors, then ran up into the mountain to hide. It's a horrible thing, and now the people are without a priest."

"Dear Lord." Tom sat down on the sofa.

"You're fluent in Spanish, Tom, so you are perfect for this assignment, and the people there need a priest who will care for their spiritual needs. There is a group of Peace Corps workers stationed there who will help you build a makeshift building for church services. As you can imagine, we can't rebuild a church in the middle of a civil war." *Genocide*, Tom thought. *There is nothing civil about genocide.*

"I understand, Father. I will go wherever God needs me to go. When do I leave?"

"In one week."

Father Tom stood to shake Father Flynn's hand and walked out of the rectory to tell Bill the news. He couldn't leave without saying goodbye. It was almost noon, and the bar was empty. Bill was happy but surprised to see his friend.

"Back so soon, my friend? What brings you here so early on a Saturday?

"I have big news, and I think I need a minute and a pint of Guinness." Bill poured Guinness for Tom and two fingers of whiskey for himself.

"How did your visit with Dolores go last night?"

"You know I can't tell you what I learned from my visit. I was there as a priest, so it's confidential, my friend. But I will tell you that Dolores brought all the children, except for the oldest, to the rectory this morning to sign up for Catechism classes. So, I believe that it is a step in the right direction."

"Well, I'll say that's a good start." Bill finished his whiskey in one long swallow and slammed the glass on the bar. Father Tom took a gulp of his lager, then took a breath before continuing.

"The Diocese is sending me to Guatemala. The priest there was murdered, along with many of the parishioners. It's a horrible thing, that war. Sometimes, I fear it will never end. The displaced people just keep coming in from Guatemala, and I worry that we will run out of resources to help them. I am also so impressed with the people and how they carry the beauty of their faith and culture here with them. Anyway, I'm leaving next week, so I wanted to say goodbye, my friend. I don't know how long I will be there, so this may be the last time we see each other." Bill went around the bar to give Tom a big hug.

"Bah! I'll hear none of that. If you have at least one hand, you can write to me. I want you to promise me that right now."

"I promise, my friend." Father Tom wiped at his tears before they fell. He stepped back and took one last look at his friend. Then he tossed two dollar bills on the bar and headed towards the door.

"How many times do I have to tell you, Tom? You're money's no good here."

⌣

GUATEMALA CITY ~ 1980

When Luz arrived in Guatemala City, there were soldiers driving through the villages armed with pistols and machine guns. The stench of death and the sound of gunfire blew hard through the air. Small cement dwellings with hatch roofs lined both sides of the street; the lime green, pink, and cobalt-blue muted by the smoke from gunfire and the dust of the traffic from trucks piled with soldiers searching for subversives. The soldiers searched every home and field until they found someone who fit the description of subversive; it was subjective. Luz walked through the streets trying hard not to be noticed by the soldiers. Born in Oaxaca, she had traditional features of bronzed skin, long black hair, straight as a sheet of obsidian, startling green eyes, and a moon face. It was her green eyes that made others stop and take notice. Some thought they were a sign of blessing from the ancestors, others thought they were a sign that she was a witch. At 36, Luz was independent with a fiery passion for life, along with an inner light that emanated and often drew people to her. Her strength was her fierce determination; once she had her mind set to do something, nothing and no one was going to talk her out of it.

On the same day she arrived, a comandante, whom they called El Perro Malo, was sitting on the back of a Jeep. He gripped his rifle as he noticed Luz walk past him. At first, she did not notice him. She was busy searching for the street signs that would guide her to her Tía Marta's home. It had been many years since she had last visited, and as she looked around, she felt sick seeing the black ashes of so many houses burnt to the ground.

"Hola, Señorita. Where are you going in such a hurry? I haven't seen you around here before. I would have surely remembered such a pretty girl." He had startled Luz, and this made him laugh out loud. Luz saw the gun in his hand and quickly averted her gaze to the ground.

"I'm going to visit my Tía Marta. She lives here somewhere. I can't remember exactly where she lives. It's been a long time since I was here last."

"Why don't you climb into my truck, and I'll make sure you get there safely."

"Do you know my Tía Marta?"

He reached into his shirt pocket for a cigar, licking the sides, then bit off the tip and spit it on the ground near her feet. "Tía Marta, Tía Rosa. These people are all the same to me. Their names do not matter. They are insurgents, and I punish them as such." There was a seething hatred in El Perro's eyes—a dark malice Luz had never seen. She saw tendrils of foul sexual energy extending from his etheric body out to hers, dirty tongues hungry for her light. El Perro smacked his lips as he continued to examine Luz. He wanted her, and he knew he would have her sooner or later. The waiting added to the thrill of the game. He forced a smile as he puffed on his cigar. He feigned kindness and spoke seductively to Luz.

"Please, allow me to escort you to your Tía Marta's. Climb in my truck and I'll take you there."

Luz stared at the ground as she carefully thought about how to answer. She looked at El Perro, veiled behind a cloud of tobacco smoke.

"Comandante, you are a very important and busy man. I couldn't possibly expect you to interrupt your duties to escort me." Then, out of the cloud of smoke, three long, sinewy, yellow-green entities with jaundiced eyes revealed themselves to Luz. The entities knew that Luz could see them, and they taunted her, flicking their long, serpent tongues, trying to feed from her light. Luz had never seen anything like these beings before. She tried to appear calm and prayed silently.

"Ayuda me, mi Divina." La Llorona appeared immediately. She stood behind Luz and ran her hands through the etheric threads of Luz's sacred shawl. She raised her arms high and snapped her red rebozo, sending a flash of lightning to illuminate the space around El Perro. She spoke into his mind.

"You have forgotten yourself. I see what you are. Return to your dwelling place." She snapped her rebozo again, and electric blue fire shot out at the entities. They let out a shrieking howl that caused El Perro to cover his ears. A sudden vertigo came over him, and a stabbing pain gripped his chest, as the entities were extricated from him. He dropped his cigar, leaning against the side of his truck, clutched his chest, and looked at Luz.

"What are you, cabrona, some kind of pinche bruja or something?"

Luz stood silent, keeping her eyes lowered, not wanting to meet his gaze. La Llorona moved behind El Perro and whispered into his mind.

"Stay away from my daughter." He turned around to see who was speaking to him, but he saw no one.

"Ahhh! Too much tequila today." Just then, a truck full of soldiers drove up beside El Perro.

"Are you alright, Comandante?" one of the soldiers asked.

"Yes. I am fine. What do you want?" he responded while studying Luz, not wanting to forget her face.

"We need your assistance. We have found a large group of insurgents." El Perro looked at Luz, grinned, and tipped his hat.

"I will be watching you, señorita. I'm sure that we will meet again."

Luz kept her eyes down and said nothing, which, normally, she did not do very well. La Llorona watched as El Perro drove off, and saw new entities that attached themselves to him and the other soldiers. The entities filled the empty space in the soldiers where the light of their souls was missing. They had traded their light for the fleeting experience of power and the illusion of importance. Power came at a great price, for it often required evil to sustain it. Llorona understood that even El Perro, in all his darkness, was still a divine creation of the One Great Heart. But he had rejected the light in himself. He hated these people who he thought of as less than people, but in truth, he was one of them. This density of his self-hatred pushed the light of his true essence out of his body. He had lived in Guatemala City his entire life. He joined the military at the age of fourteen. It was a way to ensure he could help to feed his family and protect them. Still, he hated these people. Most of all, he despised the childlike, blind faith in a god that he believed had clearly abandoned them. He understood that power was the only way to get what you wanted in the world.

⌣

When Luz finally arrived at Tía Marta's home, she was sitting at the kitchen table, staring at the wall, her face pale and expressionless. Luz went to her and put her arms around her. Her body was stiff. Luz sat beside her at the table and waited. When Marta realized Luz was there beside her, she composed herself as best she could. She stood up, smoothed her apron, and gave Luz a brief hug.

"Mija, what are you doing here? This is no place for you. You need to turn around and return to San Cristóbal."

"Tía Marta, I came to see you. Please tell me what has happened here. This place looks like a graveyard." Without any emotion, Marta moved to the stove to make tea. She motioned for Luz to sit at the table with her and conveyed all that had transpired the day before.

"Yesterday, as we were returning from morning mass, several trucks full of soldiers carrying rifles surrounded the church. They told us to hurry home and that they would come to question us. But they did not wait for us to go home. They entered the church and began to beat the men with their pistols right there in the church, in front of God and all the Saints." Tía Marta paused to wipe the silent tears that rolled down her cheeks.

"The women…they violated some of the women right there in the holy church. Then, they beat them and threw their bodies in the back of their trucks, while their children watched, frozen with terror. We grabbed the children and ran to our homes, while the soldiers laughed at us. When we got to our homes, other soldiers were waiting for us. They beat the men in front of their homes, made them beg for their lives, and then executed them in front of their wives and children. Everyone watched, frozen with terror and unable to utter a sound. There was nothing we could do. Their bodies were dragged off by the soldiers and thrown into the back of a truck that was piled with the bodies of other victims. They were taken to an unknown grave, buried without prayers or blessings of our priest. Now their souls will wander, forever without rest. Those of us who remained were warned not to speak of what we saw. We were told not to make altars or say prayers, and worse, we are not to even utter the names, or the soldiers would return and do the same to us." Tía Marta wiped at a tear before it reached her cheek. She was tired of tears.

"As weeks and months passed, the presence of the soldiers was a constant throughout Guatemala; the power of their force was made known with blood. The people were too afraid to speak to each other about their loved ones who were missing or murdered. They told themselves that it was all a terrible dream. In some of the villages, the churches had been burned down, and the priests and nuns murdered. Father Tom is our priest now. He is a gringo from El Norte, but he is a kind man who does everything he can to help. But honestly, there is nothing he can do. Each day we choke on this dry, black grief, the tears in our hearts have dried up, along with our home and my faith." Tía Marta threw her cup against the wall and stood up. She took a deep breath to compose herself. "Tomorrow, you should return home, Luzita. Nothing good can come from you being here."

Luz said nothing. She went outside, sat on the front steps, and sipped her tea. She thought about all that her tía had told her. She was enraged and heartbroken, but worst of all, she felt helpless. She had to do something. She closed her eyes and called on La Divina once more. She appeared immediately and sat down on the steps beside Luz. She pulled Luz close, wrapping them both in her red rebozo.

"Tell me what's in your heart, mija?" Luz knew that La Divina already knew what was in her heart, soul, and mind, but she wanted Luz to speak it.

"I'm furious. I want to break something. I want to do something to change what's going on here."

"I understand how you feel, but you are only one person. This war is a conflict of greed and the desire for power. It has been going on for hundreds of years. It will run its course, and the people will rise, band together, and make their voices known. The truth of what occurred here will be known. This will take time. Truth unfolds in cycles because humans live in a state of spiritual amnesia. The original people here remember that they are made of the dust of the stars and the soil of the earth. They are descendants of the great timekeepers, builders, story bringers, weavers, healers, and wise ones. The ones who have forgotten make war against this truth. They hate them and want to destroy them. Nations agree upon stories to justify their actions. Do you understand what I'm telling you?"

"No, but I'm trying to."

"That is enough for now. I want you to close your eyes, so you can see and feel what has happened here, then your heart will tell you what needs to be done." Luz closed her eyes as she was instructed, and La Divina sang a prayer to awaken the eyes of Luz's heart. Luz felt herself suddenly dizzy, as if she were spinning out of her body. Then she heard La Divina's voice, which grounded her in the waking dream. Luz looked around and saw that she was standing on a street at night, where many of the houses had been burned down. As she walked along the streets, she noticed the homes were dark. There were no candles burning for the ancestors, and the fragrance of copal was absent from the air.

Luz moved her awareness into her heart and felt the charcoal vessel of their souls, where they kept the memory of their loved ones hidden. They prayed silently for their souls to find peace. Families sat in their homes without speaking of what happened, and when vigilance finally released them, they fell into an exhausted sleep where their souls wept and wandered out into the night, searching for their loved ones. During the day, they ate little. They cooked food without joy or laughter, as if trying to make themselves small and invisible. They lived as ghost people; not yet dead, and not fully alive. The earth had stopped spinning, and the sun upon their skin offered no warmth. Even the wind had lost hope and carried only the stench of death. Luz saw Tía Marta and her friends, who lived nearby; she could see how the luminous threads of their sacred shawls were dull, frayed, and torn. She understood how she could help.

⌣

The next morning, Luz put water on the stove for coffee, then went to get a cup from the cabinet. She saw a small ceramic bowl towards the back of the cabinet. She was happily surprised that it contained several pieces of copal and charcoal. She switched off the stove and carried the bowl and matches out into the backyard. After emptying the contents of the bowl on the step, she scooped up a handful of sand from the garden and placed it in the bowl, then placed the charcoal on the sand and lit it, and waited for it to turn bright red. After a few minutes, Luz placed three pieces of copal on the charcoal and turned to the rising sun, raising the bowl to offer the sacred smoke with prayers to the Great Heart of the Sun. Luz turned to each of the directions, giving thanks for their gifts of life, then asked for help from the Ancient Ones to bring peace to Guatemala and to the souls of those who were murdered. She knelt and touched her hands to the earth, inhaling the fragrance of copal mixed with the verdant early morning mist that descended from the mountains. Finally, she stood up and lifted the copal to the sky and prayed.

"InLakesh Alakin. I am calling the Divine Ones, Tonantzin, Teteo, Ix Chel, Coatlique, Coyolxauhqui, Tlazolteotl, La Divina, and those whose names I do not know. I humbly ask for the restoration of luminous threads to the sacred shawl of these people, and for wisdom on how I can help them. Ancient Ones, shining ones, with hearts of fire, sacred goddesses of heaven and earth, air, water, and fire. I ask for your blessing, your guidance, and protection as I listen for your guidance. Enfold me in your sacred rebozo."

Tía Marta woke to the smoky fragrance of copal. She lay awake in her bed listening to Luz's prayers, then got up to call her niece inside.

"Mija. Come inside at once. If the soldiers smell the copal or see the smoke, they will come. Hurry now. Put the copal in the dirt and come inside."

Luz sat at the table while Marta made a pot of coffee. They sipped coffee in silence until Luz could no longer hold her frustration inside.

"So now it's illegal to burn copal, or to pray, Tía?"

"It's considered subversive and communist, whatever that means. Nonetheless, it's forbidden. If they catch you, it's an excuse for them to kill you, or worse."

"But Communists are atheists. These people and the soldiers are Catholic. It makes no sense."

Tía Marta slammed her fist on the table and got up from her chair. She paced back and forth, trying to calm her fear and anger.

"It doesn't have to make sense, Luzita. Do you think any of this murdering makes sense? The soldiers will do whatever the government wants them to do, and right now, they want us dead. They want the land that people here have stewarded for thousands of years. Evil doesn't have to make sense."

"But Tía, I know what I must do. I want to call the women nearby. Those whose loved ones were murdered. We must hold a ceremony. I want us to go up to the mountain, where they say the bodies were taken. Someone must know where they are."

"That would be very stupid and dangerous. You will not do this. I forbid it. The soldiers."

"I'm sick of the pinche soldiers. They have all the power now. Living in this fear is no way to live. You taught me that. Don't you remember?"

"Who are you to tell me how to live? I thought this war would be over by now, but now I understand that it will go on forever. You should go home, Luzita."

"No, it won't last forever. People are organizing in the city and towns. They are starting to fight back and stand up for their rights. Things will change, Tía. I promise you."

"I love you, mija, but you are young and foolish, and I am old and tired." Luz walked over to hug Marta, but Marta put her hand up. Luz sat back down and continued.

"I remember before you moved here to marry Tio Angelo, you taught me so much about how the spirit world works. I was amazed by your knowledge of energy and dreaming. You taught me to listen with the eyes of my heart and to feel with the eyes of my hands. You introduced me to La Llorona. Do you remember, Tía?"

Marta smiled at this fond memory. "Sí, mi amor. I remember. But I did not teach you anything. I simply helped you to remember. And you have always known La Llorona. She first came to you when you were an infant. Your heart has always known her. Your mind just needed a context to understand her outside of the ignorant superstitions people attach to her. You have always been her daughter."

"I suppose you are right. I remember the last time we sat together by the river in Oaxaca. It was Fall, and you came to visit on El Dia de los Muertos. Mi mami, you, and I sat together under the moon, and we sang to her, then we danced and prayed to Las Cihuateteo and the Ancient Ones. We gave thanks and asked for blessings for the new year. Then we went back to the house and lit candles around the yard and on the altar for our familia who had crossed over. You taught me how to make Pan de Muerto, but mine never came out quite as good as yours did. Our yard would glow with so many candles and the hundreds of Marigold petals scattered on the ground; orange and yellow sparks of light, you called them, to light the way for the ancestors to return to us. I remember we spent three days and nights making mole, tamales, frijoles, roasted corn, and pupusas for the altar. Tomorrow is El Día de los Muertos, and you don't have an altar set up. My Tío was an honorable man. He died fighting for freedom. We should honor his memory." The mention of Angelo's name was bitter, cold water thrown in Tía Marta's face. She moved to face Luz, her face red, full of anger.

"Do you think that I do not honor the memory of my husband? I honor him with each breath in my body. Don't you dare tell me about how my husband died. You were not there. You know nothing about his death." Marta went to sit at the table. Her face flushed with a rage she had not allowed herself to feel since the day the soldiers took her husband away.

"You didn't have to watch as the soldiers punched my Angelo in the face until his eyes would not open, or as they kicked and punched him all over his body, until he lost consciousness. You didn't watch helplessly as they threw his body in the back of the truck and drove away. I never knew if he was dead or alive. It didn't matter because I knew eventually, they would kill him. I also knew they would torture him first, and that part was unbearable. After they took him, I took our two boys up into the mountains to hide them. But, a week later, they found them. A neighbor boy told the soldiers where they were hiding; he wanted to win favor with the soldiers to protect his own family. They found my children and shot them in the back of the head and threw their bodies in a truck, and drove down from the mountain, the truck stacked with dead bodies. They dumped them in front of the church and sent word for the families to come and claim them.

"We ran to the church as soon as we heard the news. But when we got there, we could not believe what we saw. There were bodies of men, women, and children thrown in a huge pile on the ground, like trash. Father Tom was there waiting for the soldiers to leave, so he could bless the bodies. El Perro was also there. He watched and smiled as we helped each other to carefully line up the bodies in rows, so we could identify them. But El Perro did not want them to be identified. I will never forget what happened next. The only way I was able to identify Angelo and my boys was by scraps of clothes on their bodies. All the bodies were the same. Their faces were beaten beyond recognition. Their hands and the soles of their feet cut off, and maggots in the open wounds. We screamed with rage and grief.

"Then, El Perro fired his rifle and commanded us to move away from our loved ones. The soldiers moved in to pour gasoline over them. When the fire was ignited, I tried to run into the flames, but the soldiers stopped me. They wanted me to live with this nightmare in my mind. But my soul flew into the flames that day to be with my children and my husband. My bones are here, but my soul is gone. After the fire cooled and only ashes remained, the soldiers still did not allow us to bury the remains of our loved ones. They swept the ashes and bones up, placed them in plastic bags and drove off. One of the boys followed the soldiers. He risked his life so that he would know where his father's bones were placed. They tossed the bags of bones in an unmarked grave up on the mountain." Luz wept as she listened to Marta tell her story.

"I'm not telling you this so that you will pity me, Luzita. I want you to know that this war has turned men into monsters. This is what monsters do. This is what evil looks like. This is what they are still doing. I cannot make an altar for my husband and children, because they have not yet passed over to be with our ancestors. Their souls are trapped here, wandering without peace. Do you understand?" Luz ran over to Marta and tried to hug her, but Marta pushed her away.

"You need to hear the rest of the story. Now, please sit down."

☽

"That night, the soldiers returned here to kill me. Someone told them that I was a bruja, a witch, and that I practiced black magic. First, they beat me to get me to confess to practicing black magic, but I wouldn't, because it's a lie. When they looked in my eyes and saw that I had no fear of death, they decided they would not kill me. The things they did to me, I cannot speak of them. I was grateful mi Angelo and my boys were not alive to see it. They left me in a pool of my own blood. I was happy to die, but Rosario found me and called the other women to care for me. I begged them to let me die, but Rosario would not hear of it. I was alive, but I was dead. At first, I was angry with Rosario for saving me, but eventually I came to accept it. It was not yet my fate to die. Without my children and husband, there was nothing to live for. So now, each morning I face a new day. I cook a little. I work a little. I sleep very little. Sleep is like a small death that teases, but never comes. This life is not a true life, because there is no justice. Soon, there will be no Guatemala for us; only the military and corrupt politicians serving the rich Americans who come here to exploit the farmers and steal the land. We will all be dead. God has abandoned us; the Ancient Ones have abandoned us." Marta could no longer contain her grief. She sobbed into her hands. Luz rushed over to Marta and put her arms around her, but Marta would not be comforted. She pushed Luz away. Then she wiped her tears and stared out the window at the Marigolds in her garden.

"Ay, Tía, discúlpame, I'm so stupid. I always speak without thinking. I didn't mean to bring up painful memories. I can't imagine how you have suffered. I'm so sorry, and I'm sorry I was not here for you. But I'm here now. I want to take you back to Oaxaca to live with me," Luz said.

"There is nothing you could have done, mija. Just as there is nothing you can do now. I will not leave Guatemala. This is my home. It is where my husband and children are buried. I will not rest until their bones are returned to me, and I can lay them to rest in holy ground. You should go home, Luzita. This is no place for you. You are naïve and strong-willed, and that is a very dangerous and useless weapon here. No good can come of it. I will not help you call your own death. But if you are determined, I cannot stop you. Find Rosario. She is also young and foolish. I'm sure she will help you."

"Gracias, tía. I will find Rosario and any other women who will go with me," Luz said. Tía Marta walked to her room and shut the door.

Luz found Rosario sitting on her front steps, crushing herbs in her molcajete. She introduced herself and explained her plan. Rosario agreed to go up to the mountain and try to find the unmarked grave to bless the people for El Día de los Muertos, so perhaps the souls of those buried there could find peace and cross over. She told Luz that she knew some of the women who lost their families, as well as the boy who knew the location. They would go with her.

⏝

When the sun began to set behind the hills, Rosario and seven other women gathered in front of Marta's home. The boy refused to go, but he told Rosario where the families were buried. Luz opened the door to greet Rosario and the other women. The women decided they would wait until it was dark and most of the soldiers would most likely be asleep, as they did most of their killing during daylight for everyone to see. As night came, the women made the long trek up the mountain just outside of the city. They discovered an immense trench in the earth where the soil had been recently covered. The women stood in a circle around the grave.

Rosario sprinkled rosemary, blue cornmeal, and honey for sweetness on the ground to attract the spirits who were lost and wandering. Luz took out a ball of red thread from her shoulder bag. She wrapped a section of the thread around her wrist three times, then passed the thread to the woman on her left. Each of the women wrapped the thread around their wrist three times and passed it around the circle. When each of them had a piece of red thread, they cut the thread with their teeth and tied it around their wrists. Luz prayed.

"This thread unites us in heart and mind and connects us to the One Great Heart." Luz lit copal and fanned the smoke around the circle, praying through her tears.

"By air, by earth, by water, by fire. Holy mother, hear our heart's desire. Come to us and ease this great sorrow. Bless these bones and return these souls to the heart of the Sun, where they may find rest."

Luz invoked La Llorona by all her names. La Llorona, the goddess of lost souls, goddess of healing waters, the goddess who guides the souls of the dead through the celestial underworld, el río abajo río, to be purified and made whole. Then finally, they called her by her true name, La Divina, and a swift, cool wind blew through the grass.

One of the women, Lettie, whose husband lay somewhere on this ground, began to weep; the blade of her sorrow stabbed her heart, and she could no longer contain her sorrow. One by one, the women sobbed, wept, and wailed. They scratched at their faces and pulled at their hair. The rage that silenced them poured forth in torrents of tears, soaking the soil that covered their loved ones. Lettie fell on her knees and pounded the dirt with her fists, crying out the name of her husband. The other women bent over, so their tears would wet the earth, and the dead would know they were loved and grieved.

Then she appeared.

La Divina walked out from the swaying stalks of corn that circled the area of the grave. She wore a long, white cotton dress that touched the ground and dragged behind her. Each of the women stood and bowed as she stepped into the center of the circle. Her face was adorned with red circles painted around her eyes, and silver jewels across the lines of her brows and beneath her eyes that reflected the light of the moon. The tip of her nose was black, and her lips painted white, with black horizontal lines drawn across them, giving her the appearance of a muerto. Her tears bled down her face in red streaks. Her hair was unbraided, with thick, uncombed locks obscuring part of her face. A red rebozo covered her head. She stepped in front of each of the women and kissed them on the lips. When she came to Luz, she spoke into her mind.

"Once again, you have chosen a dangerous path in this life, mi Patli, but I will not abandon you. You will need to fight with all your soul, and with strength you do not yet possess. Me entiendes, mi amor?" Luz nodded her head, although she did not understand what her words meant, including why she called her Patli. La Llorona stood over the grave and wept, spilling her healing tears on the earth. Then she raised her arms and shrieked into the star-filled sky, her cries drifting heavy through the night, echoing down into the streets of the city. The women watched La Divina walk down the mountain. They had been certain that she would answer their prayers. They sat on the ground and wept tears of confusion and hopelessness. They continued with prayers for those who lay beneath them, without rest, in unholy ground. They spoke the names of their loved ones to the four sacred directions and called their spirits to them.

Meanwhile, down the mountain, two young soldiers were asleep from a drunken stupor after trying to outdrink each other earlier in the city. They suddenly woke when they heard screeching and wailing. They saw La Llorona walk past them, with thirteen owls flying behind her. Their skin turned to ice, and they were too frightened to move, but they knew who she was. They shivered as they prayed for protection to a god they were not supposed to believe in. They asked Jesus to protect them from the demon spirit that wailed in the darkness. Once La Llorona was far enough away and her cries faded, they stood up, holding their rifles close. Then they heard voices up the mountain, yelling and crying. They crept up the hillside to see who was in the place that was forbidden to be. The women stood and waited for La Divina to bring back the lost souls. They prayed for her to take them to the realm of the Ancestors. But this would not be the night their prayers would be answered. It would take many years for justice and healing to come. La Divina knew many more would die, and it grieved her, but she also knew humans were slow to change. She had witnessed the ways of humans for over 400 years. For now, this was the way it would be. But she also knew that someday healing would come.

The two soldiers knew they needed to capture at least one of the women and deliver her to El Perro, or they would be killed. But they knew most of these women who lived in their village. Rosario had delivered their babies, and Lettie had come to sit with one of their wives when she was sick with fever and cured her with herbs. There was one woman whom they did not know. Without speaking, they knew what they must do. The soldiers ran out from the corn field, rifles in hand, and seized Luz. The other women made no sound. They knew what would happen if they did. One of the soldiers was not older than fifteen or sixteen at most, but he had a gun, a knife, and a rifle. This was enough to make him a man. He hit Luz across the head with the butt of his rifle, and she fell to the ground unconscious. Rosario tried to run to Luz, but the other soldier moved quickly to point his rifle at her.

"If you like, you can go with her, but I really don't want to take you. You helped my wife give birth to our son last year, so I owe you a debt. Now, please move back." They warned the women not to try anything like this again. They told them they knew where they lived and that they would return, and next time they would show no mercy. Rosario fell to her knees, her last traces of hope draining into the soil beneath her. The women walked home in silence, soaked in dread of knowing what would befall Luz.

The soldiers dragged Luz through the grass, onto a truck down the mountain, where they had been asleep. They sat her between them, to make sure she would not try to escape.

⌣

Luz woke up surrounded by a cloud of cigar smoke. Her head was pounding, and when her eyes came into focus, she saw El Perro sitting in a chair a few feet in front of her. She tried to move, but her feet were tied to the legs of the chair, with her hands tied in front of her. She looked up to see El Perro smoking a cigar, sitting with his leg comfortably crossed over the other. He had several dark, formless entities dancing around in his energy field. They looked at her, laughing and jumping toward her. Just close enough to make her jump in her chair. There was a large metal desk beside El Perro, with a bottle of tequila, a shot glass, and several empty bottles of beer on it. Five soldiers stood at attention against the wall, one hand on their holsters. El Perro puffed his cigar and smiled widely at Luz. The whites of his eyes were yellow and dirty.

"Ah, good. You're awake. I remember you, chula carbona, from last week, when you first arrived in town. So beautiful; I knew you were trouble then. My soldiers tell me you tricked the other women into going with you up the mountain and that you found the place you should not have found. They saw you all crying and praying, standing around the grave. The grave that no one is supposed to know about.

How did you find it?" Luz said nothing. He slammed his fist on the desk and walked slowly in front of Luz. He moved his face so close to hers that she could smell his sour breath.

"It does not matter, because after I'm done with you, the women will not dare disobey my orders again." He walked back to his desk and threw the chair against the wall. Luz felt herself shaking in fear and hated herself for it. He spoke with a calculated, malicious calm in his voice. If Luz had believed in the devil, this is surely what he would be like.

"Now, let us continue. My men tell me that you are a bruja and that you called up a demon who walked around the grave crying, and the other women cried with her."

"Since when is crying a crime?" Luz sat up defiantly.

"It's not a crime, but there is nothing for the women to cry about, because nothing happened. Do you understand me? Nothing happened." He picked up a beer bottle from the desk and hurled it at the wall. Luz jumped in her chair.

"Hmm. Yes, yes. A real bruja, able to conjure demons. Here's the problem. I don't believe in this ignorant peasant mentality. I don't believe in demons and brujas, or superstition. I believe in what's right and the law, and you and your pince' mujeres broke the law."

Luz understood that whatever was to come would not come quickly. El Perro grabbed her hair and slapped her hard three times across the face. She tasted blood in her mouth. El Perro raised his fist, and Luz shut her eyes, so she would not see what came next. El Perro threw her to the floor and stomped on her in the stomach and kicked her back, until she spit up blood. She felt searing, hot pain burn through her body. Then the room went black. He threw his beer in her face and gritted his teeth.

"Oh, no, cabrona. You are going to be awake for this." He knelt on the floor and untied her from the chair. She tried to move away from him, but one of the soldiers quickly came to hold her arms. El Perro kneeled between her legs, then tore open her huipile and her skirt with his hands, so that the front of her body was exposed. Luz could see the entities around El Perro licking their tongues in perverse delight.

"You should not have interfered with things that are none of your business. Now, I want to hear you scream." He thrust his hand inside her without warning. She heard herself scream as her soul flew out of her body, up to the ceiling of the room. She watched as he thrust inside of her. When he was finished, he got up and let the soldiers take their turn with her. It seemed that hours had gone by. As they tore into her body, she felt the threads of her sacred shawl being ripped apart. She knew she would die. El Perro allowed her to sleep for a few hours before he threw cold beer at her face. Luz woke in a daze of pain. For just a minute, she could not remember where she was until El Perro sat down on the floor next to her. Her face was bruised beyond recognition, and she could not move her body. He touched her gently on her cheek and kissed her softly on her lips.

"Hmm. No witchcraft to save you? Where is your demon woman now?" El Perro got up and pointed to the two soldiers who had brought Luz to him.

"Get rid of her. Throw her body out with the garbage, where everyone will see her. Let her be a warning to the other women. If they try anything like that again, this is what will happen."

⏝

Father Tom was on his way to give mass at a makeshift building in the middle of the town where his parishioners met to receive communion on Sunday mornings. The soldiers had burned his parish church to the ground, and the townspeople were afraid to gather anywhere near there. The air was plagued with the smell of burnt flesh and a fearful silence. He passed an alleyway that separated two small shops when he heard someone moaning. He approached the alley with caution. At first, he did not see her, but her leg spasmed and hit against an empty glass bottle, causing Father Tom to look in her direction. Luz was covered in her own blood, urine, and vomit. She lay under a pile of trash, unable to move or speak. Father Tom gasped when he saw her. He bent down and placed his ear to her swollen and bruised face to see if she was breathing. Her breath was shallow, but she was alive.

"No. Please, father, leave me be. I'm dead already. I beg you," Luz barely croaked her words. He carefully gathered her into his arms and took her to the only one he knew could help her.

"I'm sorry, but I can't do that, Lass."

When Father Tom got to Rosario's house, he called out to her.

"Rosario. It's me, Tom. Please open the door." Rosario opened the door and saw Luz lying limp in Father Tom's arms.

"Ay, Madre de Dios. Is she alive?" She rushed him inside and motioned for him to lay Luz on her bed.

"She was conscious for a few seconds when I found her. I think she's still breathing."

Rosario hurried to the kitchen to boil water and find towels. Then she gathered dried mint and Marigold petals from the cupboard to make tea for susto, along with comfrey and arnica to make a salve for her wounds. Rosario returned with a bowl of water and several towels.

"Thank you for bringing her to me, Tom. I thought she was dead. It's a miracle. You should go, Father. I will take it from here. Please stop by Leticia's house and tell her Luz is here and to bring the women by in the morning."

"Are you sure? I can stay here and pray at least."

"The kind of prayer she needs, you cannot offer her, Father. Now, please leave us so I can tend to her wounds. This will be a long journey back for her, and that is if she decides to return."

"Very well. I will do as you ask, but if you need me for anything, please don't hesitate to call on me. You know where to find me."

"No, Father, I will not do that. I cannot risk the soldiers learning that Luz is still alive." Rosario removed what was left of Luz's clothing. She washed her wounds with Arnica water, then she bathed her and dried her, speaking gently to her in a sweet, sing-song voice.

"You can come home now, Luzita. You're safe now. I'm here, and I won't let anything happen to you ever again. Come back to me. I promise you I'm going to take us far away from here. I don't know how, but I promise you I will do it. I swear this on my life." Then Rosario gently lifted Luz and moved behind her, wiping her brow with a cold compress. Luz was burning up, incoherent, suspended between life and death.

Rosario prayed to La Llorona.

"Ay Diosa de lágrimas sagradas, goddess of sacred tears, bring Luz back to me. There is something you should know. I love this woman. I fell in love with her the moment I watched her walk around the circle when we were on the mountain. Her prayers were fierce, and the light around her bright. Yes, I know she is too stubborn for her own good, but it comes from a place of love. If you bring her back to me, I promise we will make a good life together. She doesn't know it yet, but she will love me, too." Rosario continued her vigil through the night, alternating between conversation and prayer. She fed her teaspoons of ginger-lemon tea to cool her fever and rubbed a salve of comfrey and arnica into the open wounds, where she had been bitten and scratched. The sight of Luz unconscious, broken, and bruised cut Rosario to her heart.

The next morning, Leticia arrived with the other women who had also been at the ritual. They were enraged at what happened to Luz, and they knew it could have easily been any one of them. She survived. She was alive. Barely, but alive, nonetheless. They had to bring her soul back from the underworld. They knew what needed to be done. A few minutes later, Tía Marta arrived with sacred anointing oils of copal and palo santo, bunches of Marigolds and Calla Lilies from her garden, along with a ball of red cotton thread. She moved briskly through the small house until she found Luz. When she saw her lying pale and lifeless on the bed, she fell on the bed beside her, sobbing.

"Ay mija, discúlpame, mi amor. I should never have let you go out that night. But I'm here now. I brought Leticia, Ramona, Lila, Madalena, Blanca, Jesucita with me, and Rosario is here, of course. This is her home. She's been taking good care of you. Don't you worry about anything. We are going to bring you home." Leticia made a circle of blue cornmeal around the bed for protection. Tía Marta placed the Marigolds around Luz's body. Marigolds, tiny suns to light the way for her soul to return. She fanned out four blooms at the top of her head and did the same at her feet. She pulled the blooms from their stems and placed four of them on the center of her chest and three on her womb in the shape of a downward triangle. Rosario cleared the table beside the bed and placed the candles, copal, red thread, and Tía Marta's oils on the table, near the statue of Tonantzin-Guadalupe. She filled a vase of Calla Lilies, for the power of resurrection and to give Luz strength to make the long journey home.

"Rosario, mija," Tía Marta cajoled. "You sit behind Luz and hold her close. She needs a thread of love to hold onto." Next, Jesusita took the red thread from the table and wrapped it three times around her left wrist, then passed it to Madalena, who then passed it around the circle until all the women were connected by the red thread. Then each woman cut the thread and tied it around the wrist of the woman next to her, grounding the circle for healing. Rosario had dressed Luz in a simple white cotton gown. Tía Marta slid the dress off Luz's shoulders, down to her legs. Then she took her copal oil and rubbed the small glass bottle between her palms to warm it and invite its essence into the room.

"Holy oil of copal, medicine of Mother Earth and of our Ancestors. I call you forth to bring healing and light to your daughter, Luz. Take the filth of the sins placed into her and turn them into light, as light is her true essence." She poured several drops into the palms of her hands and rubbed them together. She fanned the fragrance from the oil in front of Luz's nose and over her face and head. Luz quivered, as if something passed through her.

"Ah, good. She can feel it. It is already working," Tía Marta said. She poured several more drops into her hands, rubbed them together, and began to gently rub the oil onto Luz's bruised belly, then on her heart center. She anointed the center of her brow, the top of her head, her hands, and her feet. The women prayed and keened sweetly, while Rosario held Luz, whispering into her ear.

"You are a daughter of the light, divine and sacred. Nothing anyone does to you can soil your soul. You are perfection, made of love from the One Great Heart of creation. I'm here with you. I will never leave you again." She repeated these words over and over, softly, like a lullaby.

"Rosario, you must be the one to go and find her soul. Your love will bring her back to us." Tía Marta wiped the tears from her eyes. "Rosario, are you willing to do this?"

"Yes. I am the only one who can do it. I'm ready," Rosario said firmly. Tía Marta gazed around the circle at the women, connected by a red thread, love and prayers. The women closed their eyes and began to sway and keen. Tía Marta pulled the white cotton dress up to cover Luz. She placed one hand on her heart and the other on her womb. She felt the essence of the sacred oil begin to move through Luz, bringing life force up from the earth into her body. Rosario lay down beside Luz and held her hand. She closed her eyes and drifted into the words of Tía Marta's prayers.

"I call you forth, blessed goddess of the moon and healing waters. La Llorona, come forth and guide your daughter home." Leticia fanned copal smoke over Rosario and Luz. Rosario fell into the sacred void, her body burst into ribbons of light. Rosario floated and floated, then she fell and landed softly next to Luz, who lay curled up on the ground, hands covering her face, knees tucked to her chest. Rosario looked around and saw that they were in the Celestial Underworld.

⌣

Luz lay just ahead, by the side of the river that flowed between the underworld and the upper world. Luz was curled up on her side, like a child. She slept fitfully, flipping from one side to the other. She cried mewling sounds, lost and trying to find her way home. The sound of the river echoed around her. She prayed that death had finally taken her, and if this was where she would dwell, eternally, then she was grateful for it. She could not feel her body, yet she was cold and trembling. If she no longer had a body, then she would be glad. She could still smell the stench of trash. She breathed in the darkness around her and curled her body into yet a smaller ball of nothing. Rosario went to sit beside her, gathering her and laying her head on her lap. Then Luz heard someone weeping. She knew she would come for her, yet she had prayed that she wouldn't.

La Llorona sat on her haunches at the edge of the river. She flashed her red rebozo above her head, illuminating the space around them. The walls shimmered in golden light. The celestial underworld was her home, el río abajo río, the river beneath the river. The place where the soul descends when it has been separated from the flesh, lost, frightened—susto. Luz's sacred shawl, once strong and full of light, was now polluted by men who used her body as a receptacle for their filth and rage. La Llorona walked over to where Luz lay with Rosario and touched her hand to her face.

"I am here with you, Mija. I promised I would not forget you, Patli, and here we are once again. But this time you will live." Then she picked up Luz from Rosario's lap and carried her limp body into the clear azure river that flowed through the underworld. She moved her body back and forth through the water, whispering to her in a soothing voice.

"This is not who you are. This filth does not belong to you." She picked up an obsidian shard from the edge of the river and used it to softly scrape away the residue on Luz's body and sacred shawl. La Llorona began to weep, then her weeping turned into wailing,

"Oh, my beloved daughter. My sweet, sweet child." La Llorona cleaned the sin that leached into Luz's womb. She placed her hands upon Luz's belly and sang, prayed, and chanted. The frequency of her song compelled the sin out of Luz's womb. La Llorona caught the residue in her hands, violet light streamed from her fingers, transmuting the residue into light. Luz curled herself up into the goddess's sacred shawl, allowing herself to be enfolded in her cobalt field of light.

"Hey ya na ho. Hey ya na ho. A ye a ye hare, hare, yo no, yo na. You are made of light, a divine child, my daughter. Not even this great sin will destroy you." La Llorona continued to wade Luz slowly back and forth in the river, cleansing the darkness and releasing the terror from her womb. Then, she carried Luz out of the river and over to a large mesa, made from the trunk of an ancient Cottonwood tree. She lay her down and placed boughs of Jasmine and Lavender around her. She lit copal and blew the smoke across Luz's body.

"It is done. Come back into your body." Luz shivered and let out a long moan as her soul returned to the center of her being. Rosario walked over to the table where Luz lay. She stood beside her and placed the palm of her hand across Luz's brow.

"I will take her home, Madrecita."

"You must ask her permission."

"I want to take you home, Luzita. Even if you do not feel the same as I do, I will stay with you and keep you safe. I love you, Luz. Return with me, back to the living." Luz opened her eyes briefly and nodded. Then the goddess cupped the palms of her hands and blew the breath of life into Luz's heart center, and one more breath into the top of her head.

"Return now, mija. Return home to your body. You still have much to live for and so many to help. I bless you. Return, return, return." Luz drifted through a foggy gray mist. Her body heavy, and her mind still haunted by images of what was done to her. She had heard stories of women being taken and raped. Now she understood it in a way she never imagined she would be able to. The fog began to clear, and she found herself in the middle of a lush grove of trees. Luz looked up and allowed the sun to warm her face. She could hear Rosario calling to her in the distance. Suddenly, Luz was surrounded by a soft golden light, and a gust of wind blew her soul back into her body. Luz slept fitfully for three more days before she woke to find Rosario lying carefully beside her.

"Rosario, how long have I been gone?" Words barely croaked from her mouth.

"It's been five days since Tom brought you here." Luz reached out and cupped Rosario's cheek in her hand.

"Father Tom. Yes, I remember. Then, I was lost, and I could not find my way back. Then you and Mi Divina were there. I remember." Luz's voice was hoarse; her swollen jaw and face prevented her from speaking clearly. Rosario adjusted her pillows so she could sit up a bit. As she tried to sit up in bed, she felt like shards of glass were scraping her cervix. Her womb began to spasm, and Rosario could see the pain on her face.

"Rosario, something is between my legs. What is it? Take it out!" She struggled to reach for it, but she could not yet move.

"It's a poultice soaked in herbs that Leticia made to prevent infection. I'll remove it for you. Please allow me, Luz." Rosario pulled the covers and lifted Luz's gown. She heard Luz gasp when she saw the blackened bruises and cuts on her inner thighs.

"It's alright, Luzita. You're safe now. Breathe. Okay, I'm going to remove the poultice now." Rosario carefully moved her hand towards Luz's thighs.

"I'm going to place my hand on your thigh first. You let me know if I can keep going." When Luz felt Rosario's hand on her thigh, she began to tremble.

"Just do it. Get it out of there." She shouted, but didn't mean to. Luz knew she was safe, but it was as if the terror she experienced still leaked from her womb.

"You're going to have to spread your legs a little bit, so I can remove it." Luz spread her legs as much as she could, then closed her eyes and held her breath. Rosario reached down to remove the poultice, but as soon as Luz felt her hand, she began to scream.

"No. Don't. Please stop, stop, stop. Don't touch me."

"Open your eyes. It's me, Rosario. I'm not going to hurt, mi amor. Look at me. I'm going to remove the poultice now, okay?" Luz opened her eyes and looked into Rosario's eyes. When she saw the tenderness in Rosario's eyes, she exhaled and nodded for Rosario to proceed. Rosario removed the cloth and tossed it on the floor. She did not want Luz to see the blood.

"Lettie has been coming every day to make sure you didn't develop an infection. She is a wonderful midwife and healer." Rosario sat in the chair and took a washcloth from a bowl of cool water on the nightstand and placed it across Luz's forehead.

"I'm sorry I yelled at you. Please forgive me."

"Shhh. Try to rest now. You're still very weak, and you have a fever. I'm going to make you some tea to bring your fever down. Do you think you can drink a little?"

Luz nodded. "Actually, I'm a little hungry."

"Ah. That's a good sign. How about a little soup? Your tía brought over some chicken bone broth yesterday. I guess she thought you would be awake today, and she was right."

"That sounds good. Gracias." Rosario smiled and kissed her on the top of her head.

"You should try not to talk anymore. Your throat is red and swollen." She tried not to stare at the bruises around Luz's neck.

"I'll be right back with soup and a cup of tea. You just rest."

Luz looked around the room. Her vision was different. She saw a soft, light blue shimmer around everything, and the colors were brighter; they seemed almost liquid. Rosario went to the kitchen, took the pot of broth out of the refrigerator, and put it on the stove to heat. She took down a bowl from the cabinet when, suddenly, she was overcome with tears of gratitude.

"Gracias. Gracias, Senora," she said out loud to La Llorona, to her Ancestors, to the Universe, and to anyone else who helped bring Luz back to her. She knew Luz still had a long recovery ahead of her, and she also knew that they could not stay in Guatemala. It was not safe. If El Perro learned that Luz was alive, he would certainly come for her. She called Tía Marta to let her know Luz was awake and asked her to come the next day to sit with her while she went to see Father Tom. Marta wanted to come right then, but it was dark and dangerous. Rosario talked her into waiting until morning. When Tía Marta saw Luz awake and sitting up in bed, she burst into tears of joy.

"Oh, Mija. Gracias a La Virgen you are awake. I want to hug you so much, but I know you must be in pain."

Luz half-smiled and patted the bed for Marta to come sit next to her. Marta looked into Luz's eyes and saw the eyes of death and knowing, the eyes of someone who traveled to the underworld and returned. She understood that Luz would now be destined to walk between the worlds—a blessing and a burden. Luz was now a true daughter of La Llorona; she would never be the same. Marta spoke soothing words of comfort and held Luz's hand until she fell asleep. She was grateful to sit with her and watch her sleep. She pulled her rosary out of her pocket. She always carried it with her because it was a wedding gift from her husband. She had not prayed a single word since her family was murdered, and now, she could not find words to pray. She held her rosary in silence, filled with gratitude that Luz was alive.

◡

Rosario found Father Tom in the center of town, passing out bags of rice and beans to the people. Most of the people had been afraid to return to their homes after the soldiers had killed their neighbors or one of their own. They accepted the sacks and carried them up into the hills, or some other unknown place, where they prayed they would not be discovered.

"Hello, Father Tom. I came to let you know that our friend is awake and doing better than I expected." Rosario did not dare to utter Luz's name for fear someone would overhear. "That day you brought her to me, you said you would help us. Well, we need your help. We need to leave here. Do you understand? Can you help us?" Rosario wiped at her tears before they fell. He saw the desperation in her eyes and placed his hand on her shoulder.

"Rosario, I will do everything I can to help you both. But we will need to move quickly. I have helped others in this way, but you will have to trust me. Can you do that? I give you my word that I will not let anything happen to either of you." Rosario felt his words resonate in her heart, and she knew she could trust him.

"Yes, I will trust you for both of us. She is still very weak, so we need to be very careful."

"I understand completely. Can you be ready to move in three days?"

"If that's all the time we have, then we will be ready."

"Good. I will come in a car with Sister Teresa. She has helped me in the past. We'll come as soon as it is dark."

"We will be ready. Thank you, Father."

"Please, just call me Tom." Rosario nodded and smiled, then headed back to her house. When Rosario arrived home, she was happy to see Luz sitting up in bed. Tía Marta held a bowl of soup for Luz to sip. Rosario gave her a big smile and tried not to show her sadness at the deep bruises and cuts still visible on Luz's face. When Luz saw Rosario, her face lit up, and she smiled as much as she was able.

"Our girl ate well today. It's a good sign, no?" Tía Marta kissed them both on the forehead and said she would be back the next morning to check on Luz. Rosario reminded her that she must not tell anyone that Luz is alive.

"You know she cannot stay here. Father Tom agreed to help us. We're leaving in three days. You must come with us."

"I cannot go with you. My life is here, where my husband and my children's bones are. I live for the day I will find them and lay them to rest on holy ground."

"But it will be very dangerous if you stay here," Rosario said, hugging her.

"There is nothing more they can do to me, except kill me, and when that day comes, I will welcome it. Now, you two must go and begin a new life together. I see the love between you. It is a good thing. Life is uncertain, and you must hold on to love when you find it."

"I don't like your decision, and Luz will not be happy about it either, but I understand." Rosario walked Marta to the door and told her to come back in three days and to bring a change of clothes for Luz. Rosario closed the door and returned to her bedroom, where Luz was asleep, her arms flailing as if she were fighting off an attacker.

"No. Stop. Get away from me," Luz cried. Rosario rushed to her side and placed a cool cloth on her forehead. She gently brushed her cheek.

"Shhh, mi amor. You're safe now. I'm here, and I won't let anyone hurt you ever again. Sleep sweetly now. Rest now." Rosario lay down carefully beside Luz, but she herself could not sleep. She lay awake most of the night watching over Luz, listening to the sound of her breathing. She was afraid that if she closed her eyes, she would wake up to realize that it was just a dream, and that Luz was not alive. When the light of dawn came through the bedroom window, Rosario finally slept for a few hours. She woke to the sound of Luz calling her name. When she opened her eyes, her heart swelled with joy to see Luz smiling at her.

"Good morning, mi amor. Is it alright that I call you that? This may sound strange, but I feel that our destinies became bound to one another while we were in the underworld. Now here we are, and I can't remember how it felt not to love you."

"Yes. Exactly. I feel the same way. Like I can't imagine my life without you, and at the same time, I realize we don't know each other very well." Rosario moved closer to Luz and softly caressed her face.

"Besides, we have the rest of our lives to get to know each other.

And speaking of the rest of our lives, you know we cannot stay here. I spoke to Father Tom this morning, and he is coming in two nights to take us out of the country."

"He is? But how? That sounds dangerous. What about Tía Marta? She has to come with us, too. We can't leave her here." Rosario placed the palm of her hand on Luz's heart.

"I asked her to come with us, but she refuses to leave her family. As for Tom, I feel I can trust him. I know he will do as he promised."

"I trust him, too. He's the one who found me. I remember faintly seeing his face. He is a good man, but my Tía..."

"We must respect her decision. I understand how she feels. I would not leave you either."

Luz nodded. "Of course, you're right. We cannot force her."

"You should rest your voice now, mi amor." Rosario kissed Luz softly on the forehead, and the two of them slept a few more hours. Rosario woke first and went about packing some necessities for their trip. Tía Marta had come early that morning while Luz and Rosario were still asleep. She brought a change of clothes for Luz, along with fresh tortillas wrapped with beans and cheese, and a large jar of Manzanita tea. Rosario packed the food, clothes, herbs, salves, and bandages to keep Luz's wounds clean.

Father Tom arrived after dark, just as he promised. He drove up without headlights so no one would see him. He walked to the door and knocked softly. Rosario answered the door.

"We're ready. Tía Marta is not coming with us."

"I figured as much. Now we must hurry." He walked into the bedroom to greet Luz, but they had no time to chat. He pulled out two nuns' habits from a bag and left the room while they changed. Rosario had to help Luz dress. She gently patted makeup on Luz's face to try to make the bruises less noticeable. When they were dressed, Father Tom returned and wrapped Luz in a blanket, then carefully carried her out to the car, with Rosario following quickly behind. Once inside the car, he gave each of them the identification papers of two nuns from his parish. The sisters were happy to sacrifice their papers to save lives, even if it meant they themselves would have difficulty leaving the country. The pictures on the passports looked enough like Luz and Rosario that no one would question them.

"These papers will get us to Chiapas. After that, there is a network of people who will get us to the states. We have a long drive. You should both try to sleep. I'll wake you when we get to San Cristobal. I know your home is in there, Luz, but we will not have time to stop."

"It's fine. I don't want my mother to see me like this. I will write to her when we are settled." They drove through the night and the next day. They passed through two checkpoints on the road, but their papers, along with a wad of quetzals, satisfied the soldiers who were happy to see them leave.

⌣

The sun was setting when they crossed the border into Chiapas. They still had a long drive ahead of them until they reached Father Tom's friend Sister Guadalupe's home. She was a nun and a Nurse Practitioner. She had been a member of the convent at St. Peter's in San Francisco, where she and Tom had met and become good friends. She worked at a free clinic on Valencia Street in the Mission District. Many of the women who came to the clinic were lesbians, and during their visits, they shared some of the ideas of the feminist movement. Sister Guadalupe was interested in anything that supported equal rights for women. She started attending consciousness-raising meetings at the Women's Building once a week. But when she began sharing the ideas of the movement with the other nuns in the convent, Father Flynn quickly intervened and sent her on assignment to serve in a small parish in San Cristobal. He thought living among traditional Catholic women might humble her.

Sister Guadalupe had been living in San Cristobal for the last ten years. She had become a part of the community, and the women loved and trusted her. She provided basic health care and prenatal services to the people of the community. Because of her connections in San Francisco, she became part of an underground network that helped those who needed political asylum relocate to the United States. St. Peter's, along with several other Catholic parishes, was part of the Sanctuary

Movement in San Francisco. Giving sanctuary meant that immigration authorities could not enter the church to detain or deport the people under the auspices of the Church. It was a haven for people escaping Mexico and Central America. The Sisters of St. Peter's worked closely with social service organizations in the Mission District, who helped the newly arrived families to secure housing, medical care, and other necessary social services. They worked with El Centro del Corazon, which had created a true community where women gathered in weekly circles to share their experiences, ask questions, and learn English. El Centro, as everyone called it, also had employment connections. They had a resident artist who offered art classes to children and young people, bringing awareness to the stories of genocide and immigration through her murals.

Father Tom had sent word to Sister Guadalupe that they would be arriving tonight. He had been driving for over twelve hours when they finally arrived at Guadalupe's house. Luz was asleep in the back seat, but Rosario was wide awake. Tom knew that knocking on anyone's door so late at night would cause anxiety and fear, so he called her by the nickname he had for her.

"Lupita. It's me, Tom." She opened the door and immediately threw her arms around him.

"Tom! I'm so happy you made it safely. Where are your friends?" He pointed to the car.

"Please, bring them inside." Rosario woke Luz, and Father Tom carried her inside the house. Sister Guadalupe led them to her bedroom and gestured for Father Tom to lay Luz on her bed.

"Sister Lupita, these are my friends, Rosario and Luz." Rosario hugged Sister Guadalupe—she was so grateful to be out of Guatemala.

"Thank you for having us in your home, Sister. You don't know how much this means to both of us; to know that Luz is safe from…" Rosario could no longer contain the tears she had been holding in since Luz was first captured. Sister Guadalupe held Rosario and let her cry.

"There now. It's alright. You're safe, and as soon as Luz is well enough, the two of you will be on your way to start a new life in San Francisco. Father Tom and I will arrange everything. You don't have to worry about anything. You will be safe. I promise you both on the blood of Christ. And while you're here, mi casa es su casa, so please make yourself at home." Rosario moved out of her embrace and walked to the small bedroom where Tom had taken Luz and laid her on the bed.

"I have no words to express how grateful we are to you, Tom. Thank you." Rosario hugged him and then went to sit beside Luz. Sister Guadalupe interrupted the sudden awkward silence.

"Well, you all must be starving. I have a pork shoulder in the oven. Would you care to give me a hand, Tom?"

"Happy to." Before he left the room, he walked over to Luz and gently took her hand in his. Luz was feeling so much better just knowing she was far away from El Perro and that he could no longer hurt her. She looked at Father Tom.

"Thank you for helping us, Father Tom."

"You're quite welcome. I think we're all past the father title, aren't we? Please just call me Tom." Luz smiled and nodded. Father Tom went into the kitchen to help Sister Lupita prepare dinner.

Luz opened her arms to Rosario, who was standing at the foot of the bed, staring at Luz with a dazed look on her face.

"Come, mi amor." Rosario went to sit on the side of the bed, but Luz pulled her to lie down with her and held her close, smoothing her hair while she cried.

"Shhh. It's alright now. Let it all go. You've been so strong through all of this. We wouldn't be here if it weren't for you." Rosario looked up at Luz and touched her still bruised cheek and kissed her very softly on her lips.

"How do you feel about going to San Francisco?"

"I don't care where we go, as long as we're together. My home is with you, now. I never want us to be apart. Besides, I think it will be exciting to start fresh, somewhere. Tom and Lupita have connections with people there who will help us get political asylum. She says it's a good place for women like us. Now, will you help me get up from this bed? I'm tired of feeling like an invalid."

"Ahh. Your fire is coming back. It's a good sign. But are you sure you can walk?"

"Let's find out." Rosario helped Luz sit up and swing her legs to the side of the bed, so her feet touched the floor. She bent over towards Luz so she could put her arms around her neck.

"Okay. Try to stand up slowly. Put weight on me, while I pull you up." Luz still felt sharp pain in the walls of her uterus when she stood up, but she was determined not to let El Perro take anything more from her, so she moved through the pain.

"Okay. That's good. Now take a few steps." Rosario put her arm around Luz's waist as she took a few steps. Her legs were weak, but she was sure it was because she had been in bed for so long. She wanted her strength back. She didn't want everyone to have to take care of her anymore.

"I'm fine, really. I want to keep walking. Let's go to the kitchen with the others." Rosario did as she asked.

"Okay, but you tell me if you need to stop, or if you're in too much pain."

"I'm fine, Rosario. It feels good to move again. Besides, you can't carry me all the way to San Francisco."

"I will if I have to."

"I'm sure you would." They laughed at their mutual stubbornness.

"We are a match made in heaven." Luz squeezed Rosario.

"Claro que si mi amor." Rosario kissed her on the forehead.

They stepped into the kitchen to find Father Tom and Sister Guadalupe standing near the stove, in the middle of a serious conversation.

"It feels way too serious in here," Luz announced, trying to lighten the mood. Sister Guadalupe and Father Tom turned in surprise to see Luz standing there.

"Good Lord, you're walking." Father Tom rushed over to Luz, but she put her hand out in front of her to stop him.

"Don't. I'm fine, Tom. I need to get my strength back."

"She's right, Tom. The sooner she gets her strength back, the sooner you can leave for San Francisco," Sister Guadalupe said. Rosario helped

Luz sit at the table, then sat down next to her.

"I'm so proud of you." Rosario brought Luz's hand up to her lips and kissed it.

"Okay. What can we do to help?" Luz said.

"There's nothing to be done. I have a pot of pozole on the stove. It will be ready soon." Sister Guadalupe poured the contents from a pot on the stove into a cup and set it on the table in front of Luz.

"Herbal tea to help your body heal."

"Gracias, but I think I've had a lifetime full of tea. What I could really use is a shot of Tequila." The others laughed in surprise.

"I think I can help with that request." Sister Guadalupe went to the cupboard and took a bottle of Agave from the shelf." She poured a shot for each of them. "Agave. Elixir from the Ancestors. Good for the soul. Besides, we have a lot to celebrate." She lifted her glass to make a toast, and the others raised their glass, as well.

"To Luz and Rosario. Bendiciones! Here's to the new life waiting for you in San Francisco." Father Tom drank his shot in one gulp, then slammed it down with joy.

"We'll stay here for a couple more weeks, until you're well enough to travel the distance. I'm coming with you. It will be safer that way. Then I can get you settled and introduce you to the community in the Mission. My home parish, St. Peter's, is there. So many people from Mexico and Central America have found a new home with their help. Besides, I have a surprise for you both once we get there."

Luz's eyes widened at the mention of a surprise. "A surprise? That word makes me nervous, Tom. Will you just tell us what it is?"

"You must know by now that I only want the best for you both. I would do anything for you. You will love my surprise, I promise. Trust me."

Rosario put her arm around Luz's shoulders and gave her a gentle squeeze. Before leaving Guatemala, Tom had written a letter to Bill O'Donnell. He explained Luz and Rosario's situation and asked Bill if they might be able to stay in his flat above the restaurant on 24th Street. He had not yet received a reply, but he knew Bill would want to help in any way he could.

"Of course, we trust you, don't we, Luz?" Rosario said.

"Claro. I trust you, Tom. I think the agave went to my head."

"You need to eat, and you'll be right as rain." Sister Guadalupe put a bowl of pozole with corn tortillas in front of Luz. Then she served the others and sat down to enjoy their meal. Father Tom entertained everyone with stories of Lupita's feminist rebellion in San Francisco.

"This is sabrosa, Sister. Thank you for your generous hospitality and the wonderful food. Suddenly, I'm so sleepy." Rosario stood to help Luz to bed.

"Buenas noches, you two. You'll be on your way before you know it. Duerme con los ángeles," Sister Guadalupe said.

Over the next two weeks, Rosario and Sister Guadalupe worked together to help Luz regain the strength in her hips and legs, where her ligaments had been injured, making it difficult for her to walk. Rosario and Sister Guadalupe also picked local herbs to make a salve to continue to heal the wounds in Luz's vagina and cervix. At the end of the two weeks, Luz felt strong enough to walk on her own. The bruises on her face were barely noticeable, and the swelling in her jaw and left eye were almost completely healed. She was anxious to begin their journey. On their last morning in San Cristobal, Sister Guadalupe woke early and prepared a breakfast of handmade flour tortillas, frijoles y arroz. She spread the rice and beans in several flour tortillas; enough so they wouldn't have to worry about food until they reached Mexico City. When she rolled the last burrito in aluminum foil, Luz walked into the kitchen on her own.

"Sister, you have done so much for us. We can never thank you enough."

"You can thank me by starting your new life with Rosario and loving each other well. There are some women whom I have written to about the two of you. They will contact you after you are both settled. Father Tom has their number. Don't worry, they are gringas, but good friends of mine. They speak Spanish and are very trustworthy. They are also lesbians, so they can help you to understand the culture there in the Mission. It is a very exciting time for gay people."

"Gay people? Is that what they call us? That's a much nicer word than jotas or mariconas, or especially sinvergüenzas. It sounds so harmless and happy. I like it." Just then, Rosario appeared in the doorway of the kitchen.

"What sounds harmless? This I want to hear about."

"Gay. It's what they call us in San Francisco," Luz said.

"Gay? Como feliz? Happy?"

"Yes. Isn't it wonderful?"

"Yes. I would love to feel happy and gay." They couldn't help laughing at the irony of a word that seemed almost ridiculous, compared to their life where thousands had been murdered without reason. It just didn't make sense to them, yet. A few moments later, Father Tom walked through the front door.

"What are we laughing about?"

"We'll tell you in the car," Luz replied.

"It's good to see you both laughing. Are you ready? It's a long drive, so I want to get an early start. Do I smell breakfast, Sister?"

"Yes. But you can eat while you drive. These two are anxious to get on the road."

"Perfect. I've already loaded your bags in the car. So, let's go!" Father Tom felt jovial, as well. He hadn't been sure if this day would ever come. He loved Luz and Rosario like they were his younger sisters. He was determined to give them everything they needed to begin their lives together in San Francisco.

They said their goodbyes, promising Sister Guadalupe that they would write as soon as they were settled. She had come to care for Luz and Rosario in the short time she had known them. She admired their devotion to one another, along with their refusal to let what happened destroy their faith in love.

⌣

Tom drove straight to Mexico City, stopping only to pick up airline tickets from a contact in the city. Luz slept on the plane, while Rosario gazed out the window, transfixed by the clouds and the clear blue sky. Up until that point, she had not been outside of Guatemala.

They were free.

Five hours later, they landed at San Francisco International Airport, and Luz and Rosario began their new life. Father Tom guided them outside the airport, where a car was waiting to drive them to the convent to spend the night. The next morning, Father Tom went to visit Bill. He walked into O'Donnell's to find Bill washing glasses behind the bar.

"What does a fella have to do to get a drink around here?" Bill turned around and saw Tom standing at the bar. He ran to the front of the bar and gave his old friend a bear hug.

"Tom! It's good to see ya, my friend. When did you get back? How was your trip? Tell me all about it." Bill poured two cups of black coffee and sat beside Tom.

"It's a big story to tell, Bill. It was all in the letter I wrote to you. I don't really want to rehash it all, except to say that I'm grateful to the Lord for bringing Luz and Rosario safely here."

"Well, be sure to include a little gratitude for your love and care for those two women. They are lucky to know you."

"So, will it be alright for them to stay in your flat?"

"Well, sure. It will be good to have some life in the building again. Do you have a job for them yet?"

"No. We just arrived last night. I was hoping someone at El Centro might know of a job for them."

"Can they cook?"

"It just so happens that Rosario is an amazing cook. She makes the best mole I've ever had."

"Maybe they will want to reopen the restaurant? My Ma would be so happy on the other side to know women were running the restaurant. Ask them and let me know what they want to do. Anyway, I have something for you." Bill went into his office, came back with an envelope, and handed it to Tom. Tom opened it and gasped when he read what was inside. It was the deed to the restaurant and the flats above it.

"You can't be serious, Bill. You can't just give your property away like this."

Bill sighed and took a sip of his coffee. "I can, and I must. I'm sick, Tom. I've got cancer in my liver. The doctor says I've got less than six months. I can't think of anything better to do with that property than to give it to Luz and Rosario, who will bring life and love into that old building. I don't have anyone else to leave it to." Tom looked closely at his friend and noticed that he had lost quite a bit of weight, and the whites of his eyes were yellow.

"Oh, Bill. It's a bit of a shock. I'm so sorry, my friend. I wish I could have been here for you," Tom said, wiping his tears.

"Well, then, you wouldn't have been able to help your friends now, would you?"

"I suppose you're right. God has his own plans. Thank you for this, Bill. You will be helping to improve their lives a hundred-fold."

"I took the liberty of asking some of the sisters to clean and prepare the third-floor flat for them. They were overjoyed to help. They said they would bring some furniture from the rectory storage to make it cozy for them. So, I'm not sure how good nuns are at decorating, but you'll find out soon enough." Tom laughed and imagined the flat filled with only a twin bed and a crucifix on the wall.

"Off with you then. Let me know if they want to open the restaurant, and I'll contact my lawyer to get all the paperwork in order. But there's just one condition. I want to remain anonymous."

"But why? I don't understand. They will be so grateful to you."

"That's exactly why. I don't want them to feel beholden to me."

"Very well, then. Anonymous you will be, but I will always be grateful for this, but most of all for your friendship. I'll come by and tell you how it went tonight, my friend." He hugged Bill for a long time, then left to meet Rosaro and Luz. When he got to the rectory, he called the convent and asked one of the sisters to tell Luz and Rosario to meet him in front of the church. Thirty minutes later, they appeared with bright smiles across their faces. One of the sisters had lent Luz a cane to help her walk. Father Tom was filled with mixed emotions. He could not fully contemplate a world without Bill in it. He would pray on it later, but for now, he was going to fully enjoy the morning with Luz and Rosario. He gave them each a hug.

"Are you hungry? I know this great place where we can get breakfast right there on the corner." He pointed to La Victoria's Panaderia.

"Sounds perfect," Luz squealed with delight. They decided on breakfast burritos to go, so they could eat while they walked down 24th Street. Luz and Rosario savored their food as they took in the bright colors of the murals that lined the streets, the aroma of food, and the music that blared out of the windows of the passing cars. As they crossed 24th and Capp Street, Tom stopped to wave at a woman on the other side of the street. She was standing behind a table piled high with brightly colored textiles. She had copal burning in a black ceramic copalera. She was dressed in the traditional huipil and cinta from Guatemala City. Rosario recognized the pattern of her skirt as being from her same village and laughed out loud with joy.

"That's Milagro. I want you to meet her. Hola, Milagro, Buen Dia." Father Tom waved at her as they approached her table. Rosario did not wait for an introduction but began talking to Milagro in K´iche´, their indigenous language. The two women hugged, and Rosario introduced Luz as her wife. Milagro greeted Luz with a hug and kiss on the cheek.

"My sister. Welcome to your new home." The women chatted like old friends, while Father Tom watched with joy.

"Hola, Padre." Spanish was not Milagro's first language, but she was learning it from some of the women who met in the mornings at El Centro, where they gathered to crochet or embroider after they sent their children to school.

"Hola, Querida Milagro." Father Tom and Milagro had become good friends over the last three years after he helped her escape from Guatemala. She played a crucial role in helping newly arrived families integrate into this new culture. Father Tom promised he would bring Luz and Rosario to El Centro in a few days, after they had a chance to settle into their new home. Luz heard him say "new home" and wondered what he meant.

⌣

Father Tom guided the women back across and down the street to the corner of Balmy Alley. There was a vacant storefront with windows that had been whitewashed, so you could not see inside. He took out a key from his pocket and opened one of the two doors on the side of the storefront. It had stairs that went up three flights. Tom offered to carry Luz up the stairs, but she refused. She was determined to regain her strength and independence. She told Rosario and Father Tom to go ahead of her and that she would meet them at the top of the stairs. When she got to the top of the stairs, they were waiting for her. Father Tom unlocked the door.

"This is your new home, my friends," he said.

Luz and Rosario stepped inside. They were expecting a room or two, at the most, but this flat was completely furnished with Spanish-style antique dark wood furniture. The room was filled with textiles from Guatemala and Chiapas. Milagro had helped to make the flat feel like a home. Luz and Rosario looked around the flat. They could not believe their eyes.

"I hope you like it. Sister Ana María and some of the other nuns worked together to make it cozy for you. I'm certain the textiles are from Milagro."

Luz and Rosario were speechless. Tears flowed down both of their faces.

"This is where we are going to live? It's so beautiful and so big. I've never seen any place like this," Rosario exclaimed.

"Let me show you the rest of it." Father Tom was giddy as he showed them the rest of the flat that consisted of the living room, a large kitchen with a big open dining room, tall windows in each room, a fireplace in the living room and bedroom, and a back porch that led down to a garden, with an old Redwood tree in the middle of the yard.

"The yard is so big. Perhaps I can plant some herbs?" Rosario asked.

"Absolutely. There is one more thing I want to show you, and I think you will be pleased. Okay?" Luz and Rosario could not imagine what more he could possibly show them, but they were excited to find out. Father Tom led them through a narrow path, back out to the front of the building. When they were outside, Father Tom opened the door to the storefront. They stepped inside and gasped in delight. Inside was a small restaurant and bar.

"Is this where we will work?" Rosario still could not grasp everything that was happening.

"You may do anything you like with this place. Although I was hoping you would like to open a restaurant. It's a bit self-serving on my part, I'm afraid. I would love to be able to enjoy your magical cooking, Rosario, and I know folks around here would love it, too. Something you should know about this city is that people love to eat!" Father Tom laughed.

"That would be a dream come true. This is all like a dream. A wonderful dream."

"I think the two of you are due for a magical dream after all you've been through."

"How will we ever repay you, Tom?" Luz asked.

"Why, with food of course, and with your happiness. That's all I want." Tom took the envelope with the deed out of his coat pocket. He took the papers out and showed the women. They looked at it with a puzzled look on their faces.

"This is the deed to this building and the restaurant. It's yours if you want it. You can open the restaurant and have your own business. It is a gift from someone who wishes to remain anonymous. This property has been in their family, but now there is no one left to leave it to. The only thing the owner of the building wants in return is your happiness. He is an old friend of mine and I told him your story. He was very happy to know it will go to both of you, and that the legacy of the family restaurant will go on." Tom handed Luz another envelope. She gasped when she saw it contained a large sum of cash.

"It's just to help you get on your feet and to get what you need to reopen the restaurant." Rosario and Luz were stunned at the miracle of this gift.

"Tom, I don't know if we can accept such a tremendous gift as this," Rosario said.

"Of course you can, and you will. My friend was very clear that he wanted you to have it. If you don't accept it, this building will simply be absorbed by the state, and his family's restaurant will be lost. So, you are giving something back to him. Besides, Rosario, your gift of making healing food is something that should be shared, and Lord knows this community could use healing." Rosario was already dreaming of ways the restaurant could serve the community.

"When you put it that way, we have an obligation to accept and keep your friend's legacy alive. We humbly accept, Tom, and please tell your friend that we will make this restaurant into a place that will honor his family." Luz held Rosario's hand.

"Yes, Tom. Tell your friend that we are eternally grateful, and we will make his ancestor proud."

"Good, then it's settled." He handed them the keys to the building and left to retrieve their belongings from the convent. After Tom left, Rosario jumped up and down and danced around the restaurant. She noticed an old photograph of the family that had owned the restaurant. She picked it up and showed it to Luz.

"Oh my. This is the family. How beautiful. We will leave this photograph on the wall to honor them and this gift. Si?" Luz's heart overflowed at seeing Rosario so happy. Suddenly, Luz was utterly exhausted from all that had happened.

"Rosario, I suddenly feel very tired. I think I should lay down for a bit. Can you help me back upstairs to our new home? Then tomorrow we must make a ceremony and give thanks to La Divina and La Virgencita for this miracle. Even though we don't have copal or candles to make an offering," Luz said as she made her way up the stairs.

"I'm sure our new friend Milagro will have what we need. I will go to see her in the morning," Rosario responded.

"That's a wonderful idea," said Luz.

"Si, mi amor. I love hearing you say, our home. Vamonos, let's go home."

Luz and Rosario spent their first night in their new home. Rosario cradled Luz on her shoulder, careful not to cause her pain, as she was still healing from her injuries. Luz reached up and touched Rosario's cheek, bringing her face close to hers. Rosario kissed her softly at first, then she felt her desire for Luz ignite like a flame from deep within her, but she pulled away.

"I don't want to hurt you, amor," said Rosario.

"I'm not broken anymore. I'm just very sore. Let's just kiss and cuddle for now."

"That sounds good to me. Also, I was thinking, what should we name our restaurant?"

Luz thought about it for a moment. "It seems there is only one fitting name for it. How about Dos Almas, two souls? To honor the meeting of our souls."

"Oh! I love it. Perfecto!" Rosario said, pulling Luz closer to her.

"Hmm. Where were we?" Luz kissed Rosario.

"No more talking." They kissed tenderly until they fell asleep in each other's arms, and for the first time in months, they slept soundly, without fear.

⌄

SAN FRANCISCO ~ 1981

La Divina had no use for pennies. It was the love from spoken prayers that she craved. Prayers from women who understood that she lived between the visible and unseen world, where whispers of prayers, hopes, and dreams drifted in the plumes of copal smoke; they were sweetness to her soul. Although most of the women called her La Llorona when they prayed, it made no difference to her. She was accustomed to both names. Copper pennies, small containers that held prayers for protection, and precious words of a heart's desire. She was a loving goddess—something not everyone understood or believed about her, so these nightly devotions sated her longing for love and connection.

She stood on the corner of 24th Street and Balmy Alley watching the women as they stopped on their way home from work or from the market. Women of all ages, some carrying bags of groceries, holding the hands of their children, whispering to them what they were about to do. Some of the women could see La Llorona and bowed their heads in respect, crossing themselves as they walked past her. Many of the women believed she had followed them to the United States from their homeland, holding sorrow they could not express.

Stories of La Llorona dressed in a tattered white gown were part of the legend people told about her. But in truth, she loved the vibrant textiles of Chiapas and Oaxaca. On this night, she appeared dressed in a traditional white huipil embroidered with Marigolds and hummingbirds, a bright red rebozo around her shoulders, and a pair of faded blue jeans, which were practical for walking around the city. She wore no shoes, for she had no need of them. Her long black hair hung in two long braids. They were adorned with red yarn, tiny golden bells, two owl feathers, and a fat marigold at the end of each one.

She watched the women walk to the end of the alley. Each woman waited her turn, as if they were participating in an unspoken, collective ceremony; their shared grief became a communal offering. One by one, each woman reached into the pocket of her purse, took out a shiny copper penny, and held the coin between their palms. They crossed themselves, then whispered a prayer, and bent down to carefully place the penny on the edge of the curb. The sun began to set over the hills of Twin Peaks, and the pennies were laid out on both sides of the sidewalk curbs. The sunlight danced hues of orange and yellow from the light of the pennies and the mural of Tonantzin-Guadalupe painted on the wall in the alley. Some of the women lit candles in glass jars, which turned the alley into a kind of permanent shrine. Some nights when the candles burned particularly bright, people said they saw the ghosts of loved ones in the reflection of the flames. Others said they saw angels, or La Virgen de Tonantzin-Guadalupe herself.

La Llorona had no use for these small, material tokens, except for the heart's desires held within them. Women prayed for protection for their families, to find work, but mostly they prayed for the souls of their loved ones. The souls who still wandered, thousands of miles away, their bodies that were burned, beaten, then thrown in a trench, along with hundreds of other bodies. Disposed without love or blessing. The families lived with the emptiness that haunted them, a secret shared but never spoken of. There was no need, for they had learned the commandment of never speaking of those who had disappeared. They rose early each morning and went to bed late at night, stretching the days out so they would not feel the ache of their loss.

No one dared to disturb the rows of pennies, no matter how desperate their need. Everyone knew who they were for and what they represented, even if they did not speak her name. The Goddess walked up and down the alley collecting the copper coins. She held each one in her hands just long enough to breathe in the heartache it contained, then she kissed each penny and placed them in the pockets of her huipil. After she had collected all the pennies, she placed her hands on the center of her chest and breathed deeply, and anger and sorrow rose from her belly. She coughed and coughed until she vomited a small pool of brown sticky substance and spat it on the ground.

La Llorona moved her vision inward and saw images that each woman held in the luminous threads of their sacred shawl, now torn, in need of mending. Sorrow overcame her, and she began to wail. She rubbed the tattoos of Monarch butterflies on her forearms, warming her skin to invoke their presence. They flew out from her arms, fluttering around her, following the delicate movement she made with her fingers as she wove and mended the luminous threads of the women. The butterflies infused the threads with light and love from the Ancient Ones. As she wove the luminous threads, she felt the pain of their loss and sorrow, as well as the hope of their dreams. Then she sang a song to seal the threads with golden light.

"Oh ley, oh ley, ah na na na oh way. A shaaa eesh eesh ahhh, oh ley, oh ley na na." The song transmuted the sorrow from the pennies into light. The sound of her weeping trailed on the edge of the fog as it moved through the Mission. Women crossed themselves and whispered, "Gracias, Senora."

⌣

La Llorona wiped her tears on the hem of her huipil and made her way around the corner to Dos Almas. She stepped inside and turned to the left of the doorway, where there stood a four-tiered altar made of shelves attached to the wall by brackets. On the highest shelf, there was a large statue of Tonantzin-Guadalupe carved from basalt wood and hand-painted by an artist from Chiapas. Fresh red roses and several white candles surrounded the statue. The other shelves of the altar had several vases filled with dozens of roses in every color, along with prayers written on paper, folded up into small squares. On the bottom shelf were plates of mole, frijoles, arroz, cups of coffee, cigars, cigarettes, and, of course, a shot glass filled with Agave. On the last shelf, there was a large red ceramic bowl filled with pennies, dollar bills, and other coins that sat on the floor beneath the altar with tips from the patrons. Llorona took the pennies from her pockets and added them to the bowl. Rosario used the money to make large pots of arroz, frijoles, and menudo each evening for anyone who was hungry but had no money. There was a plague of alcoholism and heroin addiction that was visible as you walked along 24th Street; men and women, their faces swollen or emaciated from too many drugs and not enough food. Most people knew that the money would go towards buying more alcohol or drugs and did not want to contribute. Instead, they pointed them to Dos Almas, where they could have a delicious, hot meal. Warm food, cafecito, and a place to share stories and laughter was a welcome event for those who otherwise felt invisible.

La Llorona sat at her usual table next to the altar, in front of the French windows that opened towards the street. The aroma of her favorite chocolate, mole, and tortillas de maíz hechas a mano made her mouth water. She looked around the restaurant and watched as families immersed in conversations and laughter ate the food infused with loving intentions that Rosario prepared. Just then, Luz emerged from the kitchen with a tray of Mole Poblano made with extra chocolate, just the way La Llorona loved it, along with two cafecitos, two shot glasses, and a bottle of La Adelita tequila, which she kept on hand especially for the goddess. No one thought it strange that Luz sat alone at a table set for two and talked with someone only she could see. The community that frequented Dos Almas knew Luz as a wise curandera who lived between the worlds of the seen and unseen.

Luz set the food on the table, sat across from the goddess, and watched as she inhaled the aroma of the food, ingesting the fragrance and color, as spirits do. Luz poured a shot of tequila for each of them, and La Llorona lifted her glass and drank the Tequila in one gulp.

"Ahh. Qué sabrosa. There are times I wish I was human, then I could eat, but at least I can drink." The two women laughed as Luz poured them another shot and La Llorona made a toast.

"¡Qué viva la vida!" She smiled as Luz lifted her glass in return.

"It's a full moon tonight, Madrecita. You will be busy this evening."

"Ah sí. As I am every night, mija, but this full moon so close to El Día de los Muertos will be especially busy, I think."

They sat quietly, simply happy to be together. La Llorona took a last sip of her cafecito, then stood up to leave. Luz stood and kissed her on the cheek.

"I will hold you in prayer tonight, Madrecita."

"I know you will, mi amor. Gracias. Please give my gratitude to Rosario por la rica comida."

"De nada, Mi Divina. Gracias a ti siempre."

⌣

When Aurora walked into La Tazita Café, she found Sofie sitting at a corner table all the way in the back of the café. Sofie had ordered Aurora a cappuccino and was sitting with her nose buried in a book while she waited. Aurora sat down quietly, waiting to see how long it would take for her to notice she was sitting there.

"Ahem," Aurora said. Sofie looked up abruptly from her book.

"Hey, girl. I didn't hear you sit down. I swear, you walk like a cat."

"What are you reading now?" asked Aurora.

"*The House of The Spirits*, by Isabel Allende. She's a Chilean writer I recently discovered. You would like it. The lead character is very psychic, and she can see ghosts. It's a really good read, so far."

"No thanks. That's a little too close to home for me. Speaking of seeing ghosts, I'm going to visit my mom after we have coffee. I'm not looking forward to it, but I need to check in on her and make sure she's taking her meds and eating enough."

"Do you want me to go with you?"

"No. But thanks. I'm used to it by now. I don't remember her any other way. She had a nervous breakdown right after I started college, remember? Now she lives like a ghost, not fully in this world, with a part of her dancing in an imaginary world of angels and saints. All she cares about is going to mass, so she can hear the voices she believes are guiding her. Maybe she is looking for forgiveness. I don't know, Sofie. I don't have the energy to try and understand her, and I don't have forgiveness to offer her. Maybe someday, but not now."

"You know, Aurora, it hasn't been easy for our mothers. They didn't have the mental health resources that we have today. The doctors used to just dope them up, lock them up, or worse, give them a lobotomy if the doctors believed it would calm them down. If we could only guide these women back to the healing ways of our Ancestors. I know things would be different for them."

"You're right about that, Sofie. My mom's been addicted to valium and alcohol since before I was born. All she needs to do is tell her doctor that she feels nervous or can't sleep, and he'll write her a prescription for pills to calm her down or pills to bring her up. It's sad. Yet, a part of me is angry with her because I don't know exactly what she has gone through to cause her to lose touch with reality. I've asked her, but she won't talk to me about it. She says she doesn't want to dwell on the past. It scares me, too, because I don't want to end up like her, Sofie."

"You won't, Aurora. I won't let that happen. I promise."

Aurora took a sip of her cafecito and pulled her notebook out of her purse. "Speaking of crazy. Umm, there's something I want to show you, Sofie." She opened the notebook and placed it in front of Sofie to read.

~~~

October 28, 1981

Aurora,

How long are you going to keep us all locked up here? I hate you! You're a coward. The little ones are suffering, and you're just up there living your life. Help us. Get us out of this hell we are trapped in because of you. You have to remember what happened!

—M.

~~~

Sofie read the passage and looked up at Aurora, her brows knitted in concern.

"I don't understand. What is this?"

"I don't know. I went to write an idea about a painting in my notebook, and I found this. It's my writing, Sofie. I mean, what the hell is that? Am I crazy like my mother?"

"We don't know what this means. Maybe it's your subconscious trying to communicate something important to you? Or maybe you were drunk when you wrote it and just don't remember. I don't know what this means, either, but we shouldn't jump to any conclusions until you fully understand this."

"I don't know, Sofie. I just needed to show it to you. Please promise me that if I lose it, you won't let them lock me up."

"I promise you. I won't let anyone lock you up."

"Thank you, amiga. I'm going to hold you to it. Well, I should get going. If I'm late, my mom will start talking to herself in the street."

Sofie got up from the table and gave Aurora a big hug. "Love you, girl, and don't worry—we'll figure this out."

"Love you, too. Thanks for listening. Let's get together for dinner at your house later this week, okay?"

"Is that your way of asking me to make you dinner?"

"Enchiladas, please." Aurora walked out of the café. She checked her watch and realized that Dolores was still at St. Peter's church. If she hurried, she could meet her outside after mass. She walked down 24th Street and stopped in at La Victoria's panaderia on Alabama Street to buy some pan dulce for her mom. Dolores often forgot to eat, but she could not resist pan dulce and would often finish two or three pieces with a cup of coffee. She had gotten so thin from her diet of Coca-Cola, cigarettes, vodka, and valium that it took a minute for Aurora to recognize her when she walked out of the church. Dolores was wearing a black lace veil that covered her face, and she still had her rosary wrapped around the fingers of one hand. When she saw Aurora at the foot of the church stairs, her face lit up. Aurora was grateful for the smile, because she never knew what mood her mother would be in when she visited. She fluctuated between rapid non-stop talking, the inability to get out of bed, or sitting in her chair for hours, chain-smoking, and staring out of the front window. Dolores hurried down the steps and gave Aurora a big hug. Aurora froze until her mother released her from her embrace. Dolores saw the white paper bag filled with pan dulce and smiled.

"Hola, mija. I'm so happy to see you, and I see you bought some pan dulce for me. Gracias, mija. You know how I love them. Let's go home, and I'll make a pot of coffee. Si?"

"Sure, Mom. That sounds good." The two of them walked down 24th Street to Dolores' flat. Aurora listened as her mother told her about the sermon Father Flynn gave about love and forgiveness, and how she felt it was meant just for her, because she is such a forgiving person. Aurora bit her lip and politely nodded. Once inside the apartment, Aurora set the bag on the kitchen table, made a pot of coffee, and put a small pot of milk on the stove to steam.

"Mija, when are you getting married? You're almost 30, and the older you get, the harder it will be to find a good man to marry. I don't want you to be alone, like me."

What do you know about marrying a good man? Aurora thought to herself. "I don't want to get married, Ma. You got married, and what good did it do you? Besides, you have never told me why my papi left us. Why didn't he take me with him? Why did he leave me with you, Ma?" Aurora could feel a blaze of anger rising from her stomach into her chest. She crossed her arms as she waited for Dolores to answer. But she only stared at the floor and shook her head. She dabbed the corners of her eyes with her white lace handkerchief. Aurora hated it when her mother pulled out her handkerchief, especially this one with tiny red crosses embroidered on the edges. It made her seem like a pious martyr.

"There are some things better left forgotten, Aurora. I'm too old now to think about the past. You don't know what I have been through. I just want to forget it all." Aurora knew it was pointless, but she couldn't hold in her anger.

"Well, good for you, Ma. I'm glad you have the luxury of forgetting the past. But I can't forget it. It's here," Aurora slapped the palm of her hand against her chest. She was shaking, and tears were rolling down her cheeks. Dolores looked up at Aurora with no expression on her face.

"You were always such an angry child, Aurora. I have never understood why. I tried to give you everything I could." Dolores returned her gaze to the window, as she so often did when Aurora was a child. She would carry on conversations for hours with someone no one else could see.

"Your idea of giving me everything is something I could have done without." The smell of stale tobacco and alcohol that infused the air started to close in on Aurora.

"I'll be here tomorrow morning to take you to see Dr. Velazquez. You have an appointment at 9:00 a.m. He needs to check your meds to make sure they are still working."

"They are not working, because I don't take them anymore. I don't need them. When I take them, I can't hear the voices of the saints, and it makes God angry with me. I get the pills I need from Dr. Hammish." Dolores looked at Aurora, her eyes squinted, her voice harsh.

"Dr. Hammish? But he was my pediatrician. Why is he writing you a prescription? The medication that Dr. Velazquez prescribes to you is so you won't hear voices, Ma." Aurora watched Dolores' eyes shift. They became piercing and dark. She needed to get out of there, but she also needed to make sure her mother was okay. As okay as she could be. Dolores continued to ramble.

"Dr. Hammish is the only one who understands me and my condition. Besides, I talked with Father Rivera about the voices, and he told me that there have been many people throughout history who have heard the voices of angels and saints."

"You don't really think you are like the saints, do you, Ma?" Aurora ran her fingers through her long black hair. She felt an old, thick sickness seep into her stomach. The talk of voices, angels, and saints sucked the air from the room. She felt suffocated by the presence of her mother. She poured Dolores a cup of coffee and set the pan dulce on a plate in front of her.

"I gotta go, Ma. I'll pick you up tomorrow at nine. Make sure you eat something, okay?" Dolores spread her arms, waiting for Aurora to give her a hug and kiss goodbye. Aurora gave her a quick kiss on the forehead, and her mother touched the palm of her hand to Aurora's cheek.

"I love you so, mija." Aurora shrank away from her touch. A touch that had always been unpredictable, usually violent. Aurora pulled away and quickly made her way towards the door.

"You know I love you, mija, don't you?" Dolores called after Aurora in a sweet, childlike voice.

"Yeah, Ma. I know." Aurora waved her hand without turning to look at her mother. When she was finally outside, she could breathe again. She walked over to St. Peter's and sat on the steps. The streets were empty, as they usually were on Sunday afternoons, when most people were home having lunch with their families.

"Damn you, Ma. Damn you!" Aurora said under her breath. She knew it wasn't her mother's fault that she had a mental illness. Dr. Velazquez told her that manic depression could lie dormant until triggered by a traumatic event. Aurora struggled between wanting to know the truth of her mother's trauma and feeling contempt for bringing her into a world where she was sometimes unsure of what was real or imagined. She tried to quell the fear that she would someday end up like her mother. This fear was a secret she held close, guarded in her heart. Yet, she could not deny that she saw ghosts and spirits, too, but she told herself it was just her overactive artistic imagination. Yet, deep inside, she feared the loss of her sanity was inevitable. Aurora hated her mother's god. She remembered when she was five or six and Dolores was in one of her religious moods, she forced Aurora to sit for hours memorizing prayers for catechism: Our Father, Hail Mary, and the Apostles' Creed. Aurora felt nothing when she prayed. But the prayer that she hated most was the one she had to say each night before bed.

"Now I lay me down to sleep. I pray the Lord my soul to keep. If I should die before I wake..." What kind of prayer is that for a child to recite? Sometimes, there were good days. She remembered when Dolores let her try on a pair of her high-heeled shoes and walk around the house carrying one of her matching purses. She would spray some Jean Nate perfume on Aurora's wrists and paint her nails pink.

"Ay, mi princesa, how pretty you look." Dolores would say, as she watched Aurora prance sweetly around the bedroom. The memory of Dolores' face, radiant with approval and love, lived hidden in Aurora's heart like the beautiful dresses in her mother's closet that hung in darkness, never worn.

⌣

Once Aurora left, Dolores began to hear the voices again. But these were not the voices of saints or angels. These were the voices that haunted her with memories of shadows.

"Your daughter hates you, and you deserve to die for what you did to her. You are a dirty, horrible mother. Why are you still alive? What is the point of living? You have never done any good in this world. You should just end it and spare Aurora any more suffering." Dolores pressed her hands to her ears to try to quiet the voices, but it was no use. She grabbed her purse and ran out of the house, slamming the door behind her. She walked briskly down 24th Street towards St. Peter's church. She prayed out loud, sad and angry, screaming at a god who had never truly answered her prayers. As she passed people on the street, they stepped aside as if the voices might be contagious. When she arrived at St. Peter's, the doors were locked. She ran to the rectory and pounded on the door, but no one answered.

"Oh god, please help me! I beg you to take the voices away. Let the angels come. Please, sweet angels, come to me. Tell me everything is going to be alright. Tell me I should go on living, and I will. I promise." The voices continued to taunt Dolores, so she went to the place where she knew someone could help her.

⌣

The crisp Autumn evening breeze moved the fog through the streets of the Mission District. La Llorona wrapped her red rebozo around her tightly and closed her eyes to feel where the sorrow was coming from. It was close. Then she walked down the street and stopped at Balmy Alley, where she heard someone praying. She walked through the fog to the end of the alley, where Dolores was kneeling on the curb in front of the mural of Tonantzin-Guadalupe.

"Blessed Mother, please forgive me for what I am about to do. Please grant me your mercy and do not condemn my soul to hell. This life has been a living hell for me, and I just want to feel peace. Will you grant me this, Holy Mother? Just a little peace?" La Llorona recognized the woman's angry, wounded soul. It had been many years since she had seen her.

"What is your name, my daughter?" La Llorona asked.

"Dolores," the woman answered as she turned to see La Llorona standing behind her. Dolores had not seen her since Aurora was four years old, when she had appeared beneath the branches of a Willow tree in the backyard.

"I didn't think I would ever see you again, after that night," Dolores trembled as she spoke.

"You mean you were hoping you would not see me again."

"No. I'm glad to see you now. I'm ready. I am done with this life. Please take me. I want to die." La Llorona let out a heavy sigh and shook her head sadly.

"So, you imagine that I am death, and I am here to take your life from you? This is not who I am. I am here to restore your soul and to help you want to live. This life is a gift. Do you not understand this, Dolores?"

"My life has not been a gift. You most of all should know this. Look into my sacred shawl, as I know you can, and see for yourself. Then, tell me that my life is a gift." Dolores stood up and spread her arms wide, making an offering of herself. La Llorona wanted no such offering. She pulled Dolores into her embrace, but Dolores fell limp in her arms, refusing comfort. La Llorona held Dolores and peered into her sacred shawl. What she saw crushed her heart like glass thrown against the wall. She understood why this woman wanted to die so badly, but she wanted to help her find a thread of hope, just enough to hold on, so La Llorona could mend the torn threads of her sacred shawl.

Dolores' sacred shawl was dim and gray. The threads were thin, like an old string mop that had not been rinsed and left out to dry. The goddess closed her eyes and prayed for the wounds of Dolores' soul to be made visible. Then she saw Dolores in her etheric form. She was about fourteen years old, standing in a yard where she lived with her family in East Los Angeles. There were five goats feeding on dried patches of grass. Dolores wore a threadbare pink cotton dress that was two sizes too large for her, no socks, and shoes with holes in them. Her face was pale, and she was very thin. Dolores could see La Llorona standing there with her. Behind Dolores, hiding in the shadow beneath the stairs, was a tall, husky man with a five o'clock shadow and yellowed eyes filled with rage.

"Who is this man, Dolores?"

"My stepfather."

"What is he waiting for?" La Llorona knew the answer, but she wanted Dolores to tell her story.

"He wants the same thing every evening when he comes home from work, smelling of tequila and too many beers. He wants me. He hates me, so he takes pieces of me and grates me down to nothing. I am nothing. But he hates my mother more than me, because she knows what he does to me, and she is too weak to say anything about it." La Llorona continued to watch the story unfold. Dolores' stepfather called out to her to come to him. She did as he asked. He took her into a small, decrepit outbuilding behind the house. La Llorona knew what he wanted. He wanted what all men who are vacant want. They want the holy light of the womb. They know only one way to take it, feed on it, in order to temporarily fill the emptiness. But this light does not belong to them. Each human has their own light, but some have forgotten it, so they become trapped in a cycle of hunting the light of innocence to fill their emptiness. They think they are driven by their sexual desire, but men who have their own light do not hunger for the light of children in this way. It disgusts them. They desire love and intimacy, not power and destruction.

The scene played out like a movie on a screen. Dolores was numb to it. She felt only hatred for him and for all men, as she believed them to be all the same. He pushed her up against the wall and forced himself inside her. He covered her mouth so her mother, Rosa, would not hear her cry out. When he was finished, he let her fall on the dirt floor and went into the house for supper. La Llorona looked further into Dolores' story and saw that sometimes her stepfather brought friends with him from work, and they too fed on her innocence. Dolores sat alone on the dirt floor, shivering and numb, until she heard her mother, Rosa, call her. She willed herself to stand, even though all she wanted was to die. Instead, she went inside to wash herself, then went into the kitchen to set the table.

"Where have you been, pendeja? Didn't you hear me calling you? Honestly, I don't know where your mind is. You know I need your help with dinner, and you're always late," Rosa said.

Dolores said nothing. She set the table quietly, her soul dazed, floating outside in the outbuilding, shivering on the ground, her sacred shawl torn to shreds.

Dolores and Rosa put the food on the table, then stood against the wall and watched as her stepfather and five brothers feasted on roasted pork, frijoles, and corn tortillas. When her husband and sons were sated, they got up from the table without saying a word. They went outside to drink beer and trade stories about their day. After the men were out of the house, Dolores and her mother sat down quietly at the table and ate what little food was left over in silence. They gave the crumbs to the dog. Dolores cleared the plates and started to wash the dishes. The dog followed her into the kitchen and started sniffing under her dress. She shewed him away. Her mother noticed and went over to Dolores.

"What have you been doing? Why is the dog sniffing under your dress?"

"I don't know, mami."

Her mother lifted her dress up briskly and saw the damp, yellow stains on her panties. Her mother's face turned red, and her hands began to shake. She struck Dolores hard across the side of her head, grabbed her by the hair, and dragged her into her bathroom so no one would hear.

"Who is it, you little puta? Have you been messing with one of the boys from school?" Her mother slapped her hard across her face. "You tell me who it is right now, or I'll call your father."

"He's not my father. My father is dead."

"He's the only father you have right now, and you should be grateful he works so hard to put food on the table and give us a roof over our heads. Now tell me who it is, or I will call him to get it out of you, and you know he will."

Dolores felt a red-hot rage rise from her belly. She looked her mother in the eyes.

"He puts food on the table for himself and for my brothers, while we wait like dogs for scraps after they leave the table. Go ahead and call your husband. I want to hear what he will say, because he is the one who did this to me!" Dolores shouted the words, no longer able to contain her anger. Rosa's face went pale. She stood silent for a moment, trying to comprehend the words her daughter had just spoken. She let go of Dolores' hair, took three steps back, and made the sign of the cross.

"You're a filthy liar, and God is going to punish you for saying such evil things. The devil has gotten into you. You're an evil child, and I am ashamed to be your mother. I'm not going to tell your father about this filth you told me. It would hurt him badly, and he does not deserve this." A river of rage that ran through Dolores erupted, and she screamed at her mother.

"How can he be a good man when he does this to your daughter? How can he be good when he beats you? Yes, that's right. You think I don't know, but I can hear you when you're fighting, and I hear you begging him to stop. That's what you call a good man? My father was a good man. He loved us and cared for us, the way a good man should. He was kind, and he was the only one who loved me."

"You shut your mouth. Don't you talk to me about your father, God rest his soul. Go to your room and pack your things. I'm sending you to live with my sister Sandra and her family. I never want to see your face again." Rosa pushed Dolores out of the bathroom, shut the door, and cried. Dolores went to her room and packed the other three dresses she owned, along with socks and underwear. She went into the bathroom to grab her hairbrush and her toothbrush and tossed it all into an old brown leather suitcase. Then she sat on her bed and waited. Three hours later, her Tía Sandra arrived to take Dolores home with her. She felt relieved that she would finally be far away from her stepfather.

⌣

Sandra was kind to Dolores, but her husband was no better than Dolores' stepfather. He went into her room most nights, drunk and angry because his wife hated the smell of alcohol. Nine months later, Dolores gave birth to a son. Her Aunt Sandra surrendered him to the local convent, which placed him up for adoption. Dolores begged her aunt to let her keep her baby, but one morning, the baby was gone. She was inconsolable. No one talked about her baby nor offered her comfort. That was when she discovered that tequila numbed her sorrow but allowed her to express her rage. She decided that she would never trust another man and that she would be the one to decide who she gave herself to.

At 16, she ran away from her aunt's home and went to live with her best friend, Esther, and her family. One day, Esther's uncle Tony and his son Raymond came to visit. Raymond was tall, with bronze skin and short black hair, which he combed straight back. He had a thin mustache, dimples, and a twinkle in his eyes when he smiled. His skin smelled like sweet corn and warm earth. Raymond and Dolores spent many evenings sitting on the front stairs talking and laughing. She had never felt so happy before. They were in love, and after a few months, Raymond asked her to marry him. They married at city hall later that month. Dolores moved into Raymond's and his mother's home, filled with hope that she had finally found happiness.

Shortly after they were married, Dolores became pregnant. When she told Raymond, he said he was too young to be tied down. He began to spend more and more time at the local bar and often came home smelling of cigarettes, beer, and other women's perfume. When Dolores questioned him about it, he slapped her and told her never to question him. A month after their son Roberto was born, Raymond enlisted in the Army. He told Dolores that he no longer loved her and wanted the freedom to see the world. She wrote to him every night, trying to convince him to change his mind and return to her, but after the first reply telling her that he was not coming back to her, she never heard from him again. Dolores was now pregnant with her second child. When Raymond's mother learned he no longer wanted Dolores, she told her to leave her home. Dolores went to see her best friend, Esther, to tell her everything that had happened. Esther told her that her Tía Lucy lived in San Francisco, worked at the Cannery on Fisherman's Wharf, and could get them both jobs there.

La Llorona continued to view the images in Dolores' sacred shawl. She saw the path that led her to this point in her life, her sense of alienation, and her experience of constant rejection. She saw that even when she met Aurora's father, Javier, who truly loved her, she could not receive his love. She continued to drink excessively and pushed him away. She decided that she would live her life the way she wanted to, and no one would ever control her ever again.

⏝

Dolores turned from La Llorona, tossed a handful of pennies on the ground, and walked home. La Llorona followed a short distance behind her. Dolores unlocked the front door and left it open. She dropped her coat and purse on a chair, then went into the kitchen and took a bottle of Gin from the freezer, along with two bottles of Valium from the counter, and went to sit in her favorite chair in front of the window. Dolores unscrewed the caps of the pills and poured the contents into the lap of her dress. She watched the people outside as they walked down 24th Street, stopping at the panaderia across the street. She thought of how she and Aurora often enjoyed pan dulce with a cafecito and how this had been a morning ritual they shared when Aurora was a child. The memory made her smile. Now the only time she saw Aurora was when she came to drive her to see her psychiatrist, whom Dolores hated. He only cared whether she was taking her prescribed medication. He never asked her about why she was sad and could not sleep, or why she was often unable to get out of bed.

But sometimes Aurora would visit in the evening, on her way home from work. She usually brought groceries and a six-pack of Coca-Cola with her. The visit was often short-lived when Aurora became frustrated at the sink full of dirty dishes or the fact that Dolores hadn't bathed. Aurora would run Dolores a bath, do the dishes, and throw out the bottles of liquor from the freezer, then leave. She knew her mother would just buy more, but it made her feel better for the rest of the night. Dolores did not blame Aurora for hating her. She hated herself more. Dolores popped a handful of pills in her mouth and took several long gulps of vodka to wash them down. La Llorona began to wail.

"Stop your weeping! It's too late for me. I don't want your tears. You have haunted me most of my life, and what good have you done for me? You are useless, just like everyone else in my life. I'm tired of it all. People have tried to control me my entire life. Well, no one is going to control my death. Not even you, Senora, so don't waste your tears on me. My death is mine alone. Maybe I will go back to the stars, or maybe I will go to hell. I don't care." Dolores put another handful of pills into her mouth, swallowing them with vodka, and repeated this until all the pills were gone. Then she sat back in her chair and watched the people coming and going down the street below, until her head became so heavy she could not hold it up.

She laid her head against the back of the chair and drifted into quiet darkness. Suddenly, she felt a stabbing pain explode in her chest, and then her heart stopped beating. She floated above her body and watched as the light of her soul dispersed to the four winds. She could no longer feel the blood rushing through her body or hear the beating of her heart. The particles of her being dispersed in separate directions. She thought she would feel peace now that she was dead, but she felt more constricted than ever. Then a portal of light appeared before her, and La Llorona moved in front of it. She motioned for Dolores to come towards her to pass through the portal, but Dolores was plagued by guilt and shame. The portal radiated an immense loving presence and a sense of mercy that she could not comprehend.

"Come, mija. It's time to return to the One Great Heart." La Llorona reached out her hand to Dolores.

"I don't want you here. Please just go." Dolores dropped her face into her ghost hands and wept. Just ahead, she saw an empty train car and ran toward it. When she went inside, she saw a large red book on one of the seats. She picked it up and sat down, then looked around the car and realized there was no color anywhere, only shades of gray. Everything outside of the train was blanketed in a thick fog. La Llorona called to her in the distance, but Dolores covered her ears until the sound faded. She was alone, but it was quiet, a strange peace, until La Llorona appeared beside her.

"Mija, you don't belong here in this place. I want to help you go to the Ancient Ones, where you will find true peace." La Llorona took Dolores' hand and sat down beside her. Dolores yanked her hand away.

"I said I don't want to go with you. I belong here in this place with no color. I will wait here until I feel it is time for me to go. I need forgiveness you cannot offer me, Señora. Only Aurora can give me that.

When she comes, I can explain things to her and maybe she will forgive me; until then, I will stay here."

"You don't have to wait for Aurora to forgive you. You can forgive yourself right now and be free and at peace. There is no blame on the other side, and Aurora will find forgiveness in her own time," La Llorona said.

Dolores stood up and pointed to the train door. "Go away. I want you to leave me here in peace," Dolores screamed.

"Very well. But I will be close by." La Llorona got up and walked out of the train door, into the fog, tears trailing behind her.

⌣

The next morning, Aurora arrived at her mother's flat to take her to her doctor's appointment. She let herself in with her key. Calling out as she opened the door.

"It's me, Ma. Hurry or we're going to be…Oh my god, Ma." Dolores was sitting in her chair, eyes closed, her head slumped to the side as if she was sleeping. Aurora saw the empty vials of pills along with the empty bottle of vodka on the floor. She ran over to her mother to try to wake her. It was too late. Dolores was cold, and Aurora knew she was gone. Then she panicked and slapped her face several times in an attempt to wake her.

"Come on, Ma, wake up! Damn you, wake up, Ma! Damn it, you answer me. You don't get to leave like this. Why would you do this to me?" Aurora pounded the arm of the chair where Dolores' lifeless body sat, then fell to her knees, her body racked by deep sobs long held captive while Dolores was still alive. After her tears stopped, she got up and called an ambulance, then she called Sofie.

"Sofie. She did it. God damn her, she finally did. Ma's dead, Sofie."

"Oh my god, Aurora. Okay. Stay there. I'll be right there. Don't do anything, okay? Promise me, Yoya."

Aurora was drifting out of her body. She sounded like a child when she answered Sofie. "Okay, Sofie. I gotta go now."

To avoid the street traffic, Sofie rode her bicycle, weaving in and out of people along the sidewalk. When she got to Dolores' flat, she saw the paramedics placing a black bag into the ambulance. Sofie ran up the stairs and found Aurora sitting on the floor beside the chair where Dolores' body had been. She sat down beside her, wrapped a blanket around Aurora's shoulders, and took her hand. That's when she felt something wet. She looked at Aurora's hand and saw blood seeping from Aurora's wrists. Aurora's eyes were open, but she was not aware that Sofie was there. Sofie called out the window to the paramedics for help. One of the paramedics ran back upstairs. He wrapped Aurora's wrists in bandages and called another ambulance to take her to San Francisco General Hospital. Sofie rode in the ambulance with Aurora. When they arrived, Sofie filled out the admission papers and waited for the Psychiatrist to update her on Aurora's condition. About an hour later, a woman came through the locked doors.

"Hello, I'm Dr. García. Are you a family member of Aurora's?"

Sofie thought quickly. She knew if she was not in the immediate family, she would not be allowed to see her, so she lied.

"I'm her therapist. She called me when she found her mother. I live up the street, so I got to her as quickly as I could. When I found her, her mother was dead, and Aurora was conscious but in shock. When can I see her?"

"She's in shock, as you said. We gave her a tranquilizer to help her sleep. If you leave your information with the charge nurse, she will contact you in a couple of days. But, for now, Aurora needs to rest. When she is responsive, I will evaluate her mental and emotional state." Sofie knew the doctor was right, but she could not leave Aurora alone. She would be terrified when she woke up and found herself in the psychiatric unit. This was Aurora's greatest fear. Sofie decided to go home and come back early the next morning. The next day, there was an intern on the morning shift. Sofie introduced herself and explained that she was Aurora's therapist and wanted to know if she was awake. He explained that she was still not responsive. On the third morning, Sofie met Dr. Novak, an Attending Psychiatrist who was making his morning rounds. After Sofie introduced herself, the doctor sat down with Sofie and asked her for some background information on Aurora.

"I've just come from checking on Aurora. She is awake, but still unresponsive. Also, it doesn't seem like she wanted to die. There were several other superficial scars on the length of her forearm. Her recent cuts were horizontal, so I don't think she intended to cut her veins." Sofie tried to maintain her composure so she wouldn't let on that she was much more than Aurora's therapist.

"That's strange. I have never noticed any scars on her arms, but she always wears long-sleeve shirts, so I don't usually see her forearms. I think the shock of finding her mother was just too much for her. They had a strained and complicated relationship."

"Yes, that's exactly right, and at this point, she is still in shock. The best thing for her now is to rest. I'll let you know if anything changes. I have to ask: do you become involved with all your clients?"

"No, actually, I don't, but Aurora has been my client for several years. She has been seeing me to deal with issues from her childhood." Sofie lied again. If someone found out the truth, she could lose her license, but she didn't care. She was the only person Aurora could count on, and she would do whatever it took to be there for her. Later that evening, the charge nurse on duty called Sofie to let her know that Aurora was awake and had been asking to see her. Sofie rushed over to the hospital to see Dr. Novak when she could see Aurora.

"She's been asking for you. Try not to excite her. I think she needs reassurance that she has not lost touch with reality. I understand that her mother was schizophrenic."

"No, she suffered from manic depression. She was unmedicated, so she suffered from delusions."

"I see. Aurora is lucid, but she has wrist restraints on for her own protection, so don't be surprised when you see her. The best thing you can do is to suggest that she cooperate with us, so we can help her. If things go well, I'm prepared to release her on the agreement that she continues therapy with you and has monthly visits with me to make sure the medication is working."

"Yes. Absolutely. I will do that. Can I see her now?"

"Yes. She's in room 111, just down that hall on the left."

Sofie opened the door and entered the room cautiously. She didn't want to startle Aurora. When Aurora saw Sofie, her face lit up and she began to sob. Sofie rushed to the bedside. The restraints were tied to the bed rails, so Sofie pulled up one of the chairs and sat as close to Aurora as possible.

"Oh, Sofie. I'm so happy to see you. I'm so sorry, Sofie. I don't know what happened to me. I saw my mother sitting in that chair, lifeless. I was so mad at her for leaving me. She is gone and now I'll never know why…why she didn't love me, or why she was so cruel to me."

"It's gonna be okay, Yoya. You just need to rest, and we can figure out everything else after I get you out of here. I told the doctors I am your therapist, so they would let me see you. You need to cooperate with them and assure them that you aren't going to try anything like this again. You're not, are you?"

"No. Sofie. I won't. I promise. I'm so sorry. I didn't mean to scare you. I guess I cut too deep."

"Don't you worry. We can talk about that later. Right now, all I care about is getting you home. What you need is to get back to painting, and you will feel better in no time."

"That sounds good to me, Sofie. How is my Brujita?"

"She's fine. She misses you, but she is fine. I stopped by to feed her, and she jumped up on the counter full of purrs, so you don't need to worry." Just then, a nurse came in to let Sofie know that morning visiting hours were over. Sofie kissed Aurora on the forehead and promised she would be back the next day. When Sofie arrived at the hospital the next morning, Dr. Novak told her that he was going to release Aurora, and that Sofie could return later that afternoon to take her home.

"She will need someone to stay with her for a week or so, to make sure she continues with her medication and that she doesn't harm herself."

"I contacted a family member who is going to stay with her," Sofie lied again. Of course, Sofie would be the one to stay with Aurora. She was terrified at the thought of leaving her alone. She hadn't had time to process all that had happened. Suddenly, her breath caught in her chest, and she could not breathe. She ran outside to get fresh air, and as soon as the air entered her lungs, deep sobs racked her body. The thought of losing Aurora was unimaginable. They had grown up on the same street. Sofie didn't have many friends because her Mexican mother had married a black man, so the other mothers did not want their children to play with her. The other mothers did not want their children to play with Aurora either, because her mother was sinverguenza, a shameless woman, so Sofie and Aurora found each other and were best friends ever since. Sofie wiped her face on her sleeve and went home to pack what she would need to stay at Aurora's. She stopped by the grocery store on her way to make sure to pick up some groceries and several cans of food for Brujita.

⌣

When Sofie got to Aurora's flat, she found the spare key in the planter and let herself in. After she put the groceries away and fed the cat, she went into Aurora's bedroom to tidy up and was stunned to find several empty bottles of wine and vodka on the floor beside Aurora's bed. She threw the empty bottles in a garbage bag, changed the sheets on the bed, and then left to pick up Aurora from the hospital. Sofie made sure to light some sage and say a prayer before she left. When she arrived at the hospital, Sofie went to see the nurse to sign the release papers, picked up Aurora's prescription from the pharmacy, and then went to Aurora's room to find her fully dressed and pacing the floor.

"Hey, mujer! Are you ready to get out of here?"

Aurora ran to Sofie, threw her arms around her neck, and held her tight. Sofie could hear Aurora crying softly. Sofie gave her a squeeze and looked her in the eyes.

"Everything is going to be okay now. I'm going to stay with you for a while, so you don't have to worry about anything."

"Oh, Sofie! I'm so happy to see you. Please get me out of here." Aurora grabbed Sofie's hand, pulled her into the elevator, and left the hospital as fast as she could. When they arrived at Aurora's flat, she unlocked the door and as soon as she was inside, Bruja jumped into her arms, scolding her with yowls.

"Ay mi Brujita. I'm so sorry I left you alone. Can you ever forgive me?" Bruja replied by licking Aurora's face and sticking her claws into Aurora's shoulders, as if to make sure Aurora would not leave her again. Aurora went into the kitchen to feed Bruja, then went to sit down on the couch near Sofie.

"Sofie, I haven't slept very well the last few nights; I had horrible dreams. I think it was from all the pills they gave me. I'm so sleepy. Do you mind if we talk later?"

"Of course. Sleep is exactly what you need. We are going to have to wean you off those meds. You just get some good sleep, and we'll talk tomorrow. I'm going to crash on the couch." She gave Aurora a big hug.

"I'm so glad you're home. Love you, girl."

"Love you, too...You are the best friend anyone could ask for."

That night, Aurora dreamed of her mother. Dolores was sitting in a vacant train car, holding a large red book. When she saw Aurora, her face lit up.

"Mija! I knew you would find me. I told La Llorona that I was going to wait for you, and now you're here! Please forgive me for how I treated you. I want you to know that I love you." Aurora tried to walk towards her mother, but in the dream, her feet were heavy, and she was unable to move. Suddenly, she felt trapped, and panic overtook her. She stared at her mother, feeling disoriented and confused.

"Ma, what are you doing here? What is this place?" Dolores stood with her arms outstretched towards Aurora.

"Can you forgive me, Aurora? I didn't understand how much I hurt you, and now it's too late." Suddenly, rage burned through Aurora. Even in her dreams, Dolores only cared about herself. Dolores patted the seat beside her.

"Come and sit beside me, Aurora. I want to show you this book. It's filled with the story of my life. I never told you about what happened to me. I hope that when you hear my story, you can forgive me." Aurora shook her head and wiped her tears before her mother could see them.

"I will never forgive you, Ma. I hate you for the way you treated me. What did I ever do to deserve what you did?" Aurora waited, but before Dolores could answer, Aurora startled awake, screaming her mother's name. Sofie ran to Aurora's side. She turned on the light and held Aurora while she cried.

"Sofie, my mother…she was in my dream…in a place that was all gray…"

"Shhh. It's just the medication talking. It's causing bad dreams. Your mother is gone. She can't hurt you anymore."

"You don't understand what I'm saying, Sofie. I saw her so clearly. She is never going to leave me alone. Not even my dreams are safe." Aurora felt like someone had poured gray paint on the canvas of her mind, leaving her feeling hopeless and scared. She felt numb inside, unable to feel anything except sadness. Sofie held her while she cried.

"I'm not going to the funeral. I don't care what they do with her body. I won't be there. Besides, I don't want to see my brothers, especially Beto. I hate him. I haven't talked to my brothers in years. When they see me, they will act like they are so happy to see me. No thanks. I'm not going." Aurora struggled to get her words out.

"I called your mother's brother, Enrique, to tell him that Dolores passed away. I didn't say anything about you being in the hospital. He said that he would handle all the funeral arrangements, so you don't have to worry about the details. You don't have to go if you don't want to. Just try to get some sleep. I'll be right here." Sofie held her, gently stroking her hair until Aurora stopped crying and fell asleep from exhaustion. Aurora slept for the next three days, waking up only to eat a piece of toast and sip a little herbal tea, then she returned to a dreamless sleep. She willed herself to return to the dream of her mother to try to find answers, but she was unsuccessful. This only fueled her anger and left her feeling more abandoned than when her mother was alive.

Finally, on the fourth day, Aurora woke up feeling a little more like herself. She showered, threw on a short-sleeved black T-shirt, a faded pair of jeans, and then went to the kitchen. Sofie had heard Aurora turn on the shower and decided to cook scrambled eggs, toast, and cafecito. Aurora walked into the kitchen where Sofie was serving them both breakfast.

"Hey, mujer. It's good to see you up and about. How are you feeling?" Sofie said. Aurora kissed her on the cheek and sat down at the table.

"I feel great, and I'm so hungry. The food smells amazing."

"Well, that's good to hear. You haven't eaten very much since..."

"I know Sofie. I want you to know that you don't have to worry about me. I suddenly feel like I just need to get into my studio to paint. I have this sudden surge of creative energy inside me. I don't understand it, but I just want to go with it and see what happens." Sofie poured each of them a cup of coffee and sat down at the table across from Aurora, smiling as she watched Aurora devour her food.

"Wow. That's so great to hear. I'm happy for you, and I can't wait to see what shows up on the canvas." Sofie took a sip of her coffee and glanced at the pink horizontal scars above the white bandages on both of Aurora's wrists. Aurora noticed that Sofie saw her scars and tried to shift the position of her wrists, but it was too late.

"How could I not know about this, Aurora? How could you keep something like this from me? When I think about how much pain you were in to make you hurt yourself like that, it breaks my heart, and honestly, it makes me angry, too. You could have died, Aurora."

"I'm so sorry. I don't know what else to say. I feel so ashamed. That's why I couldn't tell you. I don't understand why I do it. I started cutting myself when we were in college. Sometimes I feel this pain inside of me, like something trying to claw its way out from inside me, and when I cut, it's like I'm able to release some of my pain. I feel better for a little while, but then the pain comes back again. It's an ugly, vicious cycle. I know it's stupid." Sofie tried to listen without judgment.

"Your pain is not stupid. We all have different ways of coping." But Sofie was angry and hurt that Aurora had kept such a big secret from her. She felt like she didn't know who Aurora was anymore. She also knew that now was not the time to talk about her own feelings. She just wanted to make sure Aurora was safe.

"Do you think you can stop?" Sofie asked, wiping the tears from her eyes.

"Yes. I know I can. My mother is dead, and I'm not sure why, but there is a part of me that feels relieved that she's gone. I finally feel free. Does that sound terrible?"

"Not at all. It makes perfect sense that you would feel some relief. You've had to deal with your mother's mental illness since you were a child, and it only became worse as you got older. So, no. I don't think you're terrible at all, Aurora. I just need to know that when I go back to my place, you are going to be safe."

"I'll be safe. I promise you."

"You need to get some help for this, Aurora. You need to talk to someone. I have a friend I can refer you to. She is not a therapist, per se, at least not in the traditional sense. She works from an indigenous perspective. Considering that some of what you're experiencing has to do with your mother's ghost, I think she could really help you."

"I'm not ready to talk to anyone about this. I will be safe, Sofie, and I promise that if I feel like cutting myself, I will call you, okay?"

"Okay. I do want you to call me, but I'm your friend, not your therapist."

"I don't want a therapist, Sofie. I just need you to be my friend, and I need time to figure out my feelings, and the only way I can do that is through painting. Do you understand?"

"Okay, Aurora, for now. But this conversation is not over. Call me tonight, so I know you're okay. There is food in the fridge, so don't forget to eat something."

"I will, Sofie. Thank you for keeping your promise."

Sofie kissed Aurora on the cheek and let herself out. Aurora poured herself another cup of coffee and went into her studio. She looked around the room and could not remember the last time she had worked on a painting for herself. The room felt void of color or creative energy. The canvas on her easel was blank, just as she felt inside. It didn't necessarily feel bad, just different. She wondered if it was because her mother was gone. Maybe it was all her anger trying to claw its way out of her? She lit the glass votive candles that were scattered on the floor and across the large table where she kept her paint and brushes. Then she took one of the white candles from the table and waved the flame across the white space of the canvas.

"Color, warmth, emotion hiding within me, please come forward. Inspiration, creativity, and my muse, bless me with a vision. If you can hear me, then help me. This is all I have, and I really need you right now." The process of painting on canvas; this was the only religion she knew—it had never failed her. Aurora squeezed cobalt blue, black, purple, and red dabs of paint onto her palette, without giving it too much thought. She closed her eyes and tried to feel into her belly, where the clawing sensation had come from. She closed her eyes and imagined cobalt blue color filling the space inside her, brilliant and rich, like the sky. Suddenly, she felt something move into the top of her head and swiftly down into her belly. It was electric, like the light from the stars.

When she opened her eyes, the colors in the room seemed more vibrant. She picked up a paintbrush without any thought, dipped it into blue paint, and moved the brush across the canvas. She painted through the night, as if in trance, until the cool orange and magenta light of dawn startled her back into the present time. When Aurora stood back to examine her canvas, she was alarmed to see what she had painted. The canvas portrayed a roofless red brick room, with a star-filled night sky. In the corner of the room was a little girl wearing a white dress dotted with tiny pink flowers and a mass of tangled curls. She was crouched in the corner, head in her hands, crying. There was a small window just above her head that looked out into a thick gray fog. There were words written on the brick wall:

Help me, Yoya. You have to remember.

Aurora rubbed her arms briskly to warm the chill that moved through her. The red brick room gave way to a night sky, and the sight of the child filled her with dread. "Yoya" was her childhood nickname. No one called her that, except for Sofie. Bile rose in her stomach, and the stitches on her wrists began to itch. She wanted so badly to rip the bandages off and scratch them, tear at them, make them bleed. Then she remembered her promise to Sofie. So instead, she went to the kitchen to get ice and put it on her wrists. Just then, Bruja jumped through the open window, jumped down, and curled herself around Aurora's ankle.

"Oh, Brujita. You always know when I need you." Aurora opened a can of food for Bruja, then sat back down at the table to ice her wrists. The itching finally stopped. She was going to return to her studio when she heard a child crying. It sounded so close, like it was in the next room. Aurora jumped up and hurried through her flat, trying to locate where the sound was coming from. Brujita ran in front of her and sat staring at the front door. She howled until Aurora found her—an apparition of a child about four years old, standing by the front door, dressed in a white dress with little pink flowers on it. Aurora could see right through her. The child looked into Aurora's eyes.

"Help me, Yoya. Please. You have to remember. I don't want to stay in the brick room anymore." Then, just as she had appeared out of nowhere, she disappeared. Aurora tried to quell the terror that rose up within her.

No. This is not happening. This is the leftover effects of the drugs. This is not real. She picked her cat up and went to her bedroom, crawled under the covers, and fell into a dream.

Aurora was walking down 24th Street. The streets were dark and empty. The streetlights cast a strange, flickering orange glow on the streets. She walked from York Street until she came to the corner of Balmy Alley. Clear, glass votive candles lined both sides of the alley. She felt pulled towards the end of the alleyway, where an altar was placed on the ground, beneath the mural she had painted of Tonantzin-Guadalupe. As she approached the altar, she noticed a little girl crouched in the corner. She appeared to be about four or five years old. Her face was dirty, her hair was badly tangled, and she wore no shoes. When she saw Aurora, the child stood up as if she had been waiting for her.

"Are you gonna help me?" she whimpered.

Aurora walked over to her, kneeling beside her and lifted her chin so she could see her eyes. The child held out her right hand to offer Aurora a pile of shiny copper pennies. Aurora ignored the pennies.

"Why are you crying, sweetie? What are you doing here all alone?" Aurora asked.

"I was waiting for you. Are you gonna help me? Please?" She began to

sob loudly, throwing her arms around Aurora's neck. Aurora felt darkness seeping from the child, and her breath felt like it was being sucked from her lungs. She pushed the child away, jumped up and ran from the alley. She could hear the child sobbing loudly behind her and calling her name.

"Yoya! Please, don't go. Don't leave me here. Come back, please." As Aurora ran further away from Balmy Alley, the sound of the child faded.

⌣

Aurora woke to the sound of her own voice screaming. She bolted upright in bed, her heart pounding. She ran into her studio to look at the little girl in her painting, who was crouching in the corner of the brick room. Just as she feared, it was the same child from her dream. She went into the bathroom and splashed cold water on her face. Then, she threw on a pair of blue jeans, her purple San Francisco State University sweatshirt, slipped her feet into a pair of huaraches, and rushed outside into the daylight for a walk. She decided to walk to Balmy Alley to be sure there was no evidence of the little girl from her dream. Balmy Alley was a popular art walk, as every wall of the alley was covered in murals. When she got there, she walked to the end of the alley. She had painted this mural of Tonantzin-Guadalupe with some of the youth from El Centro del Corazón. Something drew her attention to the ground, where she saw a small pile of shiny copper pennies on the sidewalk. *This can't be happening.*

Aurora ran home, called Sofie at work, and pleaded with her to come right over. Then, she poured herself a shot of tequila and went to sit on the floor of her studio, staring at the painting of the little girl in the red brick room. She heard someone pounding on her door.

"Aurora, open the door!"

"It's open. Come in, Sofie." Sofie rushed in, running through the flat until she found Aurora in her studio.

"What's happened? Did something happen?"

Aurora pointed to the painting. "That happened."

Sofie caught her breath. "You called me over here in the middle of the day to show me a painting?"

"Look, Sofie."

Sofie moved closer to inspect the painting. Then she saw the words written on the red brick wall. "I don't understand, Aurora. Talk to me."

Aurora started to cry. "I saw her. The little girl. She was here last night. I saw her. She's some kind of ghost or something. She was crying and called me Yoya, like she knew me. Then...she was gone. Just like that. She's a ghost, and for some godforsaken reason, she's haunting me!"

"But those are similar words you wrote in your journal. *You need to remember,* or something like that. Did the ghost write that in your notebook, too?"

"I don't know, Sofie. That's why I called you. I'm scared."

Sofie sat down on the floor next to Aurora and put her arm around Aurora's shoulder. "Look, I don't understand what's happening here, but we're going to figure it out, okay?"

Aurora covered her face with her hands as sobs racked her body, and the sound of her weeping turned into deep keening. She moved away from Sofie and curled up in a ball on her side in the corner of the room. Sofie moved beside her and gently stroked her hair.

"It's going to be okay, amiga. I'm not going to let anything happen to you. C'mon, let's get you to bed." Sofie took hold of Aurora's hands and guided her up from the floor, then to her bedroom. Aurora's face was pale, and Sofie was afraid that she might hurt herself again. She helped Aurora under the blankets and lay down on top of the blankets beside her.

"Shhh. I'm here. I'm gonna stay right here. You're okay now." Aurora fell asleep, and Sofie followed her shortly after. The next morning, Sofie woke to the sound of clanging pots and pans in the kitchen and the aroma of fresh coffee. She jumped out of bed, rushed to the kitchen to find Aurora in front of the stove, humming and scrambling eggs.

"Good morning, Sofie. Hey, I'm so sorry I worried you last night. I feel fine today. I think I was hallucinating, maybe from coming off the meds. Anyway, I want you to know everything is fine now. I'm just going to focus on my painting and work, you know? Hey, I was thinking about starting a series of paintings for an art show. What do you think?"

Sofie didn't know what to think. She could feel Aurora's panic floating just beneath the surface of her unwillingness to deal with what happened the night before. She was worried and she didn't know what to do.

"I have a friend, Milagro. She is from Guatemala and has been through a similar loss as you have. She is very wise, and she could give you a limpia. Maybe the spirits will leave you alone? She might be able to tell you something about why the ghost, and..." Sofie said.

Aurora was sipping her coffee, then slammed down the mug on the counter. She felt a rush of both anger and fear rise inside her. "Sofie, I told you I'm fine now. I don't want to talk about this with anyone except you, and I don't even want to talk to you about this anymore. Okay? I told you I'm fine. Can you just trust me, please?" She was yelling now. How could she yell at Sofie after everything she had done for Aurora? She felt like a piece of garbage and started to cry again.

"Oh, God, Sofie. I'm so sorry. I didn't mean to yell at you. Please don't be mad at me. I'm sorry. I didn't mean it." Sofie was exhausted from the emotional roller coaster ride that had become Aurora's life. She had no energy to argue with her or to convince her of anything. She needed to get back to work, where there were women who actually wanted her help.

"It's okay, Aurora. Really, it's fine. I need to get back to work, anyway. Why don't you just do, well, whatever... I don't know. I gotta go." Aurora watched as Sofie walked out the door. She could feel the familiar panic rising in her stomach, along with the desire to scratch at her still-healing scars on her wrists. Instead, she went to her studio and stood in front of the painting of the little girl in the red brick room. Then she grabbed her notebook from the table and opened the page to the entry from "M". She reread it, then threw it at the wall.

"Go to hell—all of you. Just leave me alone!" Aurora went into the living room and found Bruja curled up on the couch. She picked her up and carried her into the bedroom, where she crawled under the covers and fell into a deep sleep, but sleep would not let her rest, and her dreams refused to let her rest.

She is walking on the shore of Ocean Beach. The full moon is hovering brightly just over the horizon. Aurora feels a peaceful and ancient connection to the sea. She stretches her arms out to the moon. This is her mother. She is unchanging in her changing, dependable, and comforting. Then she hears a haunting cry, a woman's tears, heavy with sorrow. She turns around and sees a woman with long, black hair, braided with red ribbon and feathers. She is wearing a long white cotton dress, embroidered with orange Marigolds and Monarch butterflies around the collar. Her bronze skin, illuminated by the rays of the moon and the kind expression on her face, intrigues Aurora. She walks towards the woman, who smiles at Aurora and stretches out her arms. This woman feels familiar to Aurora, almost as if she is a part of the sea; ancient and knowing. Instinctively, Aurora moves into the woman's embrace. She smells of rosemary and sage.

"Who are you? Do I know you from somewhere? Why are you crying?"

"It is time, mija, to call the lost pieces of your soul back into remembrance. There is nothing to fear. I am here for you. You must trust the path that your heart is leading you. The tears that I cry are for you. They are to bring the shadow of forgetting into light and sorrow into healing. When you are ready, I will return your tears to you. This is my purpose."

Aurora startled awake, knocking Bruja off the side of the bed, who then immediately started meowing for breakfast.

"Okay, Brujita. Let's get you some food, and I need a strong cup of coffee." Aurora sipped her coffee and tried to recall what she knew about La Llorona. It wasn't much, except for a few superstitious stories her mother had told her. They were the same stories most of the women in the Mission told about how La Llorona wants to steal your children because she drowned them over some man who dumped her over four hundred years ago. Aurora thought these stories were created by the Church as a warning against infidelity. Then she closed her eyes and took a deep breath, trying to recall the images and emotions of her dream. The woman of her dream was no superstition. Aurora didn't know how she knew, but somehow, she knew this spirit.

She went into her studio and placed a large, blank canvas on her easel. She sketched out the woman from her dream and began painting. She painted straight into the evening, stopping only to make a sandwich, grab a bottle of merlot, a glass, and then light the many white candles around her studio. She continued painting, consumed by the desire to understand why La Llorona appeared in her dream. Finally, when she saw the first light of dawn shining through the window, she put her brush in the water and went to bed and slept through the day, until she was awakened by someone knocking on the door. Aurora knew it was Sofie. No one else visited her. She staggered to the door, head aching from too much wine. She flung the door open and motioned for Sofie to come in. She followed Aurora into the kitchen, where she made a pot of coffee.

"I was worried about you. I was on my way back from lunch, and I thought I would stop by and see how you're doing. I hope you're not still mad at me." Aurora recalled how she behaved towards Sofie the day before. She felt like an ungrateful idiot. She stopped what she was doing and went to give Sofie a warm hug. Sofie hugged her back and went to sit at the table. Aurora waited for the coffee to brew, then poured them both a cup and sat down across from Sofie.

"Oh, Sofie. I'm the one who's sorry. I'm an ungrateful idiot. I wouldn't even be alive if it weren't for you. Please forgive me for being such a jerk. I'm so sorry for the way I behaved. I haven't been myself for a while. I feel like I don't even know who I am right now."

"You've been through a lot. I understand, really. Just try to remember that I'm on your side, okay?"

"I know you are. But I need you to trust that I'm not going to hurt myself again. Please, Sofie. I need you to trust me. I know I'm going through something right now, and I don't understand it all, but in a strange way, it's helping me. I can't explain it yet. I'm going to paint it all, like a visual diary. Maybe after I've painted a dozen paintings, I will have a better understanding of what it all means. Now, come with me. I want to show you something." Aurora got up from the table, and Sofie followed her into her studio. When she saw the painting on the easel, she gasped and covered her mouth with her hand.

"Oh, Aurora. She is beautiful! Tell me about her." Aurora sat on the floor and motioned for Sofie to sit next to her. She told Sofie about her dream and her feeling that she was connected to the spirit known as La Llorona.

"I feel completely compelled to understand this woman, or spirit, whoever she is. Besides, I think this is one of the best paintings I have done. Don't you?"

"Absolutely. It's incredible. I want to plan a show at the gallery. No pressure; whenever you're ready. Listen, I'm gonna get going. If you're sure you're okay? I have a women's circle to hold this afternoon." Sofie looked over at the two empty wine bottles on the floor of the studio and looked at Aurora with a nervous smile.

"Don't worry about me. I'm great, and I feel a little hopeful. I also think I'm ready to get back to work. I'm going to come tomorrow. I miss the kids."

"That's great, because they miss you. They have been asking when you are going to come back. They'll be very happy to be painting again." Sofie kissed Aurora on the cheek and went back to work. Aurora got up from the floor and went to take a shower.

After she got dressed, she grabbed a sweatshirt, her sketchbook, and pencils, and decided to walk around the Mission to see if she found anything interesting to sketch. She walked down 24th Street until she came to Balmy Alley and turned to walk to the end of the street. She noticed that there were bright copper pennies that lined the curb, all the way around the alley sidewalk. There was something she vaguely recalled her mother telling her about pennies and La Llorona, but she couldn't fully remember. It was like a faint memory she could not fully recall. Everything was a jumble of feelings floating around inside of her that she couldn't quite make sense of. Suddenly, she heard someone calling her by her childhood name.

"Yoooo Yaaaa. Help me, please." She turned around to find the same child who had appeared to her a few days ago. She told herself to stay calm and not to frighten the child.

"Hi, little one. Who are you and how do you know me?" The child appeared to be four or five years old. Her face was dirty, and her hair was badly tangled. She was clearly neglected. The girl wiped her tears and nose on her arm.

"You have to come with me. Please! Maddie's waiting, and she's really mad at you." At the mention of Maddie, Aurora felt a wave of ice move through her entire body.

"Did you say Maddie? Who are you? Is this some kind of trick?"

"It's not a trick, I promise. Come with me." Aurora watched as the ghost child got up and walked toward the street. Afraid that she would disappear again, she ran after her, but as soon as she turned the corner, the child was gone. Aurora ran home and locked the door behind her. She didn't know what to do or who to call. She felt the sensation of something clawing at her insides, trying to escape. This was her old friend. She needed to release it. So, she did the one thing that she knew would set it free. She went into the bathroom, opened the linen cabinet, and lifted a clean white towel. Underneath the towel was her friend; shiny, sharp, and waiting. She pulled off her jeans, sat down on the cool, black-and-white-tiled floor, and then removed the razor from its paper cover. She found a spot of unmarked flesh on her very upper thigh, where no one would see. She heard a voice inside her head,

"Do it, Aurora. It will make us all feel better. Do it for us. Bleed it out." Aurora placed the blade over her skin, took a breath, and pressed down, careful not to cut too deep. She moved the blade four inches across her thigh. She watched as the rivulets dripped onto the floor in a small pool of blood. She let it flow, as the rush of endorphins flooded her body, and for a few moments, the clawing subsided. She floated in a gray fog of nothingness, feeling completely numb. Then she remembered her promise to Sofie. She looked down at her thigh. The pool of blood was much larger than she meant it to be. She jumped and ran the towel under cold water and pressed it hard to her thigh. *Too deep. Again.* Then panic replaced her numbness as she recalled her recent stay in the psych ward. *Oh God! What is wrong with me?* She reached for her first aid kit under the sink, uncapped the bottle of alcohol, and poured it over the cut, grateful for the sting. She deserved it. Then she taped a thick bandage over the cut and wrapped her thigh with gauze. Finally, she rinsed the bloody towel under water and wiped up the blood from the floor. Panic continued to seize Aurora; she didn't know what to do or who to call. She couldn't call Sofie, and she wasn't ready to tell anyone else about this. She went to her bedroom and fell onto the bed. She howled and screamed into her pillow. She wept until she fell into an exhausted sleep.

Aurora slept until 5 p.m. the next evening. She got up feeling disoriented, then the stinging pain from her thigh reminded her of the events from the previous day. She went into the kitchen, made herself a cup of coffee, fed Bruja, and refused to think about it anymore. She took her coffee into her studio. She decided that she was going to focus on painting and only painting. Sitting down on the floor, she contemplated what she wanted to paint. Then she laughed out loud, because she realized her theme was right in front of her; she would paint a series called "The Dreams of Ghosts." She thought about all the people around her who were also haunted. Haunted by ghosts, spirits, and memories of loved ones they had lost in unspeakable ways. There were ghosts everywhere, and if they wanted to talk to her, they would have to communicate with her through her paintings. She placed a fresh blank canvas on her easel, picked up a paintbrush, and waved it in the air like a magic wand.

"If you're going to haunt me, you're going to have to give me something." She was still angry, but she was even more determined not to lose her sanity. Suddenly, she was aware of something stirring inside her womb. She felt like it wanted to rise to the surface. She didn't fully understand what it was, but she sensed it moving when she spoke the words out loud. She walked back to the kitchen to pour herself another cup of coffee and grabbed the bottle of tequila off the counter, then went back to her studio. Once inside, she lit the white candles that were scattered on the floor, on the windowsill, along with one next to her brushes. She poured tequila in her coffee and raised her cup to make a toast to the air.

"Here's to you, spirits, ghosts, and to whatever else is haunting me. Oh, and to you, La Llorona, please help me remember who you are. I invite you to this painting party. Inspire me. Give me vision. Help me to make sense of all this death and loss." She took a gulp from her mug, then picked up a candle and waved the flame over the canvas, and placed it back on the table. Then she squeezed cobalt blue, quinacridone red, deep violet, and white paint on her palette. She closed her eyes and thought of the stories of the women in the Mission who talked about La Llorona. Many of the women feared her, but some of the women also talked about how she was one of the Ancient Ones, and that the church had made up the story about her drowning her children to prevent women from remembering Las Cihuateteo, the Divine Women. Aurora never had the courage to ask the women more about La Llorona, and now she regretted it. She turned the radio up loud and turned the dial until she found a song by Santana, then she dipped her brush into the blue paint and made her first stroke. She painted through the night, pausing only to step back and examine the images that seemed to appear on the canvas through no will of her own. She painted until she felt a pang of hunger. She went to the kitchen to quickly heat a couple of flour tortillas with butter. She took them back to her studio and poured more tequila into her empty coffee mug.

Aurora woke up late the next day with no memory of how she got to bed. When she looked at the clock, she saw it was 2:22 p.m. She took a hot shower, hoping it would alleviate the pounding in her head. She pulled a sweatshirt and jeans on, slipped on her huaraches, and left for work. She had just enough time to get there before her students arrived. Aurora entered through the side door to avoid interrupting Sofie and the other women who were gathered in a circle in the main room. They were sharing stories, crocheting, and offering support to each other. The women would have invited Aurora to join them, and she did not want to seem rude. When she went into her classroom, there were several students sitting around the large table. They had already set up the paint and water, and each of them had a large piece of watercolor paper in front of them. Some of them were already sketching images.

"Buenos Dias, everyone. It's so good to see you. I'm sorry I haven't been here, but I had something personal I needed to take care of. You all bring a smile to my heart. Thank you for preparing everything and getting to work on your sketches." Aurora looked around the room at the children of ages from twelve to sixteen, and she felt her heart filled with gratitude. Making art with them gave purpose to her life. She walked around the table helping where needed, but most of them were very talented and did not need much guidance. They painted images that portrayed their life back in their homeland; things they missed about it, things they didn't like while they were there, like having to walk so far to plant and harvest corn in the milpa. But now that they lived in a city, they missed living close to nature. Aurora noticed that one of the girls, Gisela, was sniffling and wiping her nose while she sketched. She went over to her and put her hand on her shoulder, then gasped when she saw the image on her paper. Then she composed herself. She didn't want to upset Gisela any more than she was.

"Gisela, porque lloras, mija?" Gisela wiped at her tears and looked up at Aurora.

"These are not my tears. They are her tears. She cries for you, Maestra."

"I don't understand what you mean, Gisela." Panic began to rise in her chest, but Aurora knew she had to maintain her composure for her students. She took another breath as she examined the image in Gisela's painting. It portrayed a woman standing under a willow tree. She had a long, flowing dress. Her facial features were not filled in, except for her eyes, which had tears pouring down her face, and her arms outstretched to the viewer.

"Is this woman someone you knew in Guatemala?"

"Si. She was in Guatemala, and now she is here with you. I can see her sometimes when she follows you here. She stands over there and watches and cries." Gisela pointed to the side door, where Aurora had entered earlier. Aurora's head began to spin, and she suddenly felt weak. She excused herself from the class and went to find Sofie, who was saying goodbye to the women of her circle.

"Sofie! Can you please watch my class for a few minutes? I need to get some air, or I'm going to pass out."

"Of course. What's going on...?" Aurora ran out the front door before Sofie could finish her question. Sofie went into the class and greeted everyone. She walked around the room, marveling at the artistic skills of the students. When she got to Gisela's drawing, she quickly put her hand over her mouth to stifle a gasp. She calmly asked Gisela about her drawing, and Gisela repeated what she had said to Aurora. Sofie stayed with the students, watching them work, until Aurora returned fifteen minutes later with a cup of coffee in hand. Sofie looked at Aurora, her eyebrows raised. Aurora mouthed the words, "I'm fine," and went back to work with her students.

"Thanks for visiting, Sofie. Let's catch up later, okay?" Sofie shook her head, took a breath, and walked back to her office.

When class was over and parents came to pick up their children, Aurora proudly showed them the work of the children. She explained that the sketches would be used to paint a mural on the front of the building. When Gisela's mother, Ana, saw her drawing, she became visibly upset.

"Que es eso? What did I tell you about talking about her or drawing her? If you draw her, she will come and try to take you away from me." Her mother grabbed her by the arm, walking briskly toward the door.

"But Mami. I told you she is good and kind. She only wants to help people." Gisela's mother looked directly at Aurora. "Gisela will not come back to this class."

Aurora tried to stop her so she could explain, but it was too late. They were gone. Aurora felt like Gisela and her drawing of La Llorona was another piece of her puzzle, but now that Gisela would not be returning, she would never find out what else Gisela knew about La Llorona. Just then, Sofie walked in.

"Aurora, what is going on, and what is up with Gisela drawing La Llorona?"

"I don't know. She said that she saw her here and that La Llorona was crying for me." I know that sounds strange, but when she said it, I knew it was true. I felt it here." She placed the palm of her hand on her womb. "It felt like something true opened here. I can't explain it any better than that."

"So, now you're telling me that La Llorona followed you here? Okay, well, at least now you must accept that you are not crazy, because you're not the only one who can see her. Right?"

"Yeah. I didn't think of that. That makes me feel a little better. I need to find out more about her. Something is telling me that the only way I am going to find out who she really is and why she is haunting me is to paint her. I'm going to paint her in every scenario I have heard about her, as well as how she appears to me. Maybe if I do, I will find some peace."

"I think that sounds as good an idea as any. I sure don't have a better one. Are you really okay with this?"

"No, I'm anything but okay, Sofie, but I need to find a way to get some control around all of this, and painting is the only way I know how. Am I making any sense?"

"Yeah. It makes a lot of sense. It's a productive way to approach it. Maybe you will get a show out of it."

"Maybe. That's not really my goal at this point, but that would be nice. I need to get home. This has been a very strange day, and I need to paint. I'm just going to clean up here, and then I'll head home." Sofie gave Aurora a hug, without saying anything, which was rare for her. Being a therapist made it hard for her not to want to give advice.

"Take care. If you need anything, I'm just a phone call away."

"Thanks, amiga. I'm okay right now." Aurora washed the brushes and put away the paints. She enjoyed tidying up the classroom. It gave her a sense of having some order during so much chaos in her life. She picked up the drawing of La Llorona that Gisela had made. She decided she would include it in the mural, even if Gisela would not be there to paint it. Aurora walked down 24th Street just as the sun was beginning to set. When she passed by Balmy Alley, something caught her attention. She noticed several women placing pennies on the curb. They crossed themselves and prayed. As she watched the women, she heard the faint sound of a crying pass in the breeze. Aurora felt her breath catch in her throat, and her instinct to flee took over. She ran down 24th Street until she came to Casa Lucas grocery, where she was far enough away and felt safe enough to stop. She went inside and bought a bottle of tequila, a package of corn tortillas, and cheese. When she got home, she picked up Bruja, who was waiting by the door as usual. She showered her with kisses and carried her into the kitchen, opened a can of cat food onto a plate, and placed it on the floor. Then she made herself a couple of quesadillas and ate them quickly. She grabbed a shot glass from the counter, along with the bottle of tequila, and went into her studio. She leaned against the wall, then slid onto the floor, and poured herself a shot of tequila. After two shots, all the emotions from the day came rushing back, and she could no longer contain her tears. She surrendered to her feelings. She curled up on her side and wept.

When her tears were done, she felt clearer. She got up from the floor and performed her usual rituals before painting. She didn't think of them as rituals. They were just her way of preparing for inspiration to come through her. It helped to shift from her thinking brain into her body, where images and color awakened from some mysterious place. She lit the candles around the room, along with a bit of copal. She loved to inhale the pungent fragrance and watch the curls of smoke dance in front of the canvas. Sometimes, the plumes of smoke morphed into images that she then sketched on the canvas. Painting was her religion. It was mysterious and filled with the grace of inspiration that she never took for granted. Aurora worked in the same way for the next eighteen months, going straight into her studio as soon as she came home from work. She ate enough to have the strength to paint through the night, then slept in until it was time to go to work at El Centro for her afternoon class.

◡

SAN FRANCISCO ~ FALL 1982

Aurora and her students were cleaning their brushes in the sink and putting the paint cans back on the shelves. They were proud of the mural they had completed on the front of El Centro. It portrayed a mix of images from the lives of the students. At the center of the mural was an abuela cooking tortillas on her comal over an open flame. There were images of children playing, juxtaposed with a military jeep and a soldier standing beside it, holding a rifle. One of the students had painted a bright green Quetzal bird that flew in the sky. The images were painted on a background of a Guatemalan-style rebozo, featuring bright blues, reds, pinks, and yellows. Aurora added texture so that it looked like actual cloth. It made her want to walk up to the mural to touch it. Aurora and the children had painted Tonantzin-Guadalupe on the right side of the mural; her form was surrounded by red roses and a sunburst, with white candles at her feet. On the left side of the mural, Aurora had painted Gisela's image of La Llorona, just as she had drawn it. She added the paint, but the image of La Llorona was all Gisela's. The mural had taken over a year to complete, but it turned out beautifully, and when Sofie walked outside to look at it, Aurora heard her squeal.

"Oh! This is so beautiful!" Sofie stood in front of the mural, examining each part closely. She could feel the love and prayers the students had placed in their work. She was deeply moved by the mural and so pleased that it was on the front of her building. She went inside to tell the children how much she loved it, but they had already left. Aurora was standing in front of the sink, lost in thought. She didn't hear Sofie come in.

"The mural is beautiful, Aurora. You should be so proud." Aurora was startled by the sound of Sofie's voice. She turned around quickly to see Sofie standing there with a huge smile, her eyes twinkling with light.

"Oh, hi. I didn't hear you. I was thinking about the mural, too. The kids did such a wonderful job on it. They are so talented. You're right, it turned out great, and most of all, I'm so happy about how it has given them confidence in their skills. As you can see, many of them are really gifted artists."

"Absolutely, and I can see your hand in it. The background of the rebozo is phenomenal, really. It makes me want to walk up and touch it, and I love that you added Gisela's drawing of La Llorona in the mural."

"It was a really good drawing, and I felt like Gisela deserved to have her artwork included. Have you heard from her mother?"

"No, she doesn't want her to come here anymore. She is afraid La Llorona will take Gisela from her."

"Has Nico seen the mural yet?" Sofie asked.

"I don't know. He might have passed by when I wasn't here. I've been busy here, and then I go home and paint all night, Sofie. I haven't exactly had time for a social life. I haven't seen him since...Besides, I'm so messed up right now. He deserves better."

"He loves you, Aurora, and he's a really great guy. He accepts you the way you are with all your little, um, shall I say, quirks. That's a rare thing. He hasn't asked you for a commitment, and you can come and go, in and out of his life, and he never questions it. Now that I think of it, maybe you're right. He does deserve better. You don't treat him very well."

"Nico's an artist, too. People pay a lot of money for his paintings. His work is in several galleries in North Beach and Sausalito. He is constantly producing work. He doesn't exactly have time for a traditional relationship either, you know?"

"That may be true, but being busy and avoiding falling in love are two different things. He told you that he loves you, and you didn't say anything."

"What was I supposed to say, Sofie? I don't know if I'm capable of loving anyone. I feel so broken inside. I care about Nico. He is important to me, but I honestly can't say that I love him."

"You can't or you're too scared to say it?" asked Sofie. Aurora threw her hands up in the air.

"That's it. I'm not talking about this anymore with you. My relationship with Nico is my business. Goodnight."

Aurora walked out of the side entrance, slamming the door behind her. As she walked down 24th Street on her way home, she thought about Nico for the first time since her hospitalization. She hadn't seen him or talked to him since before it happened. He probably thought she was done with him. Now, she realized how unfair it was of her not to tell him about what happened. It seemed like her life got turned upside down after she was released from the hospital, and ghosts and spirits began appearing in her life. She decided she would call him when she got home.

Nico was happy to hear from Aurora. He didn't question her about why she had not been in touch for so long, or anything else.

"Nico, I was wondering if I could come by later if you're not busy. There are some things I want to talk to you about; why I haven't been around."

"I don't have anything planned, except a pot of spaghetti. You know you don't have to explain anything to me. I heard that your mom passed. I'm very sorry about that. I went to the funeral, but you weren't there," Nico said.

"Thank you. Yeah. I didn't go. I don't really do funerals."

"How about you come by around eight? Does that work?"

"Perfect. I'll see you then."

"You can let yourself in. The spare key is in the usual place."

Aurora hung up the phone, feeling nervous and excited to see Nico. She hadn't allowed herself to think about him, but now she was looking forward to seeing him, even though she knew it was going to be difficult to tell him what had happened. She arrived at Nico's flat about 8:15 p.m. She found the spare key under the large flowerpot, which was tumbling over with Marigolds, and let herself in. Once inside, she could hear music playing down the three flights of stairs. When she got to the top of the stairs, the door was ajar, and Aurora saw Nico standing barefoot in front of the stove, a glass of red wine in one hand, and stirring a large pot of his famous sausage and garlic spaghetti sauce with his other hand. She stepped inside, inhaling the sweet aroma of basil, oregano, and garlic, mixed with the sweetness of Roma tomatoes. She felt relaxed. When she heard Nico singing, she covered her mouth to stifle her laughter. He was singing at the top of his lungs along with

Pavarotti to "Nessun Dorma," from La Boheme, which was playing at full volume. He was alternately conducting an imaginary orchestra with one hand and stirring the sauce while holding a glass of wine with the other. A sudden warmth filled her heart as she watched Nico. He was good to her and expected nothing from her. "No strings," as they had agreed on, and so far, it worked for Aurora, although before her mother's death, she had felt like Nico wanted more.

He was eleven years older than her. She liked that he was honest, knew what he wanted from life, and he didn't play mind games. She could have real conversations with him. Not like men her age, who thought of women as a possession to show off to their friends, expected them to cook, clean, and have sex whenever they wanted it. Even worse, they eventually wanted to marry and start a family. She had decided long ago that she would never have children. That was not in her future. Never. Aurora often spent Sunday evenings with Nico, eating whatever dish he prepared and spending hours sharing the artistic process of their paintings. They would drink wine, allowing their creativity to flow into the night, and then make love. Aurora had felt safe enough to tell Nico some of her childhood stories; the ones she could remember. Stories that no one else except Sofie knew.

She watched him for a few minutes before interrupting his night at the opera. He was wearing his favorite paint-splattered jeans. His Hazel eyes and black hair were highlighted by his moss-green shirt, which he wore loose and unbuttoned. Aurora startled him when she walked up behind him and wrapped her arms around his waist, causing him to spill his wine and splatter spaghetti sauce all over the stove.

"Cara mía! I didn't even hear you come in."

"That's because you were too busy at the opera," she laughed.

Nico tossed the wooden spoon on the stove and pulled Aurora close to him. He kissed her deeply and tenderly, and she could feel his desire against her belly.

"God, I have missed you. I'm so glad you called."

"I missed you, too, Nico. There's something I need to tell you. Can we sit down and talk?"

"Um. Sure. Would you like a glass of wine?"

"That would be great. Thanks." She sat on the couch and waited for Nico to join her. He returned with two glasses of wine. She motioned for him to sit down. He sat facing her and waited for her to say something.

"Aurora. What is it? Please just tell me. Are you with someone else?"

"No. Nothing like that. You know that my mother died. What you may not know is that I was the one who found her."

"Oh God, Aurora. I'm so sorry. You should have called me. I would have been there for you."

"I know you would have. But I couldn't because of this." She pushed up the sleeves of her white blouse to show Nico her scars. They were still quite visible, and most likely would never fade. Nico put his hands on the scars, running his fingers over them.

"I was in the hospital. They released me to Sofie's care. I was really out of it for a long time. I'm sorry, but I couldn't talk to anyone. I hope you can understand." Nico kissed her scars, then released her wrists, and moved to the end of the couch.

"I'm sorry, but you have to give me a minute to absorb all of this. I haven't seen you for months, and you come here to tell me it's because you tried to kill yourself, and you couldn't pick up a phone to call me, to let me try to help you? Wow. I'm not sure how I feel right now. I have a lot of feelings coming up right now. I think maybe you should go, and we can talk about this again after I've had a little time to process it."

He wanted her to leave. Nico had never rejected her before, and Aurora didn't quite know how to handle it. She was suddenly afraid of losing Nico. Nico stood up from the couch and began walking towards the door. Suddenly, Aurora felt she had lost all the air in her lungs. Her head began to ache, and an electric pain shot through her brain, like biting bolts of lightning. Her vision blurred, and she felt herself falling, falling inside of her mind, far away from herself, into blackness.

⌣

She woke up in a cement basement hallway, her vision clouded by a muddy brown fog that filled the space. It was lit only by a single lightbulb hanging from a thick seaman's rope. She heard a child sobbing in the distance. As she followed the sound down a long, cement hallway, the child's crying grew louder and louder until Aurora felt like it was clawing at her insides, trying to escape.

"You have to come and help us. Please. It's dark and cold here, and I'm scared."

"Where are you? Who are you?" Aurora called out. "Tell me where you are, so I can help you."

Aurora followed the voice until she came to a heavy, black wooden door. She pushed open the door and went inside. She looked around and saw she was in a red brick room. There was one small window in one corner, too high for a child's reach. The room smelled of mold and stale tobacco. There was a small, urine-stained mattress on the floor, and a pile of dried, bloody bandages on the floor beside the mattress.

"Hello? I'm here. Where are you?" The crying stopped. Aurora turned to leave, but the door had shut behind her and she could not open it. She sat on the floor, held her head in her hands, and cried.

⌣

Maddie was startled into the room by the words of Nico asking them to leave. She was furious with Aurora for once again messing this up with Nico. She took a deep breath and composed herself. She stood up and walked to Nico. She put her arms around his waist and pulled him close to her.

"Please, Nico. I don't want to go. I've missed you so much. I need to be with you. I don't want to be alone tonight."

Nico was suddenly overcome by the taste of her mouth and the scent of her skin. He had missed her fiercely. He kissed her, and he felt her softening into him. She walked him backwards until he was standing with his back against the kitchen counter. The sensation of his body pressed against her ignited her passion, swirling ribbons of crimson and gold, stirring a fierce heat within her. She relished the moments when she could surface, free of Aurora. Free to do whatever she wanted.

Maddie loved Nico. She had been with him before. She loved this game of seduction. It was her forte. She ran her fingers through the down of Nico's chest with her fingertips, then she trailed her nails down his abdomen, just enough to make him shiver. She pressed play on the remote on the counter beside Nico, and Pavarotti's voice filled the room with melancholy and desire. Maddie allowed the intense sorrow of María Callas' singing to penetrate her. She swam in it. She loved to feel; feel everything, deep and intense, not like Aurora, who pushed her feelings down, afraid to face the truth about herself. Maddie unzipped Nico's jeans. He pulled her closer, kissing her hard and deep; she moaned into his mouth. Then she pulled back, making a trail of kisses down his chest, down to his navel, kneeling in front of him, but Nico stopped her.

"Whoa. Not so fast, cara-mia." He pulled her up off her knees and back into his embrace. He burrowed his face into her neck, inhaling the scent of her skin. He kissed her face and her eyes, with care and tenderness. The sweetness of his kisses made Maddie cringe. She felt herself fading. She wanted the power that led to an explosion of ecstasy. Ecstasy that came from intense, hot sex. She needed him to love her hard.

"I want you, baby, but not like this. I want you to feel my love."

"I want you too, Nico. I want you to fuck me, now."

He took her hand and led her quickly into his bedroom. They ripped off their clothes, tossing them on the floor. Nico tossed her playfully on her back. They fell together, his body covering hers. He pressed one hand against her breast, gently kneading it, until a deep moan escaped her.

"Fuck me," she demanded.

"Not yet, love. I want to go slow."

Then, she pushed him hard inside of her. He looked at her, his eyes full of heat and disappointment. He tried to move slowly, savoring the feel of her sex, but she continued to push against him.

"Fuck me hard, Nico."

Then he was lost in her heat and the connection of their bodies. He moved fast and hard inside her. Maddie dug her nails into his back and bit his neck.

He whispered words into her neck. "Ti amo cara mia."

Then, without warning, Maddie lost her breath. The weight of his tenderness became too much. She was screaming for him to stop inside her head, but no sound came. She tried to push him off, but she could not move. From a secret place inside her mind, she heard the distant voice of a child calling to her.

"Come back, Maddie. Come back. I'm scared." The distressed pleading of a lost and frightened child. It was time for her to go. Maddie knew how to navigate this familiar labyrinth of the mind she shared with Aurora. She followed the voice of the child that would lead her back to the red brick room, where she existed along with the others, suspended in a dark and forgotten space of Aurora's mind.

Without warning, an invisible force ripped Aurora from the basement. One moment, she was in a red brick room, then she woke up to find her body beneath the weight of Nico as he was pushing inside of her. Her vision was blurred, her limbs heavy, all she could hear was the sound of her own voice off in the distance, screaming.

"Get off me. Stop. Get off." Nico was off Aurora before she could say another word.

"Aurora. What the...? Wake up, damn it!" His voice was full of fear and confusion. He shook her, trying to wake her out of whatever dream she had fallen into, but he could see that she was gone. Then, a force like a great wind pushed her back into her body, back into bed with Nico. She came to and saw that he was sitting up beside her, staring at her with a mixture of fear and anger on his face.

"Nico, I...what's wrong? What happened? Why are you staring at me like that?"

"You don't know? Jesus Christ, Aurora. You passed out, or fell asleep, or something right in the middle of making love, or fucking, as you like to call it. Then you started crying and yelling. I tried to wake you up, but every time I touched you, you just screamed louder. What the hell is going on?"

"Oh, god. I'm sorry, Nico. I don't know what happened. The last thing I remember is that we were sitting on the couch. Then, I felt dizzy, and the room went dark, and I felt myself falling into a dark place. I couldn't stop what was happening; it was like I woke up inside a dream. It was dark, and there was a little girl crying, and then there was an empty room, and I don't know." She heard herself rambling, but she could not stop herself.

She was overcome with a sick feeling, like she had swallowed the ocean, and she was drowning. She got up from the bed and ran into the bathroom. Sorrow overtook her, and she fell to the floor in front of the toilet, sobbing and vomiting water; a sea of emotion demanding release. She didn't understand why she was crying, but like the ocean, the tears and vomiting had no reason and would not stop.

Nico came up behind her, pulling her to rest in his arms. The two of them sat on the bathroom floor and wept. He wept for the ghosts of Aurora's past that were always between them. After a while, he guided her to her feet and helped her into bed. He lay cautiously behind her, not wanting to trigger another episode. He held her close and promised that everything would be fine.

"You're safe, now. I'm here, cara mia. I won't let anything hurt you." She willed his words to mean something, but she knew that she would never feel safe.

"I love you, Aurora."

"I know."

The sadness in Nico's voice brought Aurora back to the present moment. She knew what he was going to say. She felt sorry that she had hurt him. She hoped this time things would be different.

"There is something very serious going on here, Aurora. It isn't going to go away by ignoring it and pretending that it's not happening. I love you so much, but this is too much for me. You know, I never told you, but my dad used to have episodes like this after he came home from the war. He would wake up in the middle of the night, screaming and fighting some invisible enemy. One time, he almost choked my mother to death. Something more must have happened to you that you don't remember, Aurora. You need to get some help to remember. My dad never got any help, and he ended up drinking himself to death. I know you care about me, but you push me away. Do you think I don't see that you're in pain? If you won't let me help you, then find someone who can."

She caressed Nico's cheek and searched for words that would ease the hurt and confusion in his eyes. "It's not your fault, Nico. I've always been this way. It's like I don't know how to be alive. When you tell me that you love me, I just want to run. It feels dangerous."

"I know you don't feel the same way, I do. What happened last night wasn't the first time. We just never talk about it, but this has gone way past what happened before. I don't think I can do this, cara mia. I love you. You're hurting, and there's nothing I can do to help you, because you won't admit that there is anything wrong. Do you understand how that makes me feel? I want to protect you, but instead you push me away and leave me feeling useless."

"It's not your fault, Nico. You didn't do anything wrong, and there's nothing you can do to fix me," she said, and in her admission, she realized that it wasn't her fault either, but she blamed herself just the same. She was defective and empty, filled with looming darkness that exploded like shards of Obsidian, destroying what little happiness she had found with Nico. Nico was good, and now she had destroyed that, too. Her heart began to pound with fear, and she wanted to scream, *Please don't leave me. I can change. I'll be good, I promise.* But she silenced herself. The silence grated against the scarred flesh of her heart. The gates were closing.

Nico's voice was suddenly angry. "This is just too intense, Aurora. Why can't you be satisfied with the way that I love you? I really do love you, you know, but I'm done lying to myself and pretending that someday you will want to marry me and be a family. I need to be honest with myself and admit that this is never going to happen. It's as if there is a place inside of you that I can't reach, that no amount of love will penetrate." Nico rubbed his hand over his face and through his hair. It was a gesture that she had grown to love. It was something that he did when he felt deeply moved and needed time to gather his thoughts. But now, she felt a chasm split open between them. She knew this was goodbye. She felt a strange relief. She was weary of this game where there could be no winners. Nico put his jeans on, slipped on some flip-flops, and pulled a sweatshirt over his head.

"I'm going for a walk. I would appreciate it if you were gone before I get back. You can just leave my keys on the bed." Nico sat next to her and pulled her close. He kissed her softly on the forehead.

"Goodbye, Aurora." He got up quickly, and before she could say a word, she heard the front door close.

⌣

It was September, and the Magnolia trees were in full bloom all over the neighborhood. Their thick, pungent fragrance wafted through the air. Aurora inhaled their perfume as she walked home, letting it permeate her senses. She stopped to caress a low-hanging bloom. She closed her eyes and imagined that her body was the Magnolia blossom, vulnerable, without shame, confident in its own essence. She tried to imagine what it would be like to feel the sunlight shine hot on her fleshy, white blossoms, heating the crimson nectar flowing through her veins. She wondered if she would enjoy the intentional gaze upon her petals, and wondered if she experienced pleasure at sharing her fragrance so freely. She envied not knowing what it was like to fully express herself without shame. She decided that she would never know the answers to her questions and decided to return to the only love she could fully trust. Over the next six months, Aurora painted furiously, devotedly, and tirelessly. Her only companions were her cat, a child ghost, and the spirit of a woman who wanted something from her she could not figure out. She drank tequila to quell the voices and the visions. She threw the empty bottles against the wall when they appeared, and when they did not appear, she felt their absence. They were a part of her life now, for better or for worse, and if she allowed herself to push past her fear, she found that in a strange way she had come to love them.

NOVEMBER 1 ~ 1983

Aurora wiped the tips of her paint brushes with a dry cloth and placed them in an empty mason jar. As she looked around her studio at the empty easel, she could not believe it had been two years since she first began the series of paintings for this show. Exactly two years since...She pushed the encroaching thoughts from her mind. Tonight, all her paintings were hung at the El Centro del Corazón Gallery. It was a dream come true for any artist.

She thought about her students and how she loved teaching. It provided a place for the children to express the pain they held, transferring it onto the canvas using paint, instead of words, as no words could describe what they had seen; what they had lost. Before leaving their children at the El Centro each day, the mothers blessed them by marking an invisible cross on their brows, then kissing the top of their heads. Milagro lit copal and offered prayers and blessings of protection for the children. This was something useful she could do. She lost her husband and her two sons in Guatemala. They were taken one day without warning.

That evening, when Milagro returned from the market where she sold her weavings, a neighbor relayed what she had heard. Her children had been helping their father in his milpa when soldiers armed with rifles drove up in a truck. An unknown person had made a report that Miguel was hiding insurgents somewhere in the milpa. After they searched and found no one, they beat him in front of his children, who watched frozen and silent. The soldiers grabbed Miguel and the children and threw them in the back of a truck. Milagro did not need to hear any more from her neighbor. After three days with no news of where her husband and sons had been taken, or if they were alive, she already knew the answer. Families disappeared every day, with no bodies to pray over or place in sacred ground. They would not receive a proper burial; they became ghosts, names never to be mentioned for fear they would meet the same fate. Aurora choked back the tears that wanted to come as she thought of these families who had lost everything and yet somehow still knew how to love. She wished she knew their secret.

She gazed at the white candles that were scattered on the floor and on the windowsills.

Light to fill the darkness she could not name. Light to fill the darkness inside.

She bathed in the light, in silence, in secret, allowing it to illuminate the emptiness inside of her. She had spent the last two years working on this series, which she titled "The Dreams of Ghosts." Two years painting alone at night, a bottle of tequila, her black cat Bruja, and two crying spirits, her only companions. Each night around 3:00 a.m., she felt the sad presence of someone watching her from the doorway, then the soft sound of a woman and a child crying. The child pleaded for help, calling her by her childhood name.

"Help me, Yoya. Get me out of here. She won't let me come home. I'm scared and cold."

Aurora followed the voice of the child through her flat, out the front door, into the street, where the voice dissolved into night. She returned to her canvas, night after night, sleeping only three to four hours. But tonight, she hoped all that was finally over. There was a clean, white canvas on her easel, filled with hope of a new beginning. She placed the palms of her hands on the edges of the easel, closed her eyes, and whispered, "Thank you for always being here for me." She picked up a candle and moved the light around the room, then raised it as if making a toast. "To good things to come." She wiped the tears that started to fall, blew out the candles, and went to shower.

After she towel-dried her hair, she slipped on a sleeveless black velvet dress, which still had the tags on it. She had not had occasion to wear it, but tonight she wanted to look her best. She combed on a little mascara, slid red lipstick across her lips, and combed out her long black hair. She let it fall loose down her back and plucked a fat orange Marigold from the vase on her nightstand and secured it in her hair with a bobby pin.

Tonight was November 1. El Dia de los Muertos; two years since her mother had taken her own life, and two years since Aurora had been hospitalized.

Aurora walked down 24th Street from her flat on Folsom Street. She took a deep breath and allowed the crisp air, thick with the aroma of roasting chiles, and the sweet fragrance of copal that wafted out of the storefronts to fill her senses and relax her. When she passed Balmy Alley, she heard someone call her name. She looked across the street to see Milagro waving for her to cross the street.

"Aurora. Venga aqui."

"Hola, Milagro. Que tal?" She loved and admired Milagro, who not only spoke Ki´ché, her indigenous language, but also spoke Spanish and was fast learning English, too. Milagro knew the ancient prayers of her people, as well as how to use herbs for healing. But more than anything, Aurora admired the way Milagro cared for the families of El Centro, using herbs to cure empacho, mal de aire, and if she could not help them, then she sent them to see Luz and Rosario when they needed a limpia or soul healing.

"Look a dis. Dis so pretty for you." Milagro held up a soft cotton rebozo for Aurora to try on. It was a deep red, the color of pomegranate seeds. When Aurora saw the rebozo, she realized she had forgotten to cover her scars. She normally wore a long-sleeved, oversized white button-down shirt for painting. It hid her scars, so she never had to worry about covering them. Milagro placed the rebozo around Aurora's shoulders and across her forearms to hide the pink lines.

"It's perfect, Milagro. I'll take it. Cuánto?"

"It is my gift. You must hide the lines of your soul because many people no understand these things. Yes?

Aurora hugged Milagro and kissed her on both cheeks.

"Muchísimas gracias, Milagro. It's perfect. I love it and I love you. Will you come by the show later?"

"Claro que sí, mija. I want to see your beautiful pictures."

"Bueno, Milagro. Te quiero mucho." Milagro blew Aurora a kiss as she walked away.

⌣

The gallery of El Centro del Corazón was packed when Aurora arrived. She squeezed past a group of people standing in front of her largest painting, chatting about her use of colors, symbols, and mystical images in one of her paintings. It portrayed a Mexican woman with long, white hair, dressed in a gossamer turquoise dress, the color of the sky just after dawn. In the painting, the woman stood on the corner of Balmy Alley and 24th Street, where several women had told Aurora that they had seen La Llorona. In the painting, the woman stood in front of a great willow tree with hanging, lacy branches. Aurora did not want to believe that La Llorona was real, nor did she understand why so many women revered a spirit that had supposedly drowned her children, then herself. But she had an almost desperate need to paint her.

La Llorona appeared to her and her mother when Aurora was six years old. Her mother, Dolores, had believed the stories of La Llorona that told of how she stole the breath of babies, then took them to el río abajo del río, in the underworld. Dolores was terrified of La Llorona, but on the night she first appeared, Aurora felt drawn to her apparition and wanted to go to her. La Llorona appeared in their backyard, hidden between the branches of a sprawling willow tree. She was surrounded by a faint blue light. There were tears falling freely down her face. She had green eyes like shards of Jade, and there was a feeling of deep sorrow that Aurora felt from her. She thought she might be an angel. When Aurora walked towards La Llorona, her mother pulled her into the house, screaming at the apparition to stay away from her daughter.

Aurora now dismissed the memory as a childhood fantasy shared with a mother whose sanity was often in question. Still, she had felt compelled to paint La Llorona, as if invoking her presence might reveal the mystery that Aurora held inside. She painted her in various scenes as she imagined she might appear—standing in front of a river, wading in the ocean, and standing on the corner of Balmy Alley watching the people pass her by. Aurora did not fully understand her obsession with this ghost-woman in whom she tried so hard not to believe in. Besides paintings of La Llorona, Aurora also painted scenes of the families of El Centro del Corazon dressed in their traditional woven clothes from Mexico or Guatemala. Their clothing was embedded with sacred symbols that told a story of their lineage. She painted the stories they were barely able to speak about in a weekly storytelling circle with Sofie.

As each woman shared a thread of her story, it gave another woman the strength to share a thread of her own, and slowly, over months, their stories wove themselves into a rebozo of light, offered up to the Ancestors with love and hope. Sofie believed this was all they needed: to share their stories and to have them heard and believed. Several of the women gave Aurora permission to paint their stories. They wanted people to know the truth. The women had also worked on a memorial mural with Aurora to paint the names of loved ones who perished in the genocide, and whose bodies had still not been found.

Aurora walked to the back of the gallery and tucked herself into the shadow of the altar that took up the entire back wall. She found comfort in the warmth from the flames of the candles, and the pungent scent from the dozens of Marigolds on the altar, as well as the crumpled petals that covered most of the floor around the altar and made a trail of orange-golden light to the front door. The Marigolds illuminated a path for the ancestors to come and feast on the aroma of the food people placed on the altar.

Marigolds. Flowers of the dead.

She gazed at the petals scattered on the floor and wished someone would leave a trail of light for her to find her way home, back to a place she longed for, a place she had never known. Most of the time, Aurora felt as though she were half-dead, or maybe it was that she had never truly felt alive. It was only when she was painting, lost in the smells of turpentine, oil paint, with a jar full of clean brushes, and a large white canvas in front of her, that she sensed her blood moving through her veins. While she painted, she loved to listen to Linda Ronstadt, Joni Mitchell, Jimi Hendrix, and Santana turned up loud. Her brushes danced across the canvas. She was outside of time, her mind's eye filled with color, lines, and faces that manifested so clearly onto the canvas. She felt alive. Painting was all she knew. This was all she could remember of her life. This was all she wanted to remember.

Aurora looked around the gallery, watching as people viewed her paintings. She felt like all the sleepless nights of the past two years had been worth it. Her paintings that came from a place between reality and dreams were now being seen. She knew she should feel happy, but instead she felt like one of the muertos on the altar, a collection of bones, and like her skin had recently fallen off and everyone could see the empty space inside her; her insides she herself could not see. She thought of the ghost of the crying child that had recently moved in with her. She half expected the child to show up at the doorway. She prayed to the Marigolds that she would not. She prayed that no one would approach her to ask her about her work. She prayed to no one.

Sofie was the director of El Centro del Corazon, as well as her best friend and agent. Sofie quickly intercepted anyone walking towards Aurora, explaining that Aurora was shy and did not like to talk about herself, and that she would be happy to answer any questions about Aurora's paintings.

Michael was moved and intrigued as he viewed the paintings. He was a serious collector of Latina art and had recently opened his own gallery in North Beach. He wanted to create a high-profile location next to other mainstream contemporary art. He wanted to invite art collectors to take Latina art seriously, both artistically and financially.

He was captivated by Aurora's paintings. There was an otherworldly quality to them that conveyed a fierce sorrow. They touched a familiar place inside, making him want to sit quietly and listen to the whispering between the layers of paint. The skin on the back of his neck stood up when he encountered one painting in particular. He felt himself being pulled into the canvas that portrayed a beautiful Mexican woman with long black braids down the front of her body. She was dressed in a white huipil embroidered with Marigolds and Monarch Butterflies around the neck. He felt that she represented something ancient and sacred. In the painting, she wore a pair of faded blue jeans, and he knew she was from the spirit world because she wore no shoes. The woman faced the viewer, arms outstretched, holding crumpled Marigolds in her hands; orange-gold petals falling to the ground. She stood in front of a willow tree, with several Barn Owls hiding in the branches beneath a blue-black sky, illuminated by a full moon. The woman in the painting conveyed a strange mix of strength and longing that made him yearn for something he could not name. He reached his hand out to touch the woman's face, then caught himself and thought better of it. He stood with her for a moment, then he noticed she had tears in her eyes. A song his mother used to sing to him suddenly flooded his memory:

Salías del templo un día Llorona. Cuando al pasar, yo te vi. Hermoso
huipil llevabas Llorona que La Virgen te creí. Ay, de mí Llorona,
Llorona, Llorona de azul celeste...
One day, while leaving the temple, Llorona, I saw you. You wore such
a beautiful blouse that I thought you were La Virgen. Oh Llorona, my
Llorona, Llorona of the celestial sky.

Suddenly, he sensed the presence of his madrecita nearby and believed she was trying to tell him something; whatever it was, he knew it had something to do with La Llorona and possibly Aurora, too. He quickly found Sofie and interrupted her conversation with a circle of people inquiring about some of the other paintings.

"Excuse me. I'm sorry to interrupt, but I want you to put a sold sign on that painting." He pointed to the painting, pulled a signed blank check from his pocket, and handed it to Sofie.

"Whatever the price. I don't care. Just mark it sold, while you're at it, I will take the whole series of 'The Dreams of Ghosts.' Mark them all sold. Now, where can I find the artist?"

It took Sofie a moment to recover from being handed a blank check. She pointed to the corner near the altar that was piled high with pictures of loved ones and offerings of tamales, chile, tequila, cigarettes, frijoles, cerveza, and menudo. The aroma of the food wafted through the gallery. There were also hundreds of pieces of colorful folded paper scattered over the altar, with prayers for blessings and protection written on them. Michael followed the carpet of Marigold petals scattered on the floor between jars of white candles that lined the way for the ancestors. Michael spotted Aurora standing in the corner next to the altar, a glass of red wine in her hand; her red rebozo wrapped tightly around her.

Aurora noticed him walking towards her and quickly looked away, hoping he would take the hint and find someone else to talk to. He was wearing a blue Pendleton shirt, a white T-shirt underneath it, with black slacks and shoes. He wore his hair combed back with one thin, long, single braid down the middle of his back. He smiled, and his face lit up with a kindness she did not expect. Suddenly, he was standing in front of her, his hand extended.

"Hola. You must be Aurora, the artist. I'm Michael del Río, and I think I have fallen in love with your paintings." Aurora did not extend her hand, so he put his hands in his pants pockets.

"Oh. Thank you so much. That really means a lot to me."

"You should be very happy; I just bought twenty of your paintings."

"What? Oh my god. That's incredible. I don't know what to say."

"Well, I really love them all, but that one has captured my heart." He turned around and pointed to the large painting of La Llorona at Balmy Alley. The painting was 60 inches wide by 80 inches tall and took up an entire wall of the show.

"She is my favorite, too. Well, favorite isn't quite the right word. She was the most challenging for me."

"Really? Why is that?"

"My paintings come to me in dreams, which is only about 3 to 4 hours a night that I sleep. The images wake me up, and I'm compelled to paint them. So, I get out of bed and paint. If you don't mind me asking, Michael, why did you buy so many of my paintings?"

"No. Not at all. I am opening a Latina art gallery in North Beach."

"Latina art—only Latina art? That seems a little strange. What are you, some kind of feminist or something?" She laughed.

"In a way, yes. My mother was a gifted painter from East L.A., and she died when I was twelve from complications of diabetes. We barely got by from what she made from her paintings to pay rent, pay for electricity, and keep us both fed. We ate a lot of bologna sandwiches. My mother died because she could not afford the insulin that she needed. Her art was amazing, and it was worth so much more than she sold it for. No gallery would show her work, because people viewed her paintings as folk art. Hell, Frida Kahlo was so happy when she sold her paintings for a few hundred dollars. When she was at the peak of her career, her paintings sold for $300 or less. My mother sold her paintings for whatever people offered her. At her funeral, I promised her that I would work hard to promote Latina painters and to make sure their artwork sold for what it was worth. So yes. I'm a feminist for art." Michael did not mean to share such a personal story. He ran his hand through his hair and took a deep breath.

"Wow. I didn't mean to dump all that on you. I'm sorry."

"Don't be sorry. I think it's beautiful that you love your mom so much and you're keeping your promise to her. You were lucky to have a loving mother. I'm sorry she was taken from you so young. I appreciate you telling me about her."

"You're welcome. Anyway, I'm going to show your paintings in my gallery, along with my mother's paintings as part of my personal collection, and if you're okay with it, I want to take commissions for you. That is, if you are interested?"

"I might be. Let me talk to Sofie about it. Maybe we can meet for coffee and talk about it next week sometime."

Just then, Aurora looked up and saw Nico, smiling and walking towards her. She had invited him months ago, but after what happened the last time they were together, she did not think he would come. He approached her and kissed her on the cheek.

"Congratulations, Cara Mia. I knew people would love your work. I'm so happy for you." Michael stepped back, feeling like an interloper in a moment of intimacy.

"Listen, Aurora, I'm going to head out, but it was great to talk to you. How can I reach you?"

"Wait, Michael. I want to introduce you to Nico. He is also a painter. Nico, Michael bought all the paintings in my Ghost series."

"That's fantastic. Good to meet you, Michael. You're a smart man." The two men shook hands and stood quietly.

"Are you a collector of Aurora's paintings?" Michael asked Nico.

"Actually, I just bought my first painting today, but I'm looking forward to acquiring others in the future," Nico said, glancing over at Aurora and giving her a wink. Aurora suddenly felt nervous at seeing Nico again and was unsure how to respond to his playful flirting, so she turned her attention back to Michael.

"I'm here every day, Michael. You can get a card from Sofie on your way out, and thank you so much."

"Okay, Aurora. I'll give you a call. I can't wait to hang your work in my gallery."

"Bye, Michael." As he walked out, he stopped to let Sofie know that he would pick the paintings up next week. Nico took Aurora's hand and held it for a moment.

"Goodnight, Cara-Mia. I'm so happy for you."

"Thank you, Nico. I appreciate that you came to my show. Did you really buy one of my paintings?

"I did."

"Which one?

"The one of the sad little girl in a red brick room."

"That's a strange painting you picked. I'm not even sure why Sofie hung it. Originally, it wasn't for sale, but she really wanted to include it in the show. Why did you choose that one, Nico? If you don't mind me asking."

"Because I know that little girl, and I love her. I hope you can help her one day, Aurora. Take care." Nico took Aurora's hand, looked into her eyes, kissed her hand, then turned and walked towards the door. Sofie smiled at Nico as he left the gallery.

"Thanks for coming, Nico."

"I wouldn't have missed it for anything, Sofie."

She locked the door behind him, then turned around with a big grin and walked over to give Aurora a big hug.

"Hey, mujer. You did it! Your show was a success. How are you feeling?"

"I'm feeling happy, relieved, and exhausted. I'm glad to have the show over with. Thank you for all your hard work putting it together. You did a wonderful job, and I couldn't have done it without you."

"It was my pleasure. Besides, you did all the hard work. I just hung them on the wall, and they sold themselves. But um, I didn't realize Nico would be here. I thought you two were over?"

"We are. I invited him months ago. I didn't think he would come, either. I don't want to talk about Nico."

"C'mon. I saw how your face lit up when you saw him. It's obvious how much he loves you. But I won't talk about him if you don't want to. Let's talk about your show, Aurora. It's not every day that an artist sells out a show in a few hours. That guy, Michael, has his own gallery, and he gave me a pinche' blank check, girl! I'm so happy for you. We need to celebrate."

"I'm not really feeling up to celebrating, Sofie. I just want to go home and try to get some sleep, or maybe start a new painting."

"Oh, really. But you're going to meet up with Michael next week, huh? A date?"

"No. It's a business meeting, and you're going to meet him, but we can talk about it later, okay?"

"I'm just saying, it looked pretty darn cozy from where I was standing, and besides, you never sleep, and you can paint tomorrow. You need to get out and have some fun! Michael bought 15 of 20 paintings, Milagro bought two of the smaller ones, Nico bought one, and the other two sold to people I never met before. They could not stop talking about your work, Aurora. It's been a good day."

"How can I say no to that, Sofie? You're right, we should celebrate. Besides, I was too nervous to eat today, so now I'm famished."

"Great. Let me take you out. There's a restaurant that my friends Luz and Rosario own. Dos Almas, it's on the corner of 24th and Balmy Alley. I've been wanting you to meet them, and the food is too delicious for words. I am not exaggerating. Please say yes." Aurora thought about it. She really did not want to be alone. The last thing she wanted was any more encounters with ghosts or spirits or having to think about her mother.

"Okay, Sofie. It sounds like fun."

"Ay, madre de dios. Did you just say fun? Ándale' maybe we can go dancing afterwards?"

"Don't push it, girl."

"Okay. Vamos pues."

Suddenly, Aurora felt a well of sadness fill her heart. She tried not to think about the fact that it was two years ago that her mother took her own life. She pulled her rebozo around her shoulders tightly and willed away her sadness. Sofie saw the tears and looked confused.

"Hey, girl, por qué lloras?"

"Oh, I don't know. I think I just need to eat."

"You should be happy, Aurora. You just had a milestone as an artist." Aurora turned away from Sofie.

"It's okay to be scared, you know, Aurora? Hell, I would be scared, too, if I had the ghost of a little girl haunting me. Maybe it's time to talk to someone." Sofie put her arm around Aurora's shoulder, but Aurora moved away from her.

"So they can lock me up like they locked up my mother? No thanks, Sofie. I'll work through this on my own. I'm doing okay, really, and besides, my show is over, so I can move on with my life."

"But you're not moving on with your life, Aurora. You're stuck. Stuck and haunted. You're depressed, you don't sleep, and you just broke up with a great guy who is madly in love with you. You need to want to live, and not just exist like your ghosts, Aurora."

"I told you it was an accident, Sofie. I cut too deep that time."

"You said it, Aurora. You always cut too deep in one way or another. Hurting yourself is not going to bring your mother back. Why you would want her back is beyond me."

"It's not that I want her back, Sofie. It's just that I have so many questions I never had the nerve to ask her while she was alive. I want to know what made her the way she was and why it was so hard to love me. Was I so terrible?" Sofie touched her hand to Aurora's cheek.

"I'm sorry. That was insensitive of me. I know tonight is..."

"Okay, Sofie. Can we get out of here now? You promised me dinner."

Dos Almas restaurant was crowded when Sofie and Aurora arrived. They looked at the rows of tables set up parallel to the long turn of the century Oak bar, decorated with ornate carvings of roses along the edge. They spotted an empty table for two in the back of the restaurant, grabbed a menu as was the custom, and seated themselves.

"Oh, the food smells magnificent, Sofie. Suddenly, I'm starving," Aurora said.

"Rosario's cooking will do that. Girl, I can't believe you haven't been here yet."

"Ay, Sofie. You know I don't go out much. I usually just grab food to go from Las Palmas on my way home from work, but this really is a nice change, and you're right; it's good to have something to celebrate."

Just then, Aurora felt a chill, like fingers scratching down her spine, and a feeling of dread rose from her stomach. Suddenly, the edges of her vision began to dim, so she grabbed the edge of the table for balance. Then, something pulled her attention towards the restaurant door. That's when she saw her.

"Sofie. She's here. It's her! Oh my god. Oh my god." Aurora stood up.

"Aurora, what's going on? What are you talking about? Please sit down. Everyone is staring at you, and you're scaring me. Please tell me what's happening."

"Turn around, Sofie. The little girl that's haunting me. It's her. I know it is. She's standing right there in the doorway, Sofie. Turn around and see for yourself." Sofie turned to see what Aurora was talking about, but when she did, the only person she saw was Luz, who was standing by the altar staring towards the doorway. Luz saw the child, who was about six years old. Her tear-stained face was covered with a thin layer of dirt. She reminded Luz of the orphans of Mexico and Guatemala who walked the dirt roads, lost, alone, picking through piles of trash for scraps of food. The child was dressed in a dirty, faded, short-sleeved white dress with faded pink flowers. The fabric was worn, with spots that were threadbare. Her hair was matted, and the inside of her forearms were lined with vertical, bright pink scratches, once bloody, now scabbed over.

"There's no one in the doorway, Yoya," Sofie called her by her childhood name, hoping it would soothe her and help her to calm down, but Aurora only grew more agitated. Her heart was pounding, and all the fear she had been holding from sleepless nights exploded in anger. Her mind was flooded with the sound of this child crying and calling for help. She swallowed hard to choke back the tears in her throat. She did not want to cry in front of everyone. She was going to confront this ghost or delusion, or whatever she was right now. She got up from the table and marched towards the door, screaming at a child that only she and Luz could see.

"What do you want from me?" The child stared back at her without answering. She turned and walked down 24th Street. The people from the restaurant ran outside to watch as Aurora followed someone they could not see. Aurora called out for the child to stop. Some of the women crossed themselves and prayed to La Llorona for help.

Sofie ran to the door and looked at Luz, who was lighting candles on the altar. Luz nodded and mouthed the word, *Go*. It was then that Sofie understood that Aurora was not imagining this. She followed her, calling after Aurora, knowing that she appeared loca to people watching from the street. Aurora continued to call after the child, running behind her.

"Stop. Where are you going? I'm here. Talk to me."

The child turned right on Alabama Street and walked up the stairs of St. Peter's church. It was the end of choir practice, so parents were leaving with their children, and the doors were open. Aurora followed the ghost child up the steps and into the church. The little girl walked to the front of the church and knelt in front of the shrine of La Virgen de Guadalupe. Aurora kneeled quietly beside her and watched as the girl pulled a red-crystal rosary from her pocket. She laced the rosary through her fingers, closed her eyes, and mouthed a silent prayer.

As Aurora observed the child, she wondered what kind of mother would neglect their child this way. Her hair was a tangled mess and looked as if it had not been brushed in weeks. She wore an old white dress with little pink flowers, and the toes of her dirty white sneakers had holes in them. She reached out to touch her, but the child shrank back in pain. Then she turned to Aurora, eyes vacant and dark; for if her eyes had once held light, it had long been extinguished by what they had seen. Aurora was impatient now and needed to know what this child wanted from her.

"What is it that you want from me? Just tell me and I'll do it. I'll do whatever you want if it means I can find some peace."

"No, you won't," the child answered matter-of-factly. "I keep calling for you to get me out of there, but you never come. You forgot about me like everyone else did."

"I can hear you calling me, but you never tell me what you want or how you want me to help you. Please just tell me, and I promise I will help you." Aurora looked down at her forearms and saw that a bright red rash had appeared.

"I can't tell you. You need to remember me, but I know you won't. Because you gave the remember to me a long time ago and you never want it back."

"I gave you what? Stop talking in riddles and answer my questions, so I can be rid of you once and for all." As soon as she said the words, she wanted to take them back, but it was too late.

"You hate me just like everybody else because I'm bad. If you don't help me, I'll have to stay there forever, and it's cold and dirty, and we want to go home. Please, Yoya. Please take me out of bricks. I promise I'll be a good girl. I promise." The child cried and scratched at her arms until they bled; red streaks ran down her arms. Aurora felt something wet on her own arms and looked down at them to see that she had been scratching without realizing it, and her arms were bleeding, too. The child placed her red-crystal rosary in Aurora's hand. She laced it through her fingers. It felt oddly comforting. Her vision began to blur, and she felt as if she were falling into darkness. She found herself standing on the stairs that led to the basement of her childhood flat.

"I'm in here, Yoya." She heard the little girl calling in a familiar voice. She followed the sound of her voice down the stairs and through the hallway until she came to a large black wooden door that had no handle or keyhole on the outside. She banged on the door.

"I hear you, little girl. I'm here, but you need to open the door for me."

"I can't. You're the only one who can open it, Yoya. Use your remembering."

"I don't understand what you mean. Open the door, so I can help you." It was no use. The child started to cry again. Aurora couldn't bear the sound of it any longer. She put her hands to her ears.

"Stop. Just stop, please. Go away and leave me alone." She heard herself yelling and was jolted back to the church with Sofie sitting there beside her.

"Are you alright?" Sofie asked.

"Do I look like I'm alright to you? I'm sitting here in an empty church talking to a child that's a figment of my imagination. I'm losing my mind, Sofie. Oh, god help me." She crumbled on the floor, sobbing, until she couldn't catch her breath.

"You are going to be okay, Aurora. I promise. Shhh, now." Aurora quieted down as she stared blankly at the floor. She rocked back and forth, repeating in a whisper, "They're going to lock me up just like my mother. I'm crazy just like her. I'm crazy. I know it." Just then, Luz ran into the church, down the aisle, and sat down beside Sofie and Aurora. She put her hand on Aurora's brow.

"Let's take her to my house, Sofie. You can both stay, and in the morning, we will figure out how to help her." Sofie and Luz helped Aurora to her feet, standing on either side of her to walk her out of the church and back to Luz and Rosario's flat. When they arrived, the restaurant was closed, and Rosario was waiting by the door to let them in. Sofie and Luz helped Aurora up the stairs, into the living room, to a couch where Sofie sat with Aurora until she fell asleep. Sofie covered her with a blanket from the arm of the couch. Then she found another couch directly across from where Aurora was and lay down, her mind spinning from all that had occurred that night. Sofie remembered the afternoon she found Aurora, wrists bloody, and an ambulance downstairs that had taken away her mother's dead body. She thought she had lost Aurora, too. Sofie said a silent prayer, asking the Tonantzin-Guadalupe to watch over Aurora and keep her safe.

◡

Aurora woke up on a couch in the living room of a strange third-floor flat. She tossed off the indigo Mayan quilt that covered her. She was still wearing her black dress from the night before. Her head felt foggy, her limbs heavy. When she moved to sit up, she felt something small, like little stones poking at her side. When she sat up, Aurora found a ruby crystal rosary on the cushion. She picked it up, holding it to the light coming in through the windows. Her head began to clear, and memories of the night before came back to her. As she looked around the strange room, she started to panic until she saw that Sofie was asleep on the sofa across from her; if Sofie was there, it was safe. She was safe. She wanted to wake her, but the artistry of the room piqued her curiosity. There were brightly colored Oaxacan textiles placed across the coffee table, throw pillows in red, cobalt, fuchsia, yellow, and orange, along with other handwoven textiles placed carefully around the room. She grabbed her rebozo from the arm of the sofa, wrapped it around her, then walked to the far wall of the room where there stood a long wooden table that someone used as an altar. It was arrayed with vases of fresh marigolds, photos of ancestors, and plates of food, a cup of coffee, and little shot glasses filled with what she guessed was Mezcal. In the center of the table stood a large wooden statue of Tonantzin-Guadalupe that appeared to be hand-carved. The table had an ornate base, carved with butterflies and roses that extended up and around the edge of the table. There were several white candles lit in glass, and a small black ceramic bowl that had copal and cedar burning in it. Aurora felt as if she was floating through a pleasant dream, then out of nowhere, memories from the night before intruded. She remembered being at her art show and feeling so happy because all her paintings had sold. Then she felt a bile rise from her stomach, as she remembered the little girl who appeared at the door of the restaurant and then ran away to the church. Suddenly, the odor of urine and mold filled her senses, and she could not catch her breath. Her consciousness began to float from her body, up to the ceiling. Then she caught herself, falling back into her body. She ran over to where Sofie lay on the couch and shook her hard.

"Sofie. Wake up. Where are we? Sofie." Sofie startled awake, sat up, and gently put her hands on Aurora's shoulders to try to calm her.

"Don't worry, Yoya. We're at my friends Luz and Rosario's house. This flat is right above the restaurant where we were last night. Don't be scared. You're safe." Aurora pulled away.

"Sofie, how did I get here? What happened? I remember the little girl crying in the church. She was trying to tell me something. No, she was trying to show me something, then I followed her to the basement where I grew up." The pitch of Aurora's voice started to rise as she began to talk faster and faster.

"She was crying so loud, but she was trapped in the room. I tried to get in, but the door was locked, and she kept crying and screaming for me to help her. Somehow, I knew she was in danger. I wanted to help her, but I couldn't get to her. I banged on the door, then it was as if I woke from a nightmare, and I was back in the church, and she was gone. Sofie, I can't feel my bones. It's as if they are still in that basement." Tears rolled down Aurora's face. She wrapped her arms around herself and felt something rough on them. She looked down and saw bright pink scabs on her arms.

Luz, La Llorona, and Rosario had been standing in the doorway and heard everything. Aurora looked over and saw the ghost woman from her dreams standing behind Luz and Rosario. She stood in the doorway for a moment, as if waiting to be invited in. She was the woman from Aurora's paintings. Her form was transparent and ephemeral. The ghost woman stared through Aurora with ancient jade-green eyes. She, too, had tears rolling down her face. Aurora swept her arm in a grand welcoming gesture, inviting her in, certain that no one else could see her delusion.

The woman's long white cotton dress brushed against Aurora as she walked past her, leaving a stream of cold air behind her. She crouched on her haunches beside Sofie, silent and watching. Aurora did her best to avoid looking at her, telling herself that she wasn't real. Luz and Rosario carried trays of food and a ceramic pot of xocoatl, along with three mugs, and set them down on the coffee table.

"Hello, Aurora. I'm Luz, and this is mi marida, Rosario. Welcome to our home."

"It's very nice to meet you, Aurora," Rosario smiled. "I need to get back to the restaurant and prepare for our lunch crowd. I'm sure I'll see you again soon." Aurora smiled but said nothing. Luz poured the steaming liquid into the mugs and handed one to Sofie and Aurora. Then, she took a mug and went to sit beside Aurora, careful not to sit too close.

"You were very upset at the church last night. Sofie and I brought you here so you wouldn't be alone. Something important happened to you last night, Aurora, and I'm hoping that might be able to help you understand it a little better."

"Something important? What are you talking about? If this is what you call this nightmare that I had last night, I think I should leave.

I'm literally losing my mind, and you are telling me that something important happened?" Aurora looked over to Sofie with exasperation and anger in her eyes.

"Sofie. I would like to go home now."

"Aurora, please just listen to what Luz has to say. Please? She was there last night and understands more than you or I do. I really think she can help us both to understand what happened; what's happening."

Luz pointed her open hand towards the food. "Please, let's have a little food before you leave, and you can tell us more about what happened. How does that sound?" Aurora saw the food laid out so beautifully, as the aroma wafted up to her, she heard her stomach growl and remembered that she hadn't eaten anything the day before.

"Alright. Fine." She settled back against the couch, careful not to look at the ghost woman sitting next to Sofie. Luz served each of them a plate with a tamale, black beans, and a small bowl of chicken mole soup. Aurora picked up the bowl of soup, put her nose close to the rim, and inhaled the chocolate aroma. Then she sipped a spoonful, sat back, and closed her eyes for a moment.

"This tastes like fresh-planted corn, and earth, and chiles; it tastes like magic." Then she took another sip of the hot beverage.

"Oh. This is amazing. I've never tasted anything like it."

"It's xocoatl, hot chocolate as you call it here. Except it's made from pure cacao and full of medicine for the soul. Rosario blesses the nibs every morning and mixes in herbs from our garden. The cacao comes from Guatemala. I'm glad you like it."

The women ate quietly, except for Aurora, who sipped and chewed slowly, as if wanting to experience every aspect of the food's color, texture, aroma, and flavor. The food helped to ground her back into her body. When she finished eating, she looked up to see Sofie and Luz smiling at her. She felt her face flush with embarrassment.

"Oh, I'm so sorry. I must look like I've never eaten before. I got lost in the food. I didn't realize I was so hungry."

"I will be sure to let Rosario know how much you enjoyed her cooking." Luz put her plate down on the tray, and Sofie and Aurora did the same. Aurora smiled at Luz, and for a moment, she felt that Luz was seeing into her secrets. It was intimate, gentle, and Aurora moved into it a little, gazing back. She felt relaxed and a little more comfortable in her skin, as if she could rest there for a bit inside herself. A peacefulness she was unaccustomed to.

"Aurora. Tell me about the little girl in the church. You said she wants your help and that she is trapped in a basement room. Why do you think she is asking you for help?" Aurora's eyes searched inside for an answer. She shook her head, unable to answer.

"Allow yourself to go back there, to the basement. It's safe." She put her hands firmly on Aurora's shoulders.

"Look at me, Aurora. Breathe with me."

"Ay, madre de Dios. Help me," Aurora whispered. She pulled her rebozo tighter, so she could feel the parameters of her being. She felt the stitching of her skin break open and her bones come loose, floating freely around the room. She wanted to run into the bathroom, cut her thigh or her arm, and let the burn of blood call her body back into order. Just then, Luz stood up and walked in front of Aurora. She put a hand on Aurora's back, behind her heart. Aurora felt a warm, tingly sensation move through her as she allowed her breathing to follow Luz's.

"Better?" Luz asked. Aurora nodded.

"We are dreaming a medicine dream, Mija. Listen to the sound of my words. Do you understand what I'm saying?" Aurora shook her head no and struggled to move away from Luz's hands, but Luz held her firmly.

"I know you fear the things you can't explain, but the truth is you're not crazy, or insane. You are awakening to the truth of who you are. This dream is a gift from the Ancient Ones."

"It doesn't feel like a dream. It feels like a fucking curse that's slowly driving me insane. I can't sleep, I hear voices and see things that aren't there, and the only way to stop it all is to cut myself. It brings a few moments of relief from the constant clawing at my insides. I can't sleep, so I stay up at night and paint my dreams. My paintings are all part of this madness. It's why I wanted to sell them so badly. I wanted to get rid of the reminder of what I am." Aurora wiped at the tears streaming down her face, as the truth she had never completely spoken came pouring out. Luz moved closer to Aurora.

"Sofie and I are both here with you, and we will not let any harm come to you. Close your eyes and let your senses take you back. Follow the sound of the little girl crying. You can hear her clearly. You know what she wants." Luz closed her eyes and began softly chanting. "Remember, Aurora. Remember. Open the eyes of your heart. See clearly. Do not be afraid."

Aurora felt herself falling inside herself, into a familiar dream that always filled her with dread. She was back in the basement, standing in front of the door. She could once again hear the child crying.

"Hello, little one. I'm here. I'm going to help you." She banged on the door, and this time it opened. She stepped into the shadowed silence of the room. There was a dim light coming in from a small window, placed too high for a child to see out of. Searching for a light, she found a string hanging directly in front of her. She pulled the string, and a dim, yellow light filled the room. Hardly enough for Aurora to clearly see the child crouching in the corner below the window. This was not the same child from the church. She was clean, her hair freshly braided and tied with pink ribbons at the ends. She had on white ruffle socks and shiny black patent leather Mary Jane shoes. Aurora knelt on the floor close enough so the child could see her, but careful not to frighten her.

"Hello, little one. Please don't be afraid. I won't hurt you. My name is Aurora. Who are you?

"I know who you are, Yoya. I'm Mary Jane, but Lil' Yoya calls me M.J."

"I don't understand." Aurora scooted a little closer. "Where is the little girl who was at the church last night? What are you both doing in this room? Who put you here?" Aurora knew she was asking too many questions for a child to answer, but the little girl did not flinch. She looked right at Aurora and answered plainly.

"You put us here, Yoya. That's why Lil' Yoya keeps calling you. She wants you to get us out of here, but you didn't never come to get us."

"Where is she—Lil' Yoya?"

"She is with Maddie. They're sleeping. Maddie don't want me to talk to you. She doesn't like you." The walls of the red brick room began to expand and contract, breathing with Aurora's breath. Her head began to spin. Mary Jane pointed to a doorway that led to another room. Aurora took one of the candles from the floor and walked into the room. She gasped in shock when she saw a young woman and a child curled up together asleep on the floor. The young woman was the exact image of Aurora at 16 years old. Her long black hair lay in a scrambled mess around her, and even asleep, Maddie's brow was creased, her mouth pursed in anger; the scars on the inside of her forearms lay bare, without shame. Aurora didn't like to think of her past or herself at this age, but at this moment, she could not deny it.

What are you doing here? Why are you called Maddie, and how do I get you out of this place?

Then she looked carefully at the familiar child who had haunted her nights and days for so long. Then she clearly saw her. Lil' Yoya, her childhood name. How could she not have made this connection before? Was she so unwilling to see the truth? Suddenly, she felt compassion for this child, with whom she had been so eager to be rid of, and then she was filled with a sense of terror, as if someone was coming for her. She bent down to wake the child when Maddie woke up. She scrambled to her feet and stood facing Aurora.

"What the hell are you doing here? You stay away from her. Do you understand me?" She demanded in a low, steady voice that made the hairs on Aurora's neck stand on end.

"Lil' Yoya has been haunting my dreams and tells me to get her out of here. Now I'm here in this god forsaken room, so why don't you tell me what I'm supposed to do?" Aurora responded. Maddie took a step closer to Aurora and pointed a finger hard into her chest.

"The only one who has forsaken us is you. I don't want you here, you stupid bitch. I never wanted you here. You are useless. You couldn't protect us then, and you sure as hell can't protect us now. I'm the one who's been taking care of them all these years. Yeah, we're here in this basement, but at least no one can hurt us here. And besides, La Divina protects us here." Aurora took a step away from Maddie. She remembered herself as a scared, angry teenager, alone on the streets with no one to look after her.

"But Lil' Yoya has been calling me to take her out of here. That's why I'm here."

Maddie moved directly in front of Aurora's face. "There is no way I'm letting them go with you. Are we clear?"

"Oh God. I have to get out of here." Aurora ran out the door, up the steps, and out into the backyard, where she fell on the ground. Then she heard a voice calling to her. She looked up to see the ghost woman who had walked into the room behind Luz and Rosario. She stood up and looked carefully at her, who stared back at her with tenderness in her eyes. This was the woman in her paintings. The woman of her childhood—La Llorona. She was standing in front of her. Suddenly, Aurora's chest constricted, and she could not breathe. She could no longer deny who this woman was. The tightness in her chest burst open, and the river of tears rushed forward, breaking through the dam of her denial. La Llorona peered into Aurora's soul. She reached out her hand, and Aurora took it.

"It is time, mi amor. It is time for you to remember who you are." Aurora saw a flash of light, and images from her childhood filled her mind. She remembered seeing La Llorona there in her backyard as a child. She remembered telling Father Tom about La Llorona and how her mother locked her in the red brick room. Father Tom had believed her. He had seen La Llorona, too. The image of the red brick room, dark, mildewed, and cold. She suddenly remembered how the Lady of Roses had appeared to her. How could she have forgotten all of that? Then images of blood running down a child's thigh crept their way into her mind. She saw the crying child clearly now. There was no denying the truth anymore. Someone had done terrible things to her when she was an innocent and helpless child. It was time to face the truth.

A thick darkness encroached on Aurora's vision, and a searing pain gripped her head. Then, as if no time had passed, she was transported back to the room with Luz and Sofie. She opened her eyes, sat up, feeling dazed and unable to speak. Her face was wet with tears. Luz and Sofie waited patiently until she was ready to share what happened to her. After several minutes, she spoke.

"I saw her. She's real." She looked over where the ghost woman had been sitting. She was gone.

"Who did you see?" Sofie asked.

"The woman from my paintings. The woman from my childhood. La Llorona; I remember that she appeared to me as a child. I saw her standing behind you and Rosario this morning, just like I saw her when my mother locked me in the basement and left me there. The little girl, oh god, Sofie, she's me. I'm Lil' Yoya. There was another child there, too. But she said her name was Mary Jane, and someone else named Maddie, who is me when I was 16. I need to understand why this is happening to me. Maybe I'm not crazy." She looked at Luz. "I can't live like this anymore. Will you help me?"

"Yes. Aurora. It would be my honor to help you in any way I can. For now, I think you should go home and get some rest. You have been through a lot. I have a feeling you sleep a little better." Luz wrote her phone number on a piece of paper, folded it in half, and handed it to Aurora.

"Please call me anytime, night or day. I mean it." Aurora took the paper and smiled. "Gracias por todo. Especially the food. Please thank Rosario for me." Luz walked Sofie and Aurora downstairs to the front door. Aurora turned to Sofie and gave her a big hug.

"Thank you, Sofie. Thank you for always being there for me. No matter what. You are the best friend anyone could ever have. I'm so lucky to have you." Aurora kissed Sofie on the cheek and turned to walk down 24th Street, towards Folsom Street, when she saw a familiar face she had not seen in many years. She lowered her eyes, hoping he would not recognize her.

"Aurora? Is that you? Wow. It's so good to see you. How long has it been?"

"Hi, Father Tom. It's been a very long time. I don't go to church, but my mother had mentioned that you left."

"Yes. I heard about your mother's passing. I was very sorry to hear about it, Aurora. I just pray that she has found peace."

"She didn't pass. She killed herself."

"Yes, I know. Anyway, I didn't leave St. Peter's. I was sent to

Guatemala to help a priest there. I only recently returned because I brought some friends to the States from Guatemala. Maybe you know them? Luz and Rosario. The owners of the Dos Almas restaurant."

"Actually, I just met them today. I was, um, having breakfast with them."

"They are two amazing women that I am very happy to call my friends. You know, Aurora, if you ever want to talk about anything, I'm here. Back at St. Peter's, I mean."

"I appreciate that, Father Tom. I just may take you up on that sometime, but I really need to get going."

When Aurora got home, Bruja was at the door to greet her with loud meows.

"Oh, Brujita. You must be so hungry." She poured a can of food on a plate, set it on the floor, then went into her bedroom and slid under the covers. She curled up like a fawn in a warm meadow and fell into a dream.

Lil' Yoya was sitting on the brown vinyl loveseat in the living room of her childhood flat. Romper Room was playing on the television. She looked so small and insignificant alone, staring at the screen without any emotion. Then her mother came into the room singing a Beatles song and swaying her wide hips, dancing to the music playing on the record player.

"All you need is love. All you need is love..." She opened the palm of her hand to reveal a handful of pills that looked like pink hearts and triangle candies, at least Aurora thought they were candy. Her mother was smiling. She was happy. Lil' Yoya jumped up from the couch to reach for a pink heart, but before she could, her mother snatched her hand away. She popped a white triangle in her mouth and washed it down with a gulp of red wine.

Aurora felt Lil' Yoya's happiness at the chance of having a piece of candy vanish when a wave of icicles moved through her body, freezing her from the inside. Next, she saw herself lying on her bed, unable to move. The room was dark, except for scarce light peeking through a small window across from her bed. Then she felt a sharp pain poking into her; it was something hard pushing between her legs. She tried to scream for it to stop, but no sound came out. Then, she felt a stale breath move close to her face, and someone rubbed his coarse beard across her cheeks.

"Be a good little girl and be quiet. You're so pretty, Yoya." He was covered in the stink of whiskey and cigar. Each word he spoke sucked the air from her lungs. In her mind, she was screaming. In her mind, she pushed him off her. In her mind, she screamed, "Someone help me!" Then she became air, floating up, up off the bed. She felt nothing. She closed her eyes and floated up to the ceiling until she was free. She opened her eyes, looked down, and saw M.J. lying in her bed. M.J. stared up at Aurora; her eyes did not blink, her body did not move. Aurora watched but did not understand why the little girl she met in the basement was in her bed, or how Lil' Yoya drifted to the ceiling. Then she saw clearly what this man was doing, and she knew who he was. It was her pediatrician, Dr. Hammish. Then, without warning, Lil' Yoya was jolted back into her body. M.J. was gone.

Aurora opened her eyes, jumped from the bed, and ran into the kitchen. It was 6 a.m. She slept for almost 18 hours. She scrambled to find Luz's number from the pile of unopened mail on the counter. When she dialed, Luz picked up on the second ring, as if expecting Aurora to call.

"Buenos días, Aurora. I was hoping you would call. How are you feeling?"

"Good morning, Luz. Something happened in my dreams. I'm hoping you can help me understand. Would it be alright if I came over?"

"Yes, of course. Come by at 8:00 and I will have everything ready."

"What's everything?" Aurora asked.

"No te preocupes. Everything will be fine, and if you are ready, then you will find the answers you seek. Please be sure you have a light breakfast, and I'll see you soon." Luz hung up the phone, and Aurora went to shower and dress.

⌣

When Aurora arrived at Luz and Rosario's flat, she rang the doorbell and heard Luz call down, "The door's open. Come up." Aurora walked up the stairs and found Luz in the living room, standing in front of the altar. She was lighting copal in her copalero and whispering prayers.

"Hola," Aurora said, feeling like she was interrupting something private. Luz turned to her and waved her in, motioning her to sit on the sofa.

"Hola, Aurora. Please come in and sit." Luz went to sit in the chair beside the sofa. There was a wooden tray on the coffee table with a teapot and cups on it. She poured tea for them both.

"I would like to offer you a ceremony today if you are open to it. I feel that you are ready. This ceremony will bring you into a place of greater self-understanding. But you must agree to it completely. It will help you to remember what you have repressed, and release some of the susto you carry in your soul. My hope is that you will uncover what you have hidden in the red brick room inside of you. When you can remember what happened to you, then you can heal the younger parts of yourself that are hiding and afraid. But it is a good sign that they are reaching out to you and calling for your help. It means you are ready. Are you willing to trust me, Aurora?" Aurora thought about it, feeling the knot twisting in her stomach. She knew there was no other way. She had to do this.

"Yes. I trust you, Luz."

"Bueno. Let us begin."

"Already? I just got here. I have so many questions. I..."

"Now is not the time for questions. It is time to move from the head into the heart. It is there you will find answers to questions you didn't know that you had. Come."

Luz walked over to her altar. Aurora followed and stood beside her. The morning fog outside the window created a soft, white veil around them, insulating them from the world outside. Luz pulled a chair up facing the altar for Aurora to sit. She lit nine white candles on the altar. Then she picked up her copalero and inhaled the pungent fragrance of copal. She fanned the smoke over her face and head with an eagle feather. Then she fanned it over Aurora's head, face, and down the front and back of her body. Aurora shuddered as the aroma of copal permeated her senses.

"I want you to place your left hand on your heart and the other hand on your womb. Breathe in slowly, close your eyes, and allow your mind to follow the fragrance of copal into your heart and into the silent space of your womb. Breathe your heart open, like a fully bloomed rose. When I ask you to open your eyes, you will remain dreaming, though you are awake." Luz touched her index finger to the center of Aurora's forehead. Aurora let out a little gasp. She felt as if her brain was disappearing.

⌣

"Open your eyes, Aurora, and see clearly." Aurora opened her eyes and looked around the room. The colors in the room were brighter and the edges around everything were fuzzy, as if it was made of billions of tiny points of light moving in constant motion. She felt the light hum and vibrate through and around her body. She took a deep breath, and a shiver of energy moved through her.

"This is the real world, Aurora. This is the waking dream. There are few people who are willing to see with the eyes of the heart. This reality is expanded and vibrates at a higher frequency of light and energy than the third-dimensional reality we exist in most of the time. This is where we find true healing. It is the dimension of reality where magic happens, where guides and angels dwell, where the Ancient Ones reside, and where the La Tierra Madre, Earth Mother, speaks to us through the natural world. Do you understand? Are you willing to see the truth of who you are, Aurora?" Tears ran down Aurora's face as she felt Luz's words begin to dissolve the bricks around her heart. They crumbled, one by one, dust falling into her womb, where they were engulfed by a vortex of golden-white light. The light transmuted them into liquid fire and released them from her womb into the earth.

"I felt the bricks move into my..." Luz placed her hand below Aurora's navel.

"This is your sacred bowl of light, where you have the power to create, destroy, and release." Aurora listened carefully to what Luz was saying. She didn't fully understand it, but she felt her womb relax, and for the first time in a long time, she could feel her breath flow freely through her body.

"See with the eyes of your heart, Aurora. Breathe into the sacred bowl of your womb." Aurora did as Luz instructed. She allowed her awareness to sink into her womb, breathing into it. Then she felt a popping sensation in her womb, a pain like menstrual cramps. Her hands immediately flew to her vulva, where she felt a wetness between her legs. She stood up and looked down at her thighs and saw blood seeping through her pants.

"This is how it should be. You are releasing old pain that you have been holding in your womb," Luz said, as she grabbed a towel from a drawer of the altar.

"Remove your pants and wrap the towel around your waist. You need to bleed freely. Asi es."

The temperature in the room dropped noticeably, causing chills to run through both Luz and Aurora. Luz pulled a blue rebozo from the back of the sofa and wrapped it tightly around herself, then grabbed Aurora's red rebozo from the sofa and handed it to her. Luz and Aurora gazed at one another for a moment, synchronizing their breathing. Like the fog outside the windows, the room was infused with a mournful blue mist, and Luz knew they were not alone. She picked up her copalero and took four steps back from where Aurora sat. She fanned copal smoke into the space between them. It created a lacy veil that curled around the edge of a slowly forming silhouette of a woman. There was an aura of pale blue light that emanated about three inches outward.

There was something familiar about the faint blue light that Aurora could not specifically remember, but she was not frightened. Then, she remembered a similar blue light from when La Llorona first appeared to her as a child. The light from the candles on the altar cast a silver shimmer upon the form.

"Come to us, La Divina, diosa de las lágrimas sagradas," Luz prayed. Then the sound of soft keening filled the room, and the keening turned into travailing moans.

⌣

Luz retrieved her owl feathers from the altar. She approached the silhouette and slowly brushed the edges of the form with the feathers and copal smoke. The shadow began to grow into a bright light that emerged from the center of the silhouette. Then Luz returned the copal and feathers to the altar. Weaving her hands through the air around the blue silhouette, her fingers spun luminous threads into a shawl of light. Luz spoke in a soothing voice.

"Come to us. Come to us, blessed mother, goddess of healing waters. I call your presence forward, out from the dreamtime." The figure shifted and moaned as Monarch butterflies flew from the center of the figure. They filled the room, then rested on the altar. Luz approached the figure, cupping her hands together, then blew three swift breaths into the center of the figure, continuing to invoke her presence into form.

"Welcome, Madrecita. It is so good to have you here with us. It has been a very long time since Aurora has seen you," Luz lovingly cooed the words, as if she were soothing a baby. Then, Luz sang a medicine song, and the figure quieted. It was an ancient song used to call the soul into the body. Luz had received this medicine song in what now seemed like a lifetime ago. Llorona had sung it to her, to call her soul back…from… She pushed the thoughts from her mind and continued to sing, using her fingers and smoke to paint La Llorona into form—transforming her from spirit into something closer to flesh and bone.

La Divina appeared fully human. Aurora watched with wide, tearful eyes; her heart filled with awe. The goddess of her paintings was standing in front of her, fully alive, flesh and bones. The center of her chest was illuminated by a magenta rose just below the surface of her skin. She had two serpents and four monarch butterflies inked around each of her forearms. She had thick, black hair that hung past her waist, smooth bronze skin, and sea-green eyes that flashed and sparkled. Luz placed both hands gently on her head. She took a deep breath and blew three swift breaths into the top of La Divina's head, who shuddered, as the last of her spirit rushed into her body. She embraced Luz and kissed her softly on each cheek. Luz wrapped La Llorona in a blanket and hugged her for a long time.

"Welcome home, Mi Divina. I have missed you in this form."

"Ah. You are the only one who calls me by name." She smiled warmly at Luz, eyes sparkling with the fire of stars.

"Well, La Llorona is more of a title, and La Divina is your name. You brought me back from the teeth of death. Even though, at the time, I begged you to let me die. I did not understand why you saved me."

"And now you do?"

"Sí, Madre Mía. I do, and I am forever grateful to you. Now, please excuse me for one moment." Luz wiped her tears of joy and rushed out of the room. She returned with clothes, a hairbrush, and red ribbons.

"I saved these clothes for you." Luz helped La Divina into a white huipil, which had embroidered Monarch and red roses around the neckline. Next, she held up a pair of faded blue jeans. La Divina smiled as she slipped her legs into the jeans.

"I like these. They're soft and practical." Aurora was awestruck as she witnessed the goddess of her painting come to life right in front of her, wearing blue jeans, no less. Luz invited La Divina to sit in a chair across from Aurora. Then she stood behind the goddess and gently parted her hair, using her hands to weave her hair into two thick braids. She finished them with a fat Marigold and red ribbons at the end.

"There. You are even more lovely than I remember. You are timeless."

The two of them laughed because La Divina was almost five hundred years old. Aurora sat dumbstruck, her mouth agape in awe, and feeling frightened. Then the goddess sat in the chair across from Aurora, who was trembling, her cheeks were wet with tears, her eyes transfixed on the goddess, who now appeared exactly as she had painted her.

⌣

La Divina looked at Aurora.

"Hello, Aurora. It is good to see you again." Aurora's mind was flooded with images of a willow tree, her mother yelling for her to come inside, Father Tom, and the red crystal rosary he had given her after they had gone down to the basement. But they were not alone. La Llorona had walked behind them, weeping her sorrow and rage for an innocent child, who was forced to endure the suffering her mother and others inflicted. Aurora began to sob uncontrollably, as memories continued to pervade her mind. Luz introduced them. Luz waited for Aurora's tears to quiet.

"Aurora, may I present La Divina, the goddess you know as La Llorona."

"It's really you. You're here. How can this be happening?" La Divina reached over and lifted Aurora's chin to meet her gaze.

"What does your heart tell you, mi amor? There is no need to fear me, Aurora. You are my beloved daughter." She touched her thumb to Aurora's brow, then took her hands and placed a kiss in each of her palms and sang.

"*Hare, hare, ka ri ya re ya so ha, so ha, so haaa.*" Her singing sparked embers of remembrance in the cells of Aurora's body.

"*Hare, hare, ka ri ya na so ha, sooo haaaa. This is your sacred fire. This is your healing song.*" As she listened, Aurora felt the vibration of the song reverberate through her, and for the first time in her life, she was filled with inexplicable joy. La Divina gently guided Aurora to lie on the rug in front of the altar. "Close your eyes, breathe into your sacred bowl of light, and allow that light to fill you. Allow your mind to drift back to the time before you came into this body. Remember, remember, remember, Aurora. Follow the song of my voice and tell me what you see." La Divina knelt beside Aurora and laid one hand on Aurora's womb and the other on her brow. Aurora followed the sound of La Divina's voice, as it swirled inside her, impelling her deep into the memories that lay hidden in the cells of her womb. Aurora felt her mind dissolving as she floated down within herself. When she opened her eyes, she was in a cave illuminated by dozens of white candles. In front of her, she saw a clear azure river flowing through the cave.

"Walk to the river and gaze into the water. Tell me what you see." Aurora did as La Divina instructed and gazed into the river.

"Tell me what you see."

Aurora stared into the flowing water as images began to form. The images shifted into the scene of her birth. "My mother is in the delivery room. She's crying because I'm not breathing. My face is blue, and the doctor keeps swatting my bottom trying to get me to breathe. I'm watching from the ceiling, looking down at myself. My body is so small, wet, and bloody, but I'm not in that body. Something is tugging at me, pulling me out of the room, up into the sky. I feel calm and peaceful, like I'm going to my true home. I float up to the sky and out to the stars."

"Bueno, mija. Now breathe deep and trust where you are going."

La Divina placed both hands on Aurora's heart center and began to sing clear, celestial tones. Aurora felt a burst of light envelop her heart, and her mind exploded into a thousand points of light, stardust moving in every direction all at once. She was breaking apart, floating in nothing and everything. She remained there, in the womb of the galaxy. Then she heard crystal bells ringing from somewhere just beyond her. She watched as the sound transformed into great spheres of light. They moved close and circled around her. She felt them to be loving and playful. The vibration they emitted excited the luminous fibers of her sacred shawl. The spherical beings slowed their movement and dropped their tone to a slow, throbbing pulse.

After a few moments, the celestial orbs quieted, and Aurora heard a woman singing. It seemed to emerge from the space between the stars, as if it contained the mystery of creation. The song shifted into a harmonious, wordless chant, which attuned her to its frequency; words, symbols, tones, and color, embedding codes of light into her cells.

From the center of the darkness, a great presence emerged. She wore an indigo velvet gown with a deep purple veil. Her face was without features and filled with the brilliance of the sun. An etheric, cobalt net of light radiated around her form, extending out to infinity. It contained all potentialities for creation, connecting all beings to Source. Then another being emerged from the shadow of the Great Mother. She moved to extricate herself from the net. She moaned and travailed like a woman in labor. With each breath, her presence expanded and contracted. Her weeping echoed through Aurora, dissolving into rhythmic chant, spiraling around her, imprinting her voice into the threads of Aurora's sacred shawl.

"*Hare, hare, kari ya no sho ha, soooo haaah. This is your sacred fire. This is your healing song.*" Ruby crystalline words fell from her mouth; she caught them in her hand and fed them to Aurora. They became petals of roses, sweet and fragrant in her mouth. Aurora fell to her knees in abject awe and wonder. She dared not peer into the woman's eyes. Then out of nowhere, a great force pushed her consciousness back to the cave, where she was still kneeling in front of the river, when she heard a voice calling in the distance.

"Come back to me now, Aurora. Return, return, return, my daughter," La Divina spoke in a calm but firm voice. Aurora returned swiftly to her body. Aurora opened her eyes to find La Divina gazing tenderly at her.

"That was incredible. I feel different, somehow."

"You are different, Mi Amor. You are remembering, which means you are healing." Luz helped Aurora up from the floor and gave her a glass of water to drink.

"You should go home and rest now. This was very deep work you did today. More medicine will come to you in your dreams. Write it all down, so you can tell us all about it when we next meet." Aurora hugged Luz and thanked her. She looked at La Divina, not sure of what to do. The goddess embraced Aurora and kissed her on her brow.

"Until the next time we meet. Dream well, Aurora."

When Aurora got home, she was full of nervous energy. She needed to process everything that she had just experienced, and the only way she knew how to process her emotions was through art. She went into her studio and grabbed several pieces of charcoal. Then she returned to her bedroom and began sketching a mural on the wall. Hours went by, and finally she felt like she had released everything onto the wall. Her body was heavy with exhaustion. She did not step back to look at what she had drawn. She was not ready to see it. She tossed the charcoal on the floor and crawled into bed.

Aurora slept for the next two days, waking only briefly to eat a piece of toast, feed Bruja, and drink the herbal tea Rosario made for her. It had been years since she slept through an entire night, without being startled awake by a bad dream, or a spirit, or the sound of a child crying. She was grateful to sleep and not have to think about anything.

Just sleep. She woke to the sound of someone pounding on the door. Aurora sat up, still half asleep. She could hear Sofie calling for her to open the door.

"Aurora! Hey. Open the door." She knocked and pounded until Aurora opened the door, disheveled, wearing an oversized, paint-splattered white shirt that belonged to Nico. Aurora opened the door to find Sofie standing with her arms crossed across her chest, staring at her with furrowed brows, as if waiting for an explanation of some sort.

"Hi Sofie," she mumbled, leaving the door open. She went back to the couch, pulling a blanket over her. "Sofie, what's wrong?"

"What's wrong? You haven't answered your phone. I've been trying to reach you, and you didn't answer when I called. You've been through a lot lately, and I wanted to make sure you're okay."

"I'm sorry I worried you, Sofie. I was so tired. I've just been sleeping. Rosario made me a remedio to help me sleep, and it worked. I didn't even hear the phone ring."

"Oh. Well, I'm glad you slept. I was just scared, you know?"

"Sofie, you don't have to worry about that. I'm not going to harm myself again. I can promise you this."

"I want that to be true, but you can't blame me for worrying about you."

"I'm sorry I made you worry, but so much has happened to me since the last time I saw you. I have a lot to tell you."

"I'm just happy to see you're okay. Anyway, I'm here to get you out of the house. It's a beautiful day and I'm taking you to the beach! You owe me that much, Aurora, and you can tell me everything in the car."

"Okay, Sofie, but I want to show you something first. It's important." Aurora got up from the couch and went to her bedroom. Sofie followed behind her, not sure what she was going to find. But when she saw the scene of a mural sketched on the bedroom wall, she let out a loud gasp.

"Oh my god. When did you draw this, Aurora?"

"I went to see Luz two days ago, and when I got home, I needed to process all that happened. I didn't plan on drawing this. It just came out of me. When I finished, I was exhausted. I went to bed, and I slept."

"I don't know what to say."

"Don't say anything. I just needed to show you. It's nowhere finished."

"Okay. I understand, but I can't wait to see when it's finished. It's going to be amazing. Thank you for showing me."

"I needed you to see it; to be my witness. I don't know. I'm going to take a quick shower, and then I'll tell you about everything. I could really use some coffee."

"Go shower. I'll make coffee." Strangely, Aurora felt lighter after showing the mural to Sofie. She felt a small spark of joy in her heart. Something she had not felt in a very long time.

Aurora walked into the kitchen, her hair still wet, dressed in jeans and a white T-shirt. She didn't bother covering her scars. Sofie poured some coffee into a mug for her. They sat at the table, quietly sipping coffee, until Sofie broke the silence.

"Aurora, are you going to tell me what's happened? You said you went to see Luz and Rosario again? Are they helping you?" Aurora took a deep breath and stared into her mug.

"Yes, and yes, Sofie. They have helped so much. I'm starting to make sense of everything that's been happening, and for the first time, I think I might actually feel hope." Sofie jumped up and hugged Aurora.

"That's wonderful news. I'm so happy for you. I knew Luz would be able to help you. I just knew it." Aurora hugged Sofie back.

"There is something else I need to tell you. Let's go into the living room." Sofie followed Aurora into the living room and sat down at the opposite end of the couch, facing Aurora.

"I don't know how to say this, Sofie, so I'm just going to say it. But before I do, promise me you won't think I've lost my mind."

"Madre de Dios, you're scaring me again. And for the record, I've never thought you're crazy, Aurora. Now just tell me, please!"

"She's real, Sofie. I saw her...I mean, she is REAL. Luz held a ceremony that brought La Llorona, I mean La Divina, that's her real name. Anyway, she brought her into the physical world. She is here walking around in a human-like body. I talked to her. She touched me and spoke to me."

"Wait a minute. I don't understand. What do you mean she is real, Aurora?"

"I mean, she was standing in front of me, like a human made of flesh and bones. She laid her hands on my head, and I felt her immense love fill me. That's kind of real, Sofie."

"But you can't just make a spirit into flesh."

"Why not? Jesus did it. Besides, she's not fully human. She just has more of a physical presence now. Milagros, Sofie. Isn't that what you keep telling me? Well, this is a real miracle. Maybe it's my miracle; what I need to finally heal."

"I've never actually seen a miracle. I've always just had faith that they could happen. To people I don't know, but you're saying it happened to you. Wow. Tell me everything."

"I remember now. She has always been with me. Not only her, but I remembered the angels, too. They used to visit me after…They appeared with her, and they were singing, and it broke my heart open, Sofie. It just broke me open, and I cried. I actually cried. I felt their love, too. I've never felt that kind of love before. Am I making any sense?" Sofie moved closer and hugged Aurora. This time, Aurora did not pull away. She let herself be held.

"I don't understand everything you've told me, but I see you, amiga." Sofie released Aurora and looked into her eyes.

"You're full of light. I've never seen or felt you like this. You're right. This is a miracle. Whatever is happening. I know it's good medicine. I feel it in my soul."

"It's not over yet. I still have a lot of healing to do, you know? I understand now that the little girl who has been haunting me is me, Sofie. It's like she's a part of my soul that got hurt and scared when I was abused. I hid the memories so I could survive, but when I locked them away in my mind, I also locked her away. Now I need to find a way to get the little ones out of the red brick room."

"Little ones? There's more than one?"

"Yes. Oh. It's a lot to try to explain. I think that's all I can talk about right now. I hope you understand."

"Of course. I'm not going anywhere, so you can tell me whenever you're ready. But right now, we are going to the beach! It's a beautiful day. I packed a picnic lunch and we're going to celebrate your miracle.

C'mon, let's get out of here." Sofie didn't wait for Aurora to answer. She grabbed her hand and pulled her up from the couch and out the door. Aurora grabbed her rebozo from the couch on the way out.

⌣

La Divina waded out with the tide until the water reached her waist. She inhaled the salty mist of the ocean spray, splashing her hands in the water, laughing with joy as she played with jellyfish and other sea creatures who came to greet her. Afterwards, she walked onto the shore. The tide chased after her and swirled around the hem of her blue jeans. Further up the shore, she picked up a stick and used it to draw a large circle in the sand around her, with lines to divide it into four quarters. She reached into the leather pouch tied around her waist and took out a small abalone shell, along with a bit of tobacco, dried cedar, and rose petals. She placed a pinch of each in the bowl of the shell and blew her breath gently over the herbs until they ignited. She plucked an owl feather from one of her braids and fanned the aroma of the smoke as a sweet ofrenda to her sisters, Las Cihuateteo.

"My beloved sisters, Tonantzin, Coatlique, Coyolxuaqui, Ix Chel, Tlazolteotl..." As she invoked the names of her sisters, a large cloud moved across the sun, obscuring light and casting a shadow over the shore. A tall wave rose from the sea, crashing against the cliffs, then rapidly ebbed back into the water, revealing the etheric presence of Tonantzin-Guadalupe floating above the water. She floated towards the shore where La Divina stood, the fire of the sun illuminating her turquoise mantle, glistening a circle of stars around her head. The Goddess stepped onto the shore to greet her sister, opening her arms in a wide embrace as she stepped into the circle.

"Mi querida hermana." She pulled her close, stroking her hair and showering her face with kisses. The sisters held hands, laughed, and danced around the circle, overjoyed to be together again.

"I have missed you, my sister, as have your other sisters." Tonantzin-Guadalupe took her sister's hand and guided her to sit. They sat quietly watching the waves crash on the rocks nearby.

"I see you have taken on this denser form. How is it to be almost human?"

"There are some things I enjoy about it, like eating, and there are other things I do not enjoy very much. It is difficult feeling their suffering more deeply than I did when I was more spirit, but I also enjoy being able to touch and be touched. It is magical to experience the world through the senses of the body."

"Hmmm, I can understand that. Yet, humans are still caught in the dream of forgetting who they truly are. They become attached to this material world and believe it is all there is. They have forgotten how to see with the eyes of their heart and how to hear the voice of their soul. They have forgotten that this is what fills the emptiness they feel."

"It hurts my heart and my soul to feel their suffering. I am doing what I can to help them to heal and to remember their divine essence. Still, there is so much darkness and suffering humans create to wound one another. Sometimes I feel weary, and yet I love them, with all of my soul and long for their remembrance."

"It has been over four hundred years that you have walked the earth. It can feel like an eternity in this dimension where they measure time. Will you be returning to us soon, or will you remain here?"

"I am not certain."

"What do they call you here, Hermana?"

"They call me La Llorona."

"But you are La Divina, the Divine One."

"Perhaps one day humans will know me as La Divina, as well." She kissed her sister on the cheek and held her close.

"I am always here for you, as are your other sisters. In La K'esh Alakin." The goddesses stood and kissed one another on each cheek, then Tonanztin-Guadalupe turned and walked back into the ocean. She stepped into the sea, the light of her spirit bursting into the rays of the sun. La Divina placed her hands on her heart, full of gratitude for her sister's love.

◡

As Aurora and Sofie drove to the beach, Aurora explained more details of how Luz had brought La Llorona into physical form, as well as what she had remembered about her pre-birth experience.

"It sounds like a dream, Aurora. Are you sure it wasn't a dream?"

"It wasn't a dream, Sofie. She was there, standing in front of me, just as real as you are. I don't know what this all means for me, and I still don't fully understand who La Llorona is. I grew up with all the stories about her being a kind of evil spirit. My mom would tell me not to go near train tracks or near the water at night, because she might try to take me. She taught me to leave a penny on the train tracks as an offering, so she wouldn't take me at night. I was to say, 'lo siento senora,' as a way of empathizing with her suffering, I guess. I never questioned it. I just did as my mother told me to do.

"But something about La Llorona intrigued me, and it made me want to go to the water even more. That's when I started sneaking out at night to go to Ocean Beach. My mom always told me that she wanted to steal me from her. She told me the story of how she followed us home from the hospital after I was born. Everyone on our block could hear her weeping, and they were frightened of her.

"She didn't follow my mother home, Sofie. She followed me home. That's why I always wanted to go to her. This is why I was so focused on painting her. Somewhere inside, I was trying to remember. I think my mother knew it, too, and she hated her for it. Then I forgot so much of what happened to me, and I forgot about her, too, but now I'm remembering. Am I making any sense, Sofie?"

"What you're saying about La Llorona makes a lot of sense, Aurora. I remember hearing my mom and her friends talking about a spirit that cried at night, but they said she was evil, and they were so afraid of her that they wouldn't utter her name. They called her La Crying Senora. It's a lot to think about." Aurora and Sofie drove the rest of the way in silence, each in their own individual thoughts. When they arrived at the beach, the sun was sitting high above the shoreline, and the sound of barking seals drifted on the ocean breeze. Aurora inhaled the cool, salty air. She felt raw and transparent, as if everyone around her could see what was inside of her. But as she gazed at the sparkling sea, she felt calm and peaceful.

"Sofie. Let's go down to the cave."

"Aww. I wanted to sit on the sand, in the sun. You know how I love the sun."

"We will, but I don't feel like being around so many people right now."

"Okay, let's go to your cave."

"Great." Aurora's face lit up with a big smile. They ran down the path below to the mouth of the cave, past the bones of the old Sutro Bath house; bones were all that remained after a fire burned it to the ground in 1966. The cave was small, more like a tunnel that let out to the slippery rocks on the other side. There was an opening in the middle of the wall on one side of the cave where the tide washed in. During the day, the tides came in low, spraying salty mist on the walls of the cave. Aurora was the first to reach the entrance of the cave, leaving Sofie running out of breath behind her.

"C'mon, Sofie." The two of them fell onto the sandy ground of the cave.

"Wow. It's nice here. I've never been down here before. I'm usually lying on the other side, baking in the sun." Aurora ran her hands along the wall of the rocky cave, as if greeting an old friend.

"I love this cave. I feel like I'm the only person in the world when I'm here. I love to just sit and listen to the sound of the waves crashing and the seals barking in the distance. This is where I come to clear my mind." The silence of the cave was interrupted by a high-pitched, melodic song that floated on the breeze into the cave.

"Do you hear that, Aurora?" Sofie rubbed the chill on her arms.

"Yeah, I hear it, but where is it coming from?" Aurora walked outside the cave and looked towards the sea, where she saw the silhouette of a woman standing on the shore in front of the bones of the old Sutro Baths.

"I don't know Sofie, but I have a feeling we're going to find out."

La Divina was facing the ocean, her arms raised, palms resting in prayer at her chest.

Aurora was transfixed by the silhouette of the woman on the shore. "What's wrong, Aurora? Do you know her?" Sofie asked, suddenly confused.

"Oh, Sofie. Your life is about to change forever. Let's go!" Aurora grabbed Sofie's hand and the two of them climbed onto the ridge of the old baths, following the labyrinthine down onto the sand where La

Divina stood. She turned to face them. Sofie stared at her, eyes wide, mouth agape. She appeared to have walked straight out of Aurora's paintings. She was unable to speak or move. La Divina stepped forward and took Sofie's hands in hers.

"Don't be frightened, mija. I won't hurt you." La Divina glanced at Aurora, nodded, and smiled, with love sparkling in her eyes.

"Come, both of you. Let's sit. You must have many questions. Yes, I'm real, Sofie." Aurora took Sofie's hand and guided her to sit on the sand with La Divina. Sofie dropped her face into her hands, then looked at La Llorona. She rubbed her face as she struggled to find words through the tightness in her throat.

"I never imagined a goddess could be real like this, I mean...are you human now?"

"No. I am not human, Sofie."

"But I touched your hands. I felt your flesh and bones. What are you if you are not human?"

"You must remember that we are all made of a series of electrons vibrating at different frequencies. Right now, I am vibrating at a slower frequency, so I appear solid, like you humans. But remember, mija. You are not solid. You are made of space, light that vibrates at a slower density and manifests in this form. Before you were human, you were one with the One Heart. You are a divine expression, pure love. This is the truth that humans cannot fully comprehend. You forget how those of us who dwell in the place of the Ancestors adore and cherish you. We are close to you, waiting to serve and assist you. In your forgetting, you experience shame, hurt, and bitterness in your heart and believe you are separate or have been abandoned by God. Then, you become attached to the story of your suffering and believe it is the only truth. Holding on to suffering makes it difficult to forgive yourself for making what you believe is a mistake. You blame yourself, and the blame turns into self-loathing and anger. When you are filled with so much anger, it is difficult to heal. Healing requires you to empty yourself and make space to receive healing light. When humans can empty themselves, they are open to allowing more of their essence into the body. Then, you can feel your connection to the universe. You contain healing intelligence in every cell of your body. Do you understand?" Sofie nodded, eyes wide, trying to comprehend it all.

"Then, are you a goddess, like Tonantzin-Guadalupe, Coatlicue, or Ix Chel?" Aurora asked.

"Yes. They are my sisters. They created me from their love."

"That is truly amazing. I can't quite understand it all. I am very grateful that you honor us with your presence here," Aurora said.

Sofie was still stunned by it all and could barely speak. "I am so grateful to meet you, Senora. Thank you for all you are doing to help Aurora. She means the world to me."

La Divina hugged them both. "You are welcome. This is my purpose. It brings me joy. You are a gifted healer, Sofie. You can sense energy, as well as the suffering of others. This is your gift. We will talk more about this another day. I am so happy to spend this time with you, but I must go now. I hear sorrow calling on the wind. I will see you both very soon." Aurora and Sofie watched the goddess walk down the shore, her silhouette fading into the light of the setting sun. They sat in silence for quite some time, staring out at the sea. Suddenly, Sofie began to sob. Aurora moved close and placed her arm around her.

"It's okay, Sofie. It will take some time to take in all of this. It's not every day that you meet a goddess in the flesh. Seriously. I'm still reeling from it, too. Let's go home. You probably need to sleep."

"Yeah. Sleep sounds good right about now." They took some deep breaths, stood up, and dusted the sand from their jeans. They walked arm in arm up the shore, back to the car, the roar of the tide fading behind them.

⌣

Rosario carried her black ceramic chalice, a copalero, into the kitchen. Milagro had recently given it to her as a gift. She was greeted by rays of white sunlight streaming through the sliding glass door. She took a piece of charcoal briquet and copal resin from a drawer. She placed the charcoal at the bottom center of the black ceramic bowl and lit it with a match. While she waited for the charcoal to turn red, she offered a prayer.

"Gracias por su medicina, Copalita."

Then she placed a small chunk of black copal on it. Closing her eyes, she inhaled deeply as the sweet, smoky aroma filled the room with plumes and curls of sacred smoke. Rosario opened her eyes and carried the copalero down the three flights of stairs into a circle of rose bushes in the center of the garden. She stood in the center of the roses and prayed, watching the smoke carry her prayers to the four directions.

"I greet this day with an open heart full of gratitude. I give thanks for my blessings, and I ask that I may be of service today. Blessed Mother, Tonantzin, bless me with your wisdom. I ask for my ancestors to walk with me today. I give special thanks to La Divina, the goddess who walks with us and helps us to heal our sorrows. May I serve you with honor and grace today. Así sea. Así es."

Rosario greeted each of her rose bushes and Marigolds, as well as the bushes of Grandfather Sage, Rosemary, and the other plants. She fanned copal smoke over each of them, saying, "Gracias por su medicina, thank you for your medicine." Then she turned to each of the directions, beginning in the East, and gave thanks to each of the elements for their blessings: fire, earth, water, air. Then she raised the copalero to the sky and gave thanks to the sacred mystery. She completed her prayers by kneeling on the ground and giving thanks to Mother Earth for abundance, love, and beauty.

When she returned to the kitchen, Luz was standing at the stove, singing a medicine song and chopping a small block of pure cacao into powder to melt over the stove. Rosario walked up behind her, kissed her neck softly, and put her arms around her waist. She joined Luz in the song to honor the spirit of the cacao and to call forth its heart-opening medicine.

Todo cura. Todo sana.
Todo lleva medicina adentro.
Cura cura. Sana sana. Cacaocita medicina del amor.

This was a ritual they had shared since they first began living together two years ago. Rosario's heart ached with a fierce love for Luz. She went to the cabinet where they kept their herbal remedios. She took a jar of rose hips from the cabinet, along with the molcajete. She placed a handful of rosehips with lavender in the molcajete and pressed the pestle into the bowl until the flowers were a fine, bright pink powder. Then, she heated water just before boiling and added the powder to the pot. Luz poured the cacao powder into another pot and added the rose tea to the cacao, a few drops at a time, watching as it melted and became a rich, dark red liquid.

"Are we having cacao this morning, mi amor, or is this for someone else?" Rosario asked Luz.

"It's for Aurora." Luz poured the cacao into a large thermos. "I thought we could stop by today. It's Sunday, and she will probably be home. I would love for you to come with me if you can take a little time away from the restaurant. I invited Sofie to join us, as well."

"I would love to. I can get Felicia and Mario to cover the lunch crowd. I was up early preparing the mole, frijoles, and tamales, and I'll be back in time for dinner. How is Aurora doing, mi amor?"

"I think she is doing very well, considering all that she has been through, but she is still not fully convinced that she is not losing her sanity. I want to sit with her and help her to understand that the insanity she fears is her soul trying to reveal the truth. I want her to understand the powerful medicine within her sacred shawl. I think she is a strong vessel, and if she can learn to harness her medicine, she will be able to heal, and perhaps, someday she will be able to help others who have suffered as she has."

"As you now help so many," Rosario said.

"Also, I think it's time for Aurora to meet the Archangels."

"Michael and Sharova? Well then, this is a very important day for Aurora. I'm ready to go when you are. I'm going to cut some of my Don Juan roses from the garden. They are blooming very fragrant right now, and marigolds, too."

"Perfecto. Will you also cut some Romero, mi amor?"

"Claro. Will La Divina be joining us?"

"If there is healing happening, you know she will be there. Aurora means a great deal to her. But, just to be sure, I asked her in my prayers this morning." Luz and Rosario laughed at the strangeness of their conversation, even though for two of them it was perfectly normal.

Aurora stood in front of the mural she had sketched on the wall. She closed her eyes and took a deep breath, trying to sense what other images might want to come through. She could feel them just beyond her reach, but she could not quite grasp them. There was a part of her that was afraid of what images might present themselves, considering everything that had occurred over the last two months. This was her first painting since her show, and she felt an almost desperate need to paint. She lit several white candles and placed them around the room. She picked up one of the candles and moved the flame across the wall. She closed her eyes and tried to pray.

"I don't know if anyone is listening, but I'm so tired of fighting this. So, I surrender to what needs or wants to come through to me. Show me something I can hold on to." She opened her eyes and gazed into the flame. She saw the image of a little girl about two years old. Maddie was holding her on her lap, rocking and singing to the child. They were in the red brick room. Aurora could hear the song so clearly.

"I hold you here. I hold you dear, little one. I'll let no harm come to you." The sounds and images were so tender and sweet—it made Aurora's heart ache. She opened her eyes, placed the candle on a table next to her art supplies. Then she picked up her oil pastels and frantically began to draw what she saw in her mind's eye. When she was finished, she stood back to see the picture fully. A little girl about two years old, asleep in the center of a peach rose. She wore a white lace dress, her hair a tousled mass of strawberry blonde curls. She looked so peaceful—a feeling Aurora could not ever recall feeling. There was a sweetness, an innocence emanating from the child. Suddenly, her chest tightened, her face flushed with heat, and beads of perspiration formed on her brow. She tried to slow her breathing and resisted an irrational urge to run outside and try to find the little girl. She needed to find her, but this time she knew that she would not find her anywhere outside. Aurora went into the kitchen to call Luz to ask for her help, but before she picked up the receiver, there was a knock at the door. She did not have many visitors besides Sofie and Nico, and she knew it was not Nico. Aurora opened the door to find Luz, Rosario, and Sofie standing there, holding bunches of flowers and bags that smelled incredible.

"Oh, my goodness, hello. What a wonderful surprise. I was just going to...never mind. Please come inside. I can't believe you're all here. I'm so happy to see you." Aurora smiled, trying to seem calm as she welcomed her friends inside. She was about to close the door when La Divina appeared in the doorway. Aurora felt a chill run down her arms as she always did when she was in her presence. She bowed her head and made a sweeping gesture with her arm to welcome the goddess inside.

"Buenos Días, Divina. I am honored to have you in my home."

"Gracias, Mija. I'm very happy to be here." She followed Aurora and Sofie into the kitchen, happy to see that Luz and Rosario had made themselves at home as they laughed and chatted, opening cabinets and drawers for plates, cups, and silverware.

"Hola, mis hijas. How are you both on this fine day?" Rosario and Luz took turns greeting her with a kiss and a hug.

"We are so happy you are here, Madrecita. I hope you are hungry," Luz said.

"Can I help with anything?" Aurora asked.

"Yes. You can help us take the food into the living room. We can put it all on the coffee table, no?"

La Divina went to sit in the chair beside the sofa. Luz, Rosario, and Aurora followed, arranging everything on the coffee table buffet style. Luz prepared a plate for La Divina with frijoles and a pork tamale topped with red mole, then she and Rosario sat down on the cobalt-blue loveseat across from Sofie and Aurora. Aurora went back to the kitchen to get the pitcher of hibiscus tea she had made the day before from the fridge. She poured a glass for each of them, then took a seat on the sofa next to Sofie. She tried to relax into the aroma of the food and allow it to calm her nerves. Still, there was a goddess in her living room eating frijoles and a tamal. Aurora watched the women as they ate and chatted. La Divina commented on how delicious the food was and about how happy she was to be able to eat again. Aurora ate a little so as not to be rude, but she did not have an appetite. She was mesmerized by watching the goddess enjoy her food. La Divina met her gaze and smiled.

"I see you are still a bit confused about me, eh mija?"

"I'm sorry. I didn't mean to stare, Señora. But, yes, I am confused. I still don't understand why you're here with me, or why you want to help me. It all feels surreal. Except that I feel a deep connection to you that I can't explain. It's as if I have always known you." Aurora wrung her hands as she tried to explain what she was feeling. La Divina reached out to take Aurora's hand, whose first response was to shirk back. But instead, she held her hand warmly.

"I think this is a good time for us to share the cacao you brought for us, Rosario. Then we will see what the medicine wants to show us, Aurora. Si?"

"Si, Señora."

Rosario went to the kitchen and poured five cups of cacao from the thermos. She carried them into the living room and handed each of them a cup. Then she sat down and took out her copalero, charcoal, and copal from a cloth bag on the floor beside her. She lit the charcoal, and when it was hot, she placed three pieces of copal on the charcoal. She passed the sacred smoke in front of La Divina, and the other women, and then herself. She placed the copalero on the table, then lifted her cup of cacao. The other women lifted their cups, as well. Luz said a prayer.

"We give thanks to the spirit of this medicine. We honor the hands that nurtured the plant and those who picked the fruit. Bless the hands of women who peeled and roasted the beans with love, so that we may have this medicine to open our hearts. We honor the land of Guatemala, where this medicine originates. We ask you, sweet Mamá Cacao, to open our hearts so that we may connect to the heart of the Earth Mother and receive her love and healing." La Divina drank first, then Luz and the others drank after her. They sat in silence; their eyes closed until they finished their cacao. After a long silence, Aurora turned to Luz.

"Luz, Sofie mentioned that you were born in Chiapas, and you lived in Guatemala for about a year, then you came here to San Francisco."

"Yes. I was born and raised in Chiapas."

"Is that how you learned to do, um, what you do?"

"Yes, my grandmother was a yerbera and a partera. She knew how to heal with herbs and how to deliver babies, but it was so much more than that. She knew how to communicate with the plants, and they taught her about their healing properties and how to use them to make remedios, cures to heal others. There was a time when all the women in the village knew this medicine, but slowly, women became afraid to be branded witches by the church. My grandmother wasn't afraid of the church. She believed God had given this knowledge to the people and that to neglect this medicine would be a great sin."

"So, are you a yerbera, too?"

"Oh no. Rosario is the yerbera. I know how to use herbs well enough, but that is not my gift. I was born with the ability to see and communicate with spirits, and the gift of healing with my hands."

"How amazing, and from what little experience I've had seeing spirits, I think it would be scary being able to see them all the time."

"It's not scary at all. Spirits of the dead are just like us: good and bad, kind and scared. The only difference is that they no longer have a physical body. They're sad mostly. Some are angry, and some are just lost. I help them to cross over to the Ancestors and find peace. Unfortunately, your Western culture doesn't honor this way of thinking. They use psychology to label other ways of seeing, feeling, and thinking as madness.

"Our ancestors had a sophisticated indigenous science that viewed a person as a multi-layered, complex being, made up of different aspects. All indigenous cultures have this knowledge. But because Western medicine doesn't comprehend the complexity of our wisdom, they reduce its value, calling it folklore and superstition. Now thousands of years later, they are just beginning to understand the wisdom of indigenous science. For example, the medical industry is only recently beginning to understand the power of hands-on healing, prayer, and the wisdom of herbal medicine. Indigenous peoples have had this knowledge for centuries."

"Sofie says you can see inside a person's soul. Is that true? Is it even possible?"

"It's not as difficult as you might imagine. You see, we all carry the story of our lives in images and words within our sacred shawl, the energy body that contains our soul in the physical body. The sacred shawl extends outside the body. It contains intelligence, healing energy into the body, and connects us to the divine aspect of our being. All humans have the ability to either see or sense images and emotions that tell the story not only of our own soul, but each other's, as well. This energy extends far beyond us and connects each of us to one another. Each luminous thread is like a strand of cosmic DNA. We are all parts of Mother-Father God. Most people are taught that we are individuals and that this kind of connection isn't possible. They label people superstitious, so we are afraid to see more than the physical world." Luz paused to take a sip of cacao. Aurora inhaled, trying to take in what Luz shared. Then, La Divina stood up from the chair and went to sit between Sofie and Aurora, and Sofie moved over to the chair.

"How are you feeling, Aurora?" she asked.

"All of a sudden, I feel warm and more relaxed, like I can breathe easier. I also feel a little lightheaded, but I really like this cacao. It's like I'm more in my body."

"That is the medicine working. I can see the threads of your sacred shawl lighting up and reconnecting themselves to the web of dreamtime. Do you feel it, Aurora?"

"I feel raw and needy, and I don't like feeling this way. I want to understand what is happening to me."

La Divina squeezed Aurora's hand, speaking in a calm and steady tone. "All creation is made of light; a sacred matrix of light particles that move and shift with our emotions and consciousness, as it expands or contracts. You have other layers of your body. They are made of more refined energy than your physical body, which is why you cannot see them with your physical eyes. You must learn to see with the eyes of your heart and align it with your dreaming eye in the center of your brow. You may call this energy your spirit or your soul. All of creation originates from an etheric matrix or design that holds the intelligence of its unique structure. Then the material form follows the intricate design and grows over it.

"For example, when a child is first conceived, the sacred geometry of cells carries within it etheric intelligence or information, so the particles will know how to organize themselves into a fetus. Each cell contains the entirety of this information. But remember, the heart is the first organ to form. It is the first intelligence. It is where the soul is anchored into the body. It is from the heart that the soul expresses itself as energy and electricity. All of the other layers of your light body grow from this expression. This is your sacred shawl. Do you understand?"

"Yes. Please go on."

"Without a human body, you would be unable to have this unique sensual experience on the earth. This is why the Ancient Ones love to visit on El Dia de los Muertos. They miss music, food, fragrance, and all things that involve the senses. The human experience is full of wonder and so much beauty. There is nothing like it anywhere else in the universe. But so many of you are so quick to want to leave your body behind when you experience heartache or loss. It is through heartache, joy, loss, and love that your heart can expand. Aurora, you have been through a great deal of sorrow, and this has allowed you to open and move between the physical and spirit worlds."

"Yes. What you're saying makes a lot of sense to me. That reminds me, there is something I want to show you all."

Aurora was a little nervous to show Luz her mural. She felt like her thoughts weren't tracking correctly, and her skin felt thin and transparent. At the same time, there was a part of her that wanted to know what they would say about it.

"I haven't really shown it to anyone yet, and it's not finished. You will probably be the only ones who will ever see it. But, well, okay." Aurora got up and led the way to her bedroom. When she turned on the light, the wall of brilliant color began to pulse. Sofie let out a gasp, but Luz didn't say a word. She stood in the center of the wall, walking back and forth several times, slowly ingesting the images of the swirling purple sky, with a full melon moon that cast an unnatural glow over a rushing river. On the far side of the riverbank stood an immense Cottonwood tree. Its tumultuous branches scraped against the swirling sky, her profuse trunk connected deep into the earth through a complex network of gnarled, tangled roots visible beneath the riverbed. One of the roots was so thick that it resembled a small tree growing in a large curve out of the ground, making it a perfect place to sit upon. A girl about four years old sat on the curve of the root. Her gaunt, pale face was expressionless, with hollow, pleading eyes. Her gaze was transfixed on the other side of the river, where a woman in a white huipil with monarch butterflies cascading down her side, torn, faded jeans, and a bright red rebozo around her shoulders stood with her back to the viewer. The fringe of the shawl floated on the surface of the water, fingers searching the river for something that could not be seen. The woman's arms extended out towards the little girl. Floating on the surface of the river were the tormented faces of children; their mouths crying out. One of these faces belonged to Aurora, a face she herself did not recognize. It was a secret she held close to her. She only had a handful of memories of her life before the age of 12, and none of them were happy ones. She moved through the world, a mirror without a reflection; blank, empty, numb.

Luz ran her hands over the image of the woman, pressing her face against the cold, painted wall. Her eyes closed, lips moving without sound, calling upon an unseen presence.

"I am calling the Ancient Ones," Luz whispered. Aurora was stunned and speechless. She had never seen anything like this in her life, except when her mother was having a psychotic episode. But this didn't feel like that. There was a hush of something holy that filled the space of the room, like what you're supposed to feel when you are in church, but never do

"Ay, madre de dios. Help me," Aurora whispered. She pulled her rebozo tighter, so she could feel the parameters of her being. She felt as if her bones had come loose and were floating freely around the room. She wanted to run into the bathroom, cut her thigh or her arm, and let the burn of blood call the bones of her body back into order. Just then, Luz opened her eyes and walked to face Aurora. She put her hands firmly on Aurora's shoulders.

"Look at me, Aurora. Breathe with me."

Aurora felt a warm, tingly sensation moving through her, calling her bones back into her body. She allowed her breathing to follow Luz's.

"Better?" Luz asked. Aurora nodded.

"This is a medicine dream, Mija. Listen to the sound of my words.

Do you understand what I'm saying?" Aurora shook her head no and struggled to move away from Luz's hands, but Luz held her firmly.

"I know you are afraid of things you can't explain, but the truth is you're not crazy, or insane. You are awakening to the truth of who you are. This dream is a gift from the Ancestors of the Dreamtime."

"It doesn't feel like a dream. It feels like a fucking curse that's slowly driving me insane. I can't sleep, I hear voices and see things that aren't there, and the only way to stop it all is to cut myself. It brings a few moments of relief from the constant clawing at my insides. I can't sleep, so I paint my crazy dreams. My paintings are all part of this madness. It's why I wanted to sell them so badly. I wanted to get rid of the reminder that I am slowly losing my mind." Aurora wiped at the tears streaming down her face.

Sofie wiped her eyes, too. In all the years that she had known Aurora, she had never seen her cry, and she had no idea that she was going through any of this. She looked around the room and saw the empty bottles of Tequila on the floor. She wanted to put her arms around Aurora and tell her that everything was going to be okay, and how sorry she was that she didn't realize what she was going through. Luz motioned for Sofie to stay where she was.

"Let her feel. Su sueño traía mucho susto, mija; this dream carries the story of the lost parts of your soul."

Aurora couldn't breathe. This was all too much for her to take in. She wanted to run, but for the first time, there was a shard of hope that maybe she wasn't losing her mind. She pinched her forearm to help her focus on what else Luz had to say. Luz pointed to the child sitting under the Cottonwood tree.

"This little girl is you, Aurora. There is a deep sadness that lives inside of you. You feel it, but you don't know what it means, so you try to ignore it, but that only works for a little while." Luz held Aurora's wrists, forcing her to look at her scars.

"You tell yourself that you don't deserve to be alive, that you have no purpose. You believe the lies that you tell yourself, because it's easier than looking at the truth. The truth is hidden from you right now, but the truth is there, hidden beneath your scars, beneath your pain." Luz pointed to the mural.

"The river is a symbol of the tears you hold inside you. It represents the deep sorrow you feel but have no words for. The children's faces represent the different parts of your soul that are lost and forgotten." Luz spoke with authority and gentleness, as if the images of the mural were speaking directly to her, or through her.

"The pain is hiding inside you. You must find it, understand it, and heal it, so you can let it go. I know this sounds simplistic, but the doing and the healing are anything but simple. It takes a great deal of courage to heal." Aurora felt dizzy, her skin turned damp and cold.

"Are you alright?" Sofie asked. Aurora shook her head. She felt the way she used to when she was a little girl, and her mother would lock her out of the house at night. Aurora would stand outside in the front yard alone, outside of her body, looking into her living room, watching her mother laughing and talking to someone only she could see and hear. Aurora tried to slow the panic she felt coming on, as the floor shifted beneath her. Luz and La Divina rushed to catch Aurora before she hit the floor, moving her quickly onto the bed.

"Is she going to be alright?"

"She has susto, Sofie. She needs a lot of healing." Luz sat beside Aurora and placed the palm of her hand across her forehead and then over the center of her heart.

"Please, Sofie, bring me my bolsa and all the candles you can find." Sofie moved quickly, handed the purse to Luz, and lit candles around the room. Luz took the bag from Sofie and emptied the contents on the bed beside Aurora. She opened a small muslin bag of blue corn meal, sprinkled a small amount into the palm of her hand, and mixed it with some of her saliva. She smeared the blue paste in the shape of a crescent moon on Aurora's forehead, then she smeared a four-quarter cross on the center of her chest.

"Take her shoes off." Sofia moved quickly, as Luz traced a four quarter on the top of each foot."

"Move those candles here at her feet." Sofia did as she was told, whispering a prayer of protection. La Divina could see that Aurora's soul had flown far from her body. She took a spirit inventory of Aurora's sacred shawl. She reached for her abalone shell and copal. She waved her hand over the charcoal, ignited the flame, and waited for the sweet, healing fragrance of the Ancestors to fill the room.

"Why are the little ones trapped in the red brick room, Señora?" Sofie asked La Divina.

"Ah. That is a very good question, Sofie. The red brick room is the Celestial Underworld, which is where you hold the emotions caused by the trauma you experienced as a child and could not possibly understand. A child has no understanding or context to make sense of sexual trauma, so Aurora's soul placed the memories of the trauma in the red brick room. A familiar place, where she would be able to access her memories when she was ready. Up until now, she had no memory of the abuse. But the pain manifested in her life just the same. This is why Lil' Yoya tells her that it is time to remember, and why the memories appear as dreams at first, and why she sometimes feels like she is going mad; to use her own words. But actually, it means she is strong enough to reclaim her memories, face her pain, and begin to heal. The psychic energy of her trauma is emerging in memories, dreams, and visions of her wounded child parts, and Maddie holds the rage she has been afraid to feel. Each person is unique, so the way soul loss manifests is unique, as well. Do you understand, Aurora?" La Divina turned to Aurora, who was now awake and listening.

"Yes. I do. What you're saying makes sense to me. I don't know if I'm ready, but I want to face this. I'm starting to feel angry about what happened to Lil' Yoya, M. J., and even Maddie. I mean, what kind of person does this to a child? It doesn't make sense, especially because it was my own mother." Aurora sat up and slammed her hand down on the bed. "When I begin to understand that Lil' Yoya, Mary Jane, and Maddie are all parts of me, then I feel like I need to find them and help them. I want to take them out of the red brick room. Can we do that? Will you help me, Señora?" La Divina smiled and turned to Luz and Rosario, nodding.

"Of course I will help you, Aurora. But only you can convince the others to trust you and leave the red brick room. I will walk with you, as I always have. I will help to illuminate the truth, but you must be willing to open your heart and to truly love the parts of you who are trapped in the red brick room. It's the only way they will trust you. More importantly, you will have to find a way for Maddie to trust you. You will have to find genuine love and compassion and open your heart to her. Do you think you can do this?"

"I don't know, but I want to try. Please tell me what to do, and I will do it. My head hurts. I'm starting to feel the pain they have been holding for me."

"Tell me, Aurora, what is the way you would say you connect to your soul most easily?"

"I never really thought about it, but I would have to say that it is through painting. It's why I created this mural. I need to get it all out of me."

"It's time for you to go to them. Si?" La Divina asked.

"Yes, it's time." Suddenly, Aurora felt a stabbing spasm in her womb. The pain bent her over.

"I feel the clawing at my insides again; something wants to get out."

Aurora felt herself becoming small, sinking into her inner dreamscape. Deeper than she had ever gone. She was surrounded in pitch-cold, obsidian space; completely alone. She pulled her red rebozo around her shoulders when suddenly she heard a familiar voice.

"That isn't going to keep you warm. You're mine now." Aurora couldn't see who the voice belonged to.

"Who are you? What do you want?"

"Oh, it's not what I want, but what you want from me."

"Who are you?" Aurora was shivering, and her voice trembled as she tried to speak. A dim candle flame barely illuminated the room. The shadowed presence moved around the space, lighting several candles, until the room was fully illumined in a warm glow. Aurora looked around to get her bearings. She was in the red brick room. There was a young woman standing on the opposite wall, with her back to Aurora. She had on ragged jeans and a worn black t-shirt. Her arms were covered with old, bloody bandages. Then Aurora understood who she was.

"Hello, Maddie," she said, trying to speak confidently. Maddie turned to face Aurora.

"It's Madrone to you."

Madrone was about 17 years old. She wore heavy black mascara and liner around her eyes, with dark red lipstick. Her black hair was parted to the side, obscuring part of her left eye.

"Hello, Madrone. Why have you brought me here?"

"You brought me here, you stupid woman. It's a wonder you managed to stay alive this long."

Madrone walked over to Aurora and yanked the turquoise earrings from her ears. Then she yanked off the squash blossom turquoise necklace from her neck and threw them on the cement floor. Finally, she grabbed Aurora's rebozo and tossed it on the floor.

"These won't help you here. Do you like it here? Look around you; look familiar?"

"Yes. It's the red brick room."

"Well, how nice of you to visit us. How nice to be able to be a visitor and leave whenever you like, while Yoya, M.J., and the Innocent One are stuck here in this disgusting room year after year. How long has it been now, Aurora? I'll tell you how long—over two decades, that's how long."

Madrone's voice was low and firm. Aurora wasn't used to feeling scared, but she was, because she was confused and seemed to have no control over what was happening to her. Then, out of the corner of the room, La Divina appeared with Lil' Yoya and M.J. on either side of her. They clung to her long, white cotton dress. Aurora's eyes grew wide with hope.

"Oh, Señora. I'm so happy to see you. Can you help me get out of this place?"

"Forget it, girl. She's here to help us. We are so tired of your excuses and your spineless confusion." Aurora's frustration was turning to anger.

"You know La Divina?" Madrone threw her head back in a disgusted laugh. She moved her face close to Aurora's face.

"She is the one who has been taking care of us. She's the only one who has ever loved us. She promised us she would help you to remember, so we can leave this godforsaken place. That's why you're here, you idiot." La Llorona sat the little ones down on Aurora's rebozo in the corner of the room. Then she stood up and walked over to Madrone, putting her arm around her shoulder.

"Come, Mija. Go sit with the children. They are frightened. I will talk with Aurora." Madrone realized her anger frightened Lil' Yoya and M.J. She immediately went to their side to comfort them.

"Is Yoya gonna take her rememories back now?" Lil' Yoya asked.

"I don't know, mija. I hope so. La Divina is going to help her." Madrone sat down with the children, holding them close, waiting to see what La Divina would do next. She turned to Madrone and motioned for her to come back.

"Think of the little ones, Maddie. You will know what needs to be done. I trust you." La Divina went to sit with the little ones on the floor. Maddie lit several more candles and placed them around Aurora's feet.

"Take your clothes off." At first, Aurora thought she had misunderstood Madrone.

"I'm sorry. What?"

"You heard me. Take your clothes off. Do you think your clothes are going to protect you? Your clothes are a part of who you think you are. Along with your paintings and all the attention you get for being such a wonderful artist. You wouldn't be able to do any of that without us. We live down here holding the pain and sorrow that you so eloquently paint into images, but you don't know where they come from. They come from me! And from Lil' Yoya and from M.J."

Madrone unwrapped the bandages from her arms and let them fall to the floor. Her forearms were covered in cuts, some still bloody and some scabbed over. Madrone continued. "All those angels that you painted in your murals; those come from the Innocent One. But you don't care about us. You just take what you think is yours alone and leave us here, alone, without light, without anyone to care about us. I hate you, Aurora. Do you hear me? I hate you! Now take your clothes off, or I will rip them off you." Aurora slowly removed her white T-shirt and jeans, then her underwear and bra. She stood before Madrone completely naked, shivering in fear of what was to come next. The red brick walls began to contract and expand, matching Aurora's breathing.

"Good," Madrone said. "Now turn around and face the wall." Aurora turned around slowly to face the wall. There were words and sentences scratched into the bricks.

"Move closer and read them out loud," Madrone commanded. Aurora moved closer to the brick wall until she could read the words clearly. She stood dumb as she read the words silently.

"I said, read them out loud. Do it! Read them so we can all hear you. We've been living with these words for decades; they have leached into our insides. We look at them every day, and even though the little ones don't understand what all the words mean, they know that they are bad. They can feel the energy of the words, and they cause them to suffer. Now read them, you fucking coward!" Aurora began to read; her voice was shaky. As she read each phrase, she felt her bones loosen from her body, like she was disappearing into the walls of the room.

"Shhh. It's only a dream…If you tell, I'll kill you…This is our secret…Don't lie. You liked it…You're a bad girl, and bad girls go to hell to live with the devil." Aurora's voice caught in her throat, so she paused for a minute.

"Keep reading. Don't stop," Madrone said firmly. Aurora continued.

"You're a liar and liars burn in hell…Be still, this won't hurt…This is how you know I love you…You won't remember this in the morning." The writing on the bricks began to blur and shift.

"That's enough. Turn around." Aurora turned around and looked at La Divina. She mouthed the words, *Help me.* "This may not be the help you want, but this is the help you need, Aurora. It's time for you to remember all that happened to all of you," La Divina said. Madrone picked up the red rebozo from the floor and tossed it to Aurora.

"Cover yourself."

"I want you to imagine what it was like for us to be reduced to a thing to be used for the pleasure of others. We became objects to be used at will by anyone who offered our mother something she needed: a sink repair, an envelope full of pills, money. Our bodies were violated, raped, beaten, infused with the rage and sin of others. We were left alone without understanding what had happened to us. It left us feeling bad. Dirty and full of shame. Empty of light, receptacles for darkness and dirty secrets. We had no comfort, except for La Señora and the angels. They were our witnesses; they cared for us down here until you were ready to come for us. I became the mean one, the tough girl, the one who didn't give a shit. But on the inside, I ached for my own light. I was invisible. Silence was my world. So, I cut their secrets into my arms, in a code that only I understood. Lil' Yoya, M.J., had no words to describe what was done to them, to me, to us, and no understanding of what was taken. They believed they were bad. They had nowhere to be safe, except the niche of a vacant church; quiet, peaceful, beautiful, with a goddess to pray to, surrounded by the light of candles. They felt safe. Then you grew up and forgot us, and we became trapped in this reality.

"Later, as a teen, I grew to understand what they took from me; what they desired from me. My sacred bowl of light, sweet womb nectar, hidden in my sex. I traded my body for ashes and crumbs, in search of a way to fill the hole inside. Then I found a way to take it back. I reclaimed it, my sword of iron, my sexual power. I discovered that men found me attractive, desirable. I had the power to decide who I gave my sex to. I felt powerful in the moment, but afterwards, I was empty. I fed my light to others and asked for nothing in return, because I believed I deserved nothing. Some told me they loved me, while others found me mysterious and wanted more. I'm not mysterious. I'm vacant, unavailable, because I don't know who I am, Aurora. I obscure myself, trading the only currency I have. Sex for affection. Sex for a warm bed with arms to hold me. I just wanted to be loved, even though I knew it wasn't real. But you don't remember any of this either. When night came, I couldn't sleep. I sat up in my bed, rocking, humming, and praying for someone to save me from the filthy hands that were sure to reach for me. Maybe not tonight, but soon. Their poison branded me worthless. I ache to feel something other than what I am feeling now. I dream of feeling love. Not just smiling faces that say the words, then trick you and drag you down to a red brick room, where others come to do things that there are no words for. Real love. Nico loved me. He saw me. He loved us. I loved him too, and you ruined it, and I hate you for it. So here we are, like a bad Stevie Nicks song, but there are no paper flowers and no velvet underground. Only this damned red brick room. Now do you understand my loathsome existence, and why I hate you?"

"But I thought you said La Divina has cared for you?"

"Oh, she has. While I am trapped in this room like an animal, I can close my eyes and find sanctuary within my mind. A mind that has been broken and remade; a labyrinth with countless chambers to hide my pain. I scratch at my thighs and feel the filth seep out of me. It weeps what I have no words for. Then I dig my fingernails into my thighs harder until they bleed a crimson river down my leg, releasing the filth from my body. Finally, I can breathe, and I descend. Down into the arms of La Divina. She catches me before my bones hit the ground and carries me over to a sparkling blue river, where she cradles my body and washes me. Then she takes her obsidian blade from around her waist and gently scrapes at my skin, clearing away their sin that clings to me.

"This is not who you are. This does not belong to you. You are my beloved daughter," she tells me. Then she sings, *Hey ya na ho. Hey ya na ho. A ye a ye hare, hare, no ha.* And she weeps.

"Ay mijita preciosa, my precious daughter." Her weeping turns to wailing that vibrates the space around me. She continues to cut away the sin that has leached into my flesh. I rest in the vastness of her Being. We merge and I transform into stardust and turquoise sky." Aurora recognized the Celestial Underworld that Madrone described, because La Divina had taken her there, too, and she had sung her the same medicine song and had washed her in the river.

"Maddie, I mean Madrone, La Divina took me to Celestial Underworld, too. She washed me and cleaned me in the river, and she sang me the same medicine song." Aurora felt like an idiot as soon as she heard herself speak the words.

"Good for you, Aurora, but that doesn't really help us. The children weep and wait for a mother who will never come. So, they called you. Lil' Yoya is so brave; she hounded you and haunted you until you thought you were losing your mind. Finally, you figured it out with the help of Luz, Rosario, and La Divina. So now you think you can just show up here to rescue us, and we are just supposed to go with you? Where is Aurora? Where will you take us? How will you get us out of here? You don't even love us." Aurora realized she hadn't made a plan. She didn't know how she was going to get them out of there, and she wasn't sure how she felt about any of them. She had only thought of her own needs in all that had happened.

"I challenge you now. You are so fond of cutting yourself. I challenge you to slice open the veins of your forgetting and bleed the excuses of insanity onto the ground, once and for all. Release it. Own it. Face it. All of it; the terror, the filth, the shame, and the beauty. We have beauty in us. See us." Madrone touched her brow to Aurora's and whispered.

"Remember the truth, Aurora, and we can be free to be loved, to be renewed and holy, in sorrow and sweetness, as we were meant to be. Free us." Madrone pulled Aurora closer, so they breathed each other's breath and felt the other's heartbeat. Then, M.J. and Lil' Yoya ran up to them and hugged their legs.

"I love you, Yoya," Lil' Yoya said. She tugged on the rebozo to get her attention. Aurora looked down to see them both beaming at her with love in their eyes. They were so beautiful and innocent, and suddenly, her heart broke open. Aurora sat on the floor and hugged Lil' Yoya. Then M.J. tapped Aurora on the shoulder.

"I love you, too, Yoya." Aurora had never felt such pure love before. She held them both. She looked at them both and kissed them on their cheeks.

"I love you, too. Both of you." Then she looked up at Madrone and patted the floor beside her, inviting her to sit with them. Maddie was holding Innocent One in her arms. She was beautiful. She had soft, loose, strawberry-blonde curls that framed her face. When she looked at Maddie, she smiled big, revealing dimpled cheeks. There was a light that emanated from the child, and when Aurora looked at her, she felt a stirring in her heart.

"Please sit with us." At first, Madrone did not respond. She stood there, angry and stubborn. Then La Divina stood beside her and whispered in her ear.

"This is what you wanted, mija. This is what you have been waiting for. Go and sit with them." La Divina placed her hand in the middle of Maddie's back and breathed her love into her. It softened her, and she went to sit with Aurora and the little ones. She grabbed Aurora's T-shirt from the floor on the way. They waited as Maddie approached and sat on the floor next to Aurora. Maddie tossed her the shirt.

"You better put this on." Aurora slipped the T-shirt over her head.

"Thanks, Madrone. I was wondering why you call her Innocent One?"

"I thought that would be obvious, but I guess not. She holds our innocence. She is the part of us who was untouched by abuse. You can think of her as our soul."

"That's so beautiful." Aurora reached over and gently touched Innocent One. The child giggled and burrowed her face in Maddie's hair.

"I love you, too, Innocent One. I really do." The child turned to Aurora and stretched out her hand. Aurora held it and kissed it before releasing it.

"You have done a wonderful job protecting her, Madrone."

"You can call me Maddie. It wasn't just me. La Divina was the one who kept her from being exposed to it all. I guess in that way, being stuck down here was good for her."

All of a sudden, Aurora understood that Maddie and the others were lost parts of herself. Maddie was a powerful and fearless part of herself, and for the first time, she allowed herself to feel her grief about all the suffering they had experienced. It now felt real to her. Sorrow and rage exploded within her, and she began to wail and scream. She pounded her fists on the floor. La Divina came and put her arms around Aurora and rocked her while she wept. Lil' Yoya and M.J. scooted near Maddie and Innocent One. Maddie hugged them close.

"Is she going to be okay?" Lil' Yoya whispered.

"Yeah. She's going to be fine. She's remembering."

"Does that mean we can get out of here, now?" M.J. asked.

"I don't know. I hope so." Maddie kissed them on their brows and sat with them as they waited to see what would happen next. Then Aurora stopped sobbing. She sat quietly beside La Divina for a moment, then got up and walked over to Maddie and the little ones. She sat in front of them and took Maddie's hand.

"I'm so sorry I forgot about you, Maddie. I know who you are now, and I didn't realize it, but I missed you so much. I see now that it was your fearlessness and courage that helped me not to give up my quest for the truth. To say thank you doesn't seem adequate to express my love and gratitude to you. I love you, Maddie, and I need you, and I promise if you return to me, I will try my best to make it work with Nico. You're right. He does love us, and I was a coward and I ran from his love." With the promise of love, Aurora had Maddie's attention.

"You really promise you'll work it out with Nico? All I ever wanted was someone to love me."

"I know, Maddie, but I love you absolutely and unconditionally. But you're courageous to want to be loved. I wanted that too, but I was too scared to let myself be loved. I didn't feel worthy because I didn't love myself. I think now I can learn how."

"Doesn't everyone deserve to be loved?" Maddie asked.

Aurora took Maddie's hands and pulled her up from the floor, so they were facing each other.

"You make it sound so simple, because you're so wise. Yes. We do deserve to be loved, and I love you, Maddie. I need you. Will you please come back to me?"

"Yes. I want to, but I don't know how." Maddie looked to La Divina.

"Will you help us, Madrecita?" La Divina walked over to them and wrapped her rebozo around the two of them. She waved her arms, and suddenly they were all in the Celestial Underworld. La Divina walked to the edge of the river and motioned for all of them to step into the river. Maddie carried M.J., and Aurora carried Lil' Yoya into the water. La Divina laid Innocent One on a blanket on the ground, away from the river, then she joined the others in the river.

"Ay, mis hijas. This has been a long journey for each of you. You have travailed, and yet the sins of others have not destroyed you. You have gained wisdom and strength in spite of it. I bless you and purify you now into wholeness. You are no longer separate, but one. One heart, one mind, and one soul." She poured water over their heads and washed their hands. Then she guided them out of the river to a large circle of lavender and rosemary on the ground. She handed each of them a fully bloomed red rose and invited them into the center of the circle, then she lit copal from her hand and fanned the sweet smoke over each of us with an owl feather.

"Stand in a circle and hold hands."

They did as she said. Then she stood behind Maddie and pulled long etheric blue threads out from her body. The threads floated and curled around Maddie, but she stood there fully trusting La Divina. Then she moved behind M.J. and did the same, pulling the etheric threads from her body, and they curled and floated around her, as they did with Maddie. Next, La Divina moved behind Lil' Yoya and did the same with her etheric blue threads. Finally, she moved behind Aurora. They all looked up and could see the blue threads floating and moving above them.

"These are the threads of your sacred shawl. They have been separated, torn, and some of the threads are lost. I am going to reconnect the threads of your sacred shawls, so you will return to wholeness as one. Do you agree with this?" They said yes. La Divina sang, and a blue mist rose up from the ground and encircled them.

"A keesh, a keesh, a keesh ua le le le va." Then thirteen very old women emerged from the mist.

"These are the Thirteen Sacred Grandmothers. They are Ancient Ones who weave and reweave the threads of the Universe. They are the keepers of the stories of the soul. When the threads of your sacred shawl become lost, it is the Thirteen Sacred Grandmothers who collect the threads and hold them."

Maddie and Aurora instinctively bowed their heads in respect, and the little one followed their movement. Then one of the Grandmothers moved into the circle. She waved her hand and lightning flashed before them. The light entered into the top of their heads, infusing the cells of their bodies with light. La Divina and the Grandmothers began to pull the strands of our sacred shawls, weaving them together. They whispered secret words into the strands, and suddenly the blue strands changed into luminous colors of emerald, sapphire, ruby, orange, gold, and silver. They pulled the threads tighter and tighter, until they were in a cocoon-like enclosure filled with light. Then La Divina spoke.

"And so it is done. You are now one." There was a great flash of blue light, and suddenly they were back in the red brick room.

Aurora and Maddie felt different—lighter, cleaner, more joyful. They sat on the floor, smiling at one another. Then Aurora asked, "If we are all one, then why are we still here?"

"La Divina healed us spiritually, but you still have to figure out how to get us out of here. We need a plan. What's left for you to do, Aurora?" Maddie asked.

Aurora thought about it, and the memory of a dream about her mother came back to her. The one where she was trapped in the train car. Then suddenly, she understood what she needed to do.

"I think I understand why we're still here. There is still one thing I need to do. I have to go, but I'll be back. I promise."

"No way. You're not ever leaving us here again. We're going with you."

FEBRUARY 7 ~ 1984

Journal Entry: 222

It's been a little over two years since I began this journey to find out the truth about who I am and what I have been through. My life has changed drastically. I have changed in ways I would not have thought possible. I'm not the same person I was a year ago, and yet, I am more myself than I have ever been. My heart is now open, and I am learning to love, and more importantly, I am learning to receive love from others. This is something I have always been too afraid to do. During my childhood and teenage years, I had parts of myself, my soul, constantly taken from me. There was so little of myself to give to anyone. In a strange way, I feared that if I ever truly loved anyone, they would take away the last traces of me, and I would disappear.

Sofie is the one person who I have been able to love. Yet, I hid myself from her, too. She is the one constant in my life and has always loved and accepted me, even when she did not fully understand me. I know that Nico loves me, too, and I am learning to trust this.

The parts of myself that I had rejected and abandoned, Lil' Yoya, M.J., the Innocent One, and most importantly, Madrone-Maddie, whom I feared and hated, I now love. Mysterious parts of myself I did not want to believe were real. They held my pain, rage, terror, as well as the love I could not access. Now I can appreciate life, seeing through the eyes of my heart, a life that is filled with beauty and magic.

I have gone round and round in my head trying to find peace with the emotions I feel. My mind and body are restless. I think of all that I have been through—what we have been through, and the serpent fire ignites in my womb and rises to my throat. The place in my body where I hid my truth and tucked secrets in a blanket of fear. No more. I am ready to journey and find the truth that I need to feel at peace and move on with my life.

I give thanks to all who have guided and helped me on my path. Tonight, I ask for your protection, love, and guidance to find what my heart desires.

Así es, así sea.

Aurora set her journal on the nightstand and went to her studio. She stood in front of her altar, which was a wooden bench she had found at a garage sale. It was paint-splattered, but she liked knowing that an artist had owned it. It was covered with a simple white cotton hand towel that had embroidered pink roses along the bottom edge. Abuela Rose gave it to her when she was ten years old. It was the only thing she ever gave her. Dolores was not close to her mother, but she took Aurora with her when she went to visit her on the weekends. She was short in stature, but her presence was grounded and kind. Abuela Rosa always had a pot of pinto beans on the stove, along with a basket of handmade flour tortillas. Aurora loved to eat them warm, rolled up with butter.

As she thought about all she had been through in the last year, tears of gratitude rolled down her cheeks. She lit four white candles on the altar, as well as the tall, white votives scattered on the studio floor. Returning to her altar, she pulled out the blue zarape she kept folded beneath it, along with her red rebozo. She wrapped her rebozo around her shoulders and sat with her legs crossed in front of her. On each side of her altar were baskets of herbs, crystals, feathers, charcoal, and the black copalero Luz had gifted her after the ceremony with Maddie. She kept it wrapped in a red cloth. Aurora remembered what Luz said to her after the ceremony.

"It is time now for you to claim your medicine and all of who you are. Your medicine and magic live within you, and you have only to look within to ignite it."

She picked up the copalero, placed a small round brick of charcoal in it, and lit it with a match. Once it turned red, she placed a piece of copal on it, inhaled the pungent fragrance, fanning the smoke over her face and head with her hands, the way Luz had taught her to do. Aurora's heart ached for answers from the only person who could give them to her: her mother. Fury and sorrow choked in her throat as she sat rocking slowly back and forth, speaking her intentions out loud.

"I call upon the medicine within me to help me to find the truth I seek, to quench the unquenchable thirst only the truth will satisfy. I call upon Tonantzin-Guadalupe, Mi Divina-La Llorona, and the spirit of my mother. Be with me now and give me strength for what I need to do." She dipped her index and middle fingers in the bowl of water, then crossed herself in the old way, touching her fingers to her brow, then to her heart, her left then her right shoulder, ending with her palms meeting in front of her heart center.

"By air, by earth, by water, by fire, Ancient Ones hear my heart's desire."

Aurora pulled her rebozo tight around her and lay down on the floor, comforted by the warm glow of the candlelight. Suddenly, the room was infused with a soft sapphire blue light. She breathed the blue light into her heart and her mind quieted, and she felt her sacred shawl expand. Then she heard the comforting sound of La Divina weeping in the distance. She called her.

"La Divina, Lloroncita—ayúdame, por favor. Help me to make this journey and find the answers my heart needs." La Llorona responded with a song that resonated through Aurora.

"*Aya nay way, ya no hey way. Hare ki raya na ho. Trust your medicine, Aurora. Trust yourself. Let your heart guide the way.*" La Divina's song ignited the gold and silver fibers of Aurora's sacred shawl. Her energetic body exploded into points of light, connecting to the infinite wisdom of her oversoul. She felt the infinite divine love of her soul permeate her being entirely. Then La Divina appeared before her.

"The answers you seek now await you." La Divina pulled Aurora into her embrace, and without warning, they began to fall. They fell between time and space, traveling through the cobalt net of Dreamtime. They landed in a place that looked like San Francisco, but it was completely without any color. It was monochrome, bathed in a thick gray mist. Aurora glanced at La Divina, who nodded for Aurora to proceed.

As Aurora looked around at the city she loved, she realized that it was frozen in a time she wanted to forget. A stream of mixed emotions drummed through her. She held her stomach as an overwhelming sense of grief cut through her. As she slowed her breathing down, she realized these emotions were not her own. She was tuning into emotions that belonged to this place. When the energy of the emotions had moved through her, she heard a familiar voice call her name. She looked through the fog and saw Lil' Yoya walking towards her, along with M.J. She was happy to see that Maddie was there, too. She carried the Innocent One on her hip. Lil' Yoya tugged on Aurora's hand.

"Don't worry, Yoya. I'm here. We're all here with you." She pointed to the Innocent One, M.J., and Maddie. Aurora picked her up and kissed her on the cheek. Then she looked at the others.

"Thank you for being here with me, and for always protecting me." Aurora looked around at others standing to the side of her, waiting to see how they would respond. She extended her other arm, inviting M.J., the Innocent One, and Maddie into a group hug. They rushed to join the group hug. Then Lil' Yoya reached into the pocket of her jeans and took out a photograph. In the photo, four-year-old Aurora was sitting on Dolores' lap, beside a Christmas tree. Dolores is smiling at the camera, while Aurora's brow is furrowed, and her mouth is turned down in a pout, her hair a mass of tangled curls. Aurora remembered how confused she felt when she had woken up that morning. Everyone was excited to open presents from Santa, who had come secretly in the night. She and her mother had left a plate of cookies and a glass of milk out for him. She had stayed awake the entire night, filled with dread, thinking of the secret man who would come in the night. Maddie put her arm around Aurora's shoulders and pulled her close.

"Aurora, we can do this."

Aurora wiped a tear from her eye. "Thank you, Maddie. I really need your strength and courage right now."

Maddie felt the fire of her own rage flare in her belly. She stared into the fog and spoke. "Mother? You need to come to us now."

Maddie raised her arms, and the mist lifted. They saw La Divina just ahead, standing in front of an abandoned BART train. It was covered in graffiti, and the windows were dirty and cracked. La Divina waved her arms, and the train doors opened, and she stepped inside. Aurora and the others shadowed behind her. Then they saw her. Dolores was sitting in a chair, staring out of a window, just as she had done each afternoon when she was alive. Except this window looked out into an empty world, encased in a gray fog. Dolores was holding a large leather book in her hands. Her form was transparent, and she seemed unaware that Aurora and the others were standing there watching, as she intently examined the contents of the book.

"I know this place. She's between worlds. It's like this place is her own red-brick room. She's trapped here, like we were," Maddie said.

"Hi, Ma," Maddie said, abruptly. Dolores was startled as she looked up and saw all of them standing in front of her. She dropped the book on the floor.

"Who are you? Why are you here? Leave me in peace." Aurora felt a tinge of sadness as she noticed the lines on her mother's face that sagged from the weight of her burden. Dolores stood up, fumbling to retrieve her book from the floor. Maddie took a few steps closer to her, but Dolores looked away from her and took a cigarette from her dress pocket and lit it.

"Mom. It's me. Don't you recognize me?"

"Yes, but you look so much younger." Maddie sat down beside her. Dolores looked at her, eyes filled with shame and grief.

"Ma, I don't understand what you're doing here." Dolores opened the book on her lap, and Maddie looked over her shoulder to see the contents of one of the pages.

"I'm trying to understand what is in these pages, but I'm afraid to look. They're horrible and filled with pictures I don't want to see." Maddie motioned for the others to come closer, so they could see, too. Each page depicted a significant scene from Dolores' life, as well as what she had denied while she was alive. Dolores looked up at all of them and tried to smile, the corners of her mouth refusing to rise. Aurora and Maddie looked at each other, and Maddie moved to speak, but Aurora put her hand on her shoulder to stop her.

"Please. I need to do this." Maddie nodded in agreement and stepped back, guiding the others away with her. Dolores pulled her thoughts inward once more and stared out into the empty space of the train window. Aurora felt a twinge of sadness that this woman was never the kind of mother she needed. Then she reminded herself why they were there. She heard M.J. plead, "Ask her. Go on, ask her." Aurora began to speak, but Dolores interrupted, rambling a string of happy memories that never happened.

"Aurora, you know, I remember…"

"I don't want to hear you tell me about your fantasies, Ma. For once, I want you to just listen to me. I want to tell you the story of a little girl who was taken down to a red brick room in a dirty basement. A little girl who felt unwanted and unloved, and no matter how hard she tried, she could never get you to love her. Do you know that story, Ma? Do you? Or, what about the story about how you used to stay out all night getting drunk, while my brothers and I were home with no food? Or, what about how you used to beat me, then lock me in a dark closet? I want you to tell me how you could hurt your own children this way." Aurora felt like her rage would split her in two. She looked over to La Divina for guidance, but she only watched in silence with the others.

"I don't know what to say, Aurora. I want you to know that I did love you. I know you don't believe me, but it's true. It's like I was two people. Sometimes when I looked at you, I saw an angel, the perfect little girl I had always dreamed of having. You had a light about you, as if you came from another world. Other times when I saw your light, I became filled with hate. I wanted you to suffer the same pain that I had suffered. The voices would tell me that you were bad inside, and that I needed to punish you. It's as if I was possessed by something evil. I knew there was something wrong with me, but I didn't want to think about it. Most days, I just wanted to die. That's why I drank so much. The alcohol and pills numbed my pain and helped me forget everything that happened to me. I didn't understand why I was born into a life of suffering and loneliness."

"Those are excuses, not answers. I want to know why you did those things to me—to us." Dolores lit a cigarette, inhaled deeply, and turned back the pages of her book. Then she motioned for Aurora and the others to come and see. La Divina, Maddie, and the little ones gathered around to see the pages in the book. On the pages, Aurora and the others saw images that played like a movie of Dolores when she was a girl. They showed Dolores trapped in a shed with a man on top of her, along with other images that depicted Dolores being abused in one way or another. Suddenly, her heart broke for her mother. She was just a child when this happened, too. Somehow, it gave Aurora a little understanding of how her mother had become a woman who was able to neglect and allow others to abuse her children the way she had.

"You see. It happened to me, too. Maybe a part of me thought that abuse was just a part of life. I didn't know any different."

"That doesn't excuse what you did, but at least I understand a little better now." Aurora felt as if her body released years of sadness she had carried in her body. She felt clearer. "I forgive you, Ma. I forgive you, and I pray for your healing, and that you can move on from this place. You will never heal if you stay here. You're hiding, just as you did when you were alive. It's time to leave this place. Do you understand?" Just then, Maddie ran between them and faced Aurora.

"No. You can't just forgive her like that. You can't just let her off so easily. It's not fair." Aurora took Maddie's hands in hers. "She's not getting off easy, Maddie. Look at the book. She has suffered enough. There is no point in her suffering anymore. It's time to end it. She doesn't belong here; lost in this nothingness. Surely you understand. We must forgive her, so we can move on, so the little ones can finally be free. Don't you want that?"

"But they won't have a mother."

"We will be their mother. You are the one who has been mothering them this whole time. You have kept them safe and loved them. Now, I will be here to take over and keep you all safe. I'm not a child anymore. I will love you all and keep you safe inside. I promise, but I can't do that until our mother has passed over." Maddie pulled away from Aurora and looked over at her mother. She looked so tired and worn. She was only half a soul. It was like she was missing a big part of herself.

"Okay. I will forgive her." On hearing those words, La Divina walked over to Dolores.

"Did you hear their words, my daughter? You are forgiven. It's time to go now." She turned to her left and stretched out her arms in front of her, palms bent up. She moved her hands in a large circular motion until an enormous portal of swirling white light appeared, and the train car was filled with light. Then, La Divina reached out her hand and Dolores took her hand and stood up. She looked over to Aurora, Maddie, and the others.

"Thank you," she said and stepped through the portal. Then she was gone, the portal closed quickly behind her. Aurora, Maddie, and the little ones stood staring at where the portal had been. Then Lil' Yoya spoke.

"Where do we go now?"

"That's a great question. Where do we go now, Aurora?" Maddie asked.

"I know you're not going to like this, but I think we need to go back to the brick room." Lil' Yoya and M.J. immediately started to cry.

"No way. We're not going back there. You promised."

"I did, and I will keep my promise. But you see, I believe we need to create our next place together, kind of like making a group painting. Each of you needs to decide what you want your new home to look like, and then you can leave this place and go there. Do you understand?

"Yeah. That makes sense, I guess. I've never thought about where I would go once you came to free us."

"I know what I want," Lil' Yoya said.

"Me, too. I know where I want to go," M.J. chimed in.

"I guess I have some thinking to do," Maddie said.

"I think you don't have to go anywhere, Maddie, because you're a more grown-up part of me, and I need you. I think we just need to create some healthy boundaries and give you a chance to grow up, until we're the same age. Maybe we could be like roommates. We live in the same body, but you have your own room to go to when I have grown-up things to do, and that includes when I'm intimate with Nico. You can be around at certain times that are safe for you, but not during grown-up stuff. At least not until you're older. It's time for you to experience what it's like to be a teenager. You didn't get to have that. Besides, I have a feeling that as you get older, we will continue to merge until we're just one."

"You mean, I won't exist anymore."

"Not at all. I mean, you will be more you than ever before, and so will I."

"Okay. Let's do it." Maddie turned to leave the train.

"Are you guys coming or what?" She laughed and ran ahead of them. Aurora stopped and looked at La Divina.

"Did I speak correctly in what I said to Maddie?"

"Sí, mi amor. You have grown very wise. What you said was correct and full of love." When they returned to the red brick room, Lil' Yoya and M.J. ran to get their crayons and some paper to draw the picture of where they wanted to live. They huddled in a corner, scribbling, whispering, and giggling together. Maddie and Aurora walked over to them. La Divina sat on the opposite side of the room holding Innocent One, curious to see what Aurora would do next.

"What are you both up to?" Maddie asked playfully.

"We're making our new home."

Aurora asked if she could see their drawing. When they showed her, all that was on the paper was a very tall tree with huge branches. Then, suddenly, Aurora understood. She closed her eyes and imagined a tree house way up in the branches of an old Oak tree. They would feel safe there. She imagined the space with a playroom, big windows, and a bedroom with two beds, so they would always be near one another. She added small details she thought would make them feel happy and safe. Then Aurora opened her eyes.

"Come on, you two. Your new home is ready for you." Aurora walked to the door of the red brick room and opened it. Light shone in from somewhere outside. Maddie looked at her, confused and not sure of what to do. Aurora saw her confusion and smiled.

"Trust me. It's time to go." Aurora took Lil' Yoya's hand, and Maddie held M.J.'s hand. They followed Aurora out into the daylight. Maddie and the little ones shielded their eyes with their forearms. They had not been in the sunlight for many years. They followed Aurora through a grassy meadow until they came to a massive oak tree that had a thick rope ladder on the side of the trunk.

"Follow me." Aurora carried Lil' Yoya piggyback up the ladder, and Maddie did the same for M.J. When they reached the higher branches, Aurora stopped to unload Lil' Yoya on a wooden porch. She stepped up to the porch, then helped Maddie and M.J. onto it.

"Now, please follow me." Aurora turned to the door of a house, right here in the thick branches of the tree. She opened the door and went inside. The others stood outside, not sure what to do. Aurora turned the lights on and invited them in again. M.J. and Lil' Yoya shrieked with joy when they saw their new home. There were soft chairs for them to sit on, along with brightly colored pillows scattered on the floor. There was a large, square wooden coffee table in the middle of the room for them to draw and color on. There were boxes of toys, games, and dolls for them to play with. There were also candles tucked in safe places, because Aurora remembered they loved candles, and they made them feel safe.

"Would you like to see your bedroom?" Aurora asked. The girls squealed.

"Yes!" They ran behind Aurora to the next room, which had two twin beds, with clean white sheets and soft, fluffy blankets. The room had a large window on one side, so they could see the stars and the moon at night. The room would always be filled with sunlight during the day. Aurora never wanted them to be in the dark again. Maddie went over to stand beside Aurora, and they watched the girls as they giggled and jumped on the beds. Then they stopped suddenly and went to Aurora.

"We really get to stay here all the time?" M.J. asked.

"And we don't ever have to go back there?" Lil' Yoya asked timidly.

"That's right. You get to live here forever! You are never going back," Maddie said.

"Where are you going to live, Maddie?" M.J. asked.

"I'm going to live right here with you." Maddie looked at Aurora and winked.

"Okay. Yaaay!" The girls yelled and then ran out to the playroom.

"I don't understand, Maddie. You're going to stay here?"

"Of course. Where else would I live? They are a part of me. But I'm free, right? I can come and go whenever I want. Isn't that right?"

"Yes. Absolutely. I didn't think of it that way, but you are right. But where will you sleep?"

"Don't worry, I'll make myself a nice space the same way you made this one. I want my own studio to paint in. Aurora, do you think I could have my own art show someday?"

"Absolutely, Maddie. When this is all over and everyone, including me, is settled, we can start painting together. Okay."

"My paintings might be dark."

"Dark is okay. If there is anything that I have learned from all of this, it is that it's important to understand our darkness. Your darkness has been a gift to me, Maddie, and I want to honor that." There was a sudden shift in the air, and Aurora turned to see La Divina standing there with Innocent One in her arms.

"Hello, La Divina. Welcome. Do you like the new home we created?"

"It's perfect, Aurora. You did very well. There is one last healing to be done."

"More?" Aurora felt like she could not bear another ritual or initiation.

"The most important of all. Now call the others over." Aurora called them, and they came running over and hugged La Divina.

"I want you to stand in a circle around me and hold hands." They did as she asked.

"This child is the pure soul light that belongs to all of you. It is time to receive her back. Now close your eyes and breathe into your heart." Again, they did exactly as she asked. Then La Divina lifted the child up over her head.

"*Return. Return. Return. Receive your light. Receive your wholeness. Receive your soul.*" La Divina sang in a clear, ringing tone, like a glass bell that resonated into their bodies. Then a brilliant light exploded, and the child vanished. Aurora, Maddie, and the little ones felt the light burst into them. It was warm, sweet, and full of love. They felt like they were finally home.

⌣

Aurora woke up on the floor of her studio. Bruja was asleep beside her. She didn't know how long she had been gone. She noticed the candles had burned halfway. She figured she had been asleep for at least a couple of days. She realized she was hungry. She pulled herself from the floor and went to the kitchen to brew some coffee, with Bruja padding and meowing behind her. Aurora put a can of food on a plate for her cat, then made a pot of coffee. She scrambled three eggs and popped two slices of bread in the toaster. She felt like she needed to keep moving, because she wasn't ready to think about the incredible healing she had just experienced. She buttered the toast, then poured coffee into a mug, slid the eggs onto a plate, and sat down at the table. She lifted a forkful of eggs into her mouth, but she could not taste them. She felt numb, half asleep, as if she was in a new body and didn't know how to maneuver it. She chewed the eggs slowly, then took a sip of coffee, and the hot liquid brought her back into her body. Then it all came rushing back to her. She felt like Dorothy when she woke from her dream at the end of "The Wizard of Oz." Then she realized what she needed to do. She got up from the table and called Luz and Rosario. The phone rang several times before she heard a voice on the other end.

"Hola." It was Luz.

"Hola, Luz. It's Aurora. Can I come over, please? I have so much to tell you. It's important."

"Sí, mija. Claro que sí. I'll make a pot of cacao. Come right over. I'll see you soon." Luz hung up the phone. Aurora realized she had been asleep for at least two days. She went to shower and quickly dressed. She wove her wet hair into a single braid, slipped on her huaraches, and left out the door. When she got to Luz and Rosario's flat, she saw Rosario leaving the restaurant, holding a clay pot. Rosario saw her and smiled.

"Buen Día, Aurora. Luz said you were coming and asked me to make some cacao. She wanted to make it, but she doesn't have the patience to let the cacao melt slowly, so it's silky and sweet. Go ahead. The doors open." Aurora tried to open the door, but it was locked.

"No, not that door. The other door. It leads to the yard. We thought it would be nice to sit in the garden. It's a beautiful day, no?" Aurora hadn't even noticed that it was a warm day, and the sun was shining brightly.

"Yes. It is a beautiful day." Aurora opened the side door for Rosario and followed behind her. When they reached the garden, Luz was sitting at the table waiting for them. She stood up to greet Aurora.

"Ah, mija. It's so good to see you. You look well. I haven't seen you for a few days." Aurora kissed her on the cheek, then greeted Rosario properly with a kiss on the cheek, as well. Rosario sat down and poured them each a cup of cacao. There was also a plate of warm pan dulce on the table.

"Now tell us what you have been up to." Aurora took a sip from her cup and began to tell them everything that had happened. Luz and Rosario listened carefully to everything Aurora shared, stopping to ask her to clarify details. Two hours later, Aurora finished telling her story. Afterwards, they sat in silence for a long time. No one said anything. Then Luz finally spoke.

"I'm so proud of you, Aurora. This is truly a milagro. Do you understand how rare it is for someone who has suffered the way you have to achieve this kind of healing? And you journeyed there on your own."

"I didn't do it on my own. You helped me so much. You and Rosario and La Divina. Oh, and Sofie, too. I couldn't have done it without all of you."

"You know, Aurora, I myself have not done this level of self-healing yet."

"You? I don't understand."

"It's been almost three years now. I was held captive and brutalized and held for several days by the military in Guatemala. I should have died. I wanted to die, but Rosario refused to let me die. She saved me, and Father Tom helped us escape, and that's when we arrived here. You have inspired me to delve deeper into my own healing."

"Oh, Luz. I had no idea. I'm so sorry that you went through something so terrible. Thank you, Rosario, for saving her. It's so interesting how our lives are interconnected. If Rosario hadn't saved you, then maybe I wouldn't be alive today."

"That is the beauty of life. Everything is connected," Rosario laughed.

"There seems to be one more area that needs healing, mija."

"What do you mean?" Aurora felt a slight panic.

"I mean your artist friend, Nico. Maybe it's time to stop running and learn to trust that someone can love you in a good way."

"Yes. I think you're right. I promised Maddie that I would try to make things right with Nico. I do miss him. I'm going to think about it for a few days, and then I'll call him."

"That sounds like a good plan," Luz said.

"Aurora, have a piece of pan dulce. I baked it this morning." Aurora picked up a concha and took a big bite. The women sat together laughing and telling Aurora about what was happening in the Mission.

Nico went into the kitchen and poured himself a glass of red wine. He grabbed a black sweatshirt with a bright orange Marigold Aurora painted on it. He hung on the back of the kitchen chair. It had been a gift from Aurora, and tonight it was the only part of her that he could have close to him. He cracked a window and inhaled the crisp air. He loved the cool, long nights of Autumn, because he preferred to paint at night, when the air was quiet, and he could better feel into the silence to discover what wanted to come through. He took a sip of his wine and walked over to the latest painting on his easel.

The painting depicted a beautiful woman with long black hair, floating on waves of the ocean. She had a flowing light blue gown with a circle of stars around her hair. The painting was Nico's interpretation of the traditional painting known as the "Star of the Sea," a goddess revered and loved by cultures around the world. The difference in this painting was that the goddess in the painting was Aurora, and she had tears falling from her eyes into the ocean. He had not planned to paint her, but she appeared on the canvas, so he went with it. This was the first painting in a series he called the "Night Muse."

He thought about the last time he held Aurora in his arms. The night started out in the kitchen; homemade spaghetti sauce simmering on the stove, and Puccini's La Boheme filling the room with the story of a love destined to fail. No matter how much he tried, he could not stop thinking about her. He closed his eyes and could smell the fragrance of her hair and taste the skin of her neck. He ached to hold her, but he was angry, too. She had pushed him away and pulled him in more times than he cared to remember, and the last time had gone too far.

He remembered when he last saw her at her art show, standing alone in the shadow of the altar. The warm glow of the candlelight cast an otherworldly glow on her face, along with the piles of marigold petals scattered around her. She looked like a goddess. He ached to take her in his arms, kiss her, and tell her how much he missed her, but he pushed those feelings down inside. Then when Michael approached her, he was jolted back to the reality of their relationship. She was no longer his love. They wanted different things; he wanted a commitment, and she wanted the freedom to come and go, without the need to define what they were to each other, which meant he was left settling for less than he truly wanted. He was older than Aurora, and he wanted to marry and start a family. With all the time that had passed, he still could not get her out of his heart, nor deny how deeply he cared for her. They had been seeing each other for a little over two years, and after all that time, he felt as if he would never truly know her. He could never get past the walls around her heart.

The painting he purchased from her show hung on the wall in the living room. He studied it now; he knew those red brick walls. He knew what it felt like to come up against them and not get past them. He also knew the frightened little girl in the painting. He had seen her emerge from within Aurora on more than one occasion. It was as if the little girl was a part of Aurora that was asking for help, but as soon as he reached for her, she pulled away, and the little girl disappeared.

Nico accepted that Aurora was a creative and complex woman, and he loved that about her. He remembered how, while they were making love, Aurora suddenly started screaming for him to get off her. He loved her, but he didn't trust her, and without trust, they had nothing. He was exhausted just thinking about it. He was in love with her and hated that he missed her so much. He wanted to be able to move on, but she had gotten under his skin like no other woman ever had.

He had to let her go.

Just then, the doorbell rang and startled Nico out of his introspection. He looked at the clock and saw that it was 10 p.m. He stuck his head out of the front window to see who was at the door, and saw Aurora standing there, holding a bunch of white roses in her hand. He felt a sudden mix of anxiety and excitement that she was at the door. He hit the buzzer to unlock the door and quickly tossed a sheet over his painting. When Aurora got to the top of the stairs, Nico was waiting with the door half ajar. When he saw her, his breath caught in his chest, and he felt his face flush. He wanted to pull her into his arms, but he caught himself, took a step back, and invited Aurora inside. She was wearing Nico's paint-splattered, white button-down shirt over a red tank top. She took off the shirt and handed it to Nico.

"I thought you might want this back."

"Aurora, I know you didn't come over at this hour just to give me back my shirt. What do you want?"

"I'm sorry to just come over without calling Nico, but I needed to talk to you, and I was afraid that if I called, you wouldn't want to see me." She gave him the roses and waited for him to ask her to sit down, but he didn't.

"These are for you. I picked them from a friend's garden. I know how much you like to have fresh flowers in your kitchen." Nico took the flowers and tossed them onto the coffee table. He took three steps back and folded his arms. He tried to breathe through the anger he felt rising from his gut.

"You are the one who didn't want me; you screamed for me to get off you. You broke my heart."

"That's why I'm here, Nico. I want to explain. Can we please sit down? I have something important I want to tell you." He motioned for her to sit on the couch, the same couch where they had made love so many times. It was the only piece of furniture in the living room, besides a coffee table, his easel, and a tall table where he kept his paint and brushes. They sat down at opposite ends of the couch. He took a sip of wine.

"Do you want a glass?"

"No thanks." Aurora glanced at the covered canvas on the easel.

"I'm glad to see you're working," she said, as she struggled to find the words to tell him about all that had happened to her.

"Painting is my life, Aurora. It helps fill up some of the space where you used to live." He touched his hand to his heart, his hazel eyes glaring at her. "I'm working on a new series I'm calling the 'Night Muse.'" Aurora wanted to see the painting, but she knew she didn't have the right to ask.

"Congratulations again on the success of your show. You sold every painting, didn't you? That's every artist's dream." Nico raised his glass.

"Yeah, that's what Sofie said. I'm happy about it. I feel very lucky."

"Luck has nothing to do with it, Aurora. You are an amazing artist. It's one of the things I lo…appreciate about you. So, Michael, huh? Is that new?" The words flew from his mouth before he could stop them, and he felt like a fool for saying them.

"What? Michael? Oh no, no. He's a patron, that's all. He has a gallery in North Beach."

"Sofie mentioned that he bought all the paintings in your ghost series. He recognizes quality art. Good for him." They sat in awkward silence until Nico spoke.

"Aurora, why are you here? I haven't heard from you in months, and now suddenly you show up here out of nowhere, with flowers, no less." He ran his hand through his long black hair and gulped his wine.

"What do you want from me, Aurora? I'm weary of this game of 'you love me, you love me, not.'"

"Nico, I came to tell you that you were right. I needed help. I thought I could avoid what was happening to me by ignoring it, but I was wrong. It all blew up after the night of my show. I see now that you were trying to help me, and I pushed you away. Then I totally freaked out the last night we were together. Nico, I want you to know how sorry I am for how I behaved that night."

"Okay, but it doesn't change the fact that you and I want different things, Aurora. I want a commitment, and you don't. Hell, you can't even commit to being present when you're with me. One minute you're here and then you're gone, lost in some nightmare from your past." Nico's words cut Aurora's heart with truth.

"You're right, Nico, I don't blame you for being angry with me. I want you to know that I have been getting the help I need. That's where I've been these past months. I'm working with a woman named Luz."

"Oh yeah, I know Luz. She and Rosario have a restaurant on 24th Street. She is a very wise woman."

"You know Luz? Wow, it seems that I was the only one in the entire Mission who didn't know her. Anyway, she is helping me to get to the source of my pain. I understand now why I pushed you away, and I don't want to do that anymore." Nico felt a sudden spark of hope, and for a moment, he dropped his guard. He wondered if they might have a chance after all.

"I'm glad to hear that Luz is helping you. I've only ever wanted for you to be happy, Aurora. Maybe now you will be able to let someone beyond your walls to love you." His words stung her. She had assumed that Nico still loved her. She was wrong. She felt confused, scared, and wasn't sure what to say next. She started to tremble, and tears welled in her eyes. Then all she wanted to say to him spilled out.

"I hoped that someone would still be you, Nico."

Nico moved closer to her and touched his hand to her cheek. "I will always love you, Aurora, but I can't fully love you, because you won't let me. I can't reach behind your brick walls." Then he felt himself pulled in again. He wanted to bring her close, kiss her face, and touch her hair, but he caught himself. It was so easy for her to pull him back. He stood up to break the spell and walked over to the kitchen counter.

"Why are you saying this now, Aurora?" He dropped his head in his hands. "Did you come over just to torment me?"

This was not how she had wanted this conversation to go. She walked over to Nico and lifted his chin, then brushed away the hair that had fallen over his eyes, and their eyes met. She felt the familiar clawing pain in her stomach. She heard Maddie's voice in her head.

"You're going to fuck it up again. Don't take Nico away from me again." Aurora took a deep breath and spoke in her mind to Maddie, Lil' Yoya, and M.J. *It's alright. Whatever happens, we will all be alright. I promise.* She brought herself back to the present moment with Nico. She allowed her heart to expand the way Luz had taught her.

She let him see her; she let him in.

"I love you, Nico. I know that now. I was afraid to love you before. I was afraid that if I let you see who I truly am, you wouldn't want me. I felt ugly and ashamed. I wanted to hide from you, so I wouldn't lose you. But, in the end, I pushed you away." Aurora waited for Nico to say something. Instead, he just stood there, as if waiting for her to convince him that she had changed.

"Something amazing happened to me, Nico. I've changed. It's like I wasn't fully alive before, and now I feel like I'm here, inside my body." She took his hand and placed it on her heart.

"I can't fully explain it, yet. I'm still trying to understand it all myself. I have more healing to do, but I want to share it all with you. If you still want me?"

Nico felt her open to him. He sensed a part of her that he had never felt before. He felt something in her shift.

Her walls had crumbled.

"I've never stopped loving you, Cara mia. I just don't know if I can trust you. I don't want to let you back in, for you to crush my heart again. I don't think I could survive that. Do you understand how much you hurt me?" Aurora kissed Nico softly on the lips, but he did not respond.

"I know I hurt you, Nico. I am so sorry for how I treated you. You deserve better."

"You're right. I do deserve better. I want to be loved, needed, and wanted, Aurora. Am I a fool for wanting that?"

"No. You absolutely deserve that. I want that too, and I want it with you. I want there to be an us. I promise you I won't run anymore when things get scary. I'll tell you everything that's happening for me." Nico had waited to hear these words from Aurora for two years, and now he wasn't sure how to respond.

"Will you give me another chance, Nico? Can we start over? Maybe take things a little slower?" He listened to what Aurora was saying, and despite how she had hurt him, he was a romantic in the true Italian sense. He believed love was the most important thing in life, and that without it, life was not worth living. He pulled her to him and kissed her softly. Maddie was watching and listening. She wasn't sure if she could trust either of them, or if Aurora would really keep her promise to make things work with Nico. But as she listened to them, she could feel the love between the two of them. Tears welled up from her chest. It was a river of clean water that washed away a little of the fear she had about not being lovable. Aurora was making good on her promise. Maddie began to merge with Aurora. She had a hundred different thoughts about what her life outside of the red brick room could be like. She could finally have an art show of her own. She realized this feeling was hope. She made herself small, curling up on her bed in the tree house, and fell asleep.

In the same moment, Aurora felt a wave of energy pass through. Nico felt it, too.

"What was that? Are you okay? Do you want me to stop?"

"No, please don't stop. I'm fine, really." She kissed Nico and allowed herself to surrender to his love. She felt herself connect with him in a way she had not been able to before. Then he cupped her chin, so their eyes met, and for the first time, she did not feel shame when he looked at her. She held his gaze.

"A fresh start sounds good to me, mi amore. But I want to hear you say it again." He showered her face with kisses, inhaling the scent of her hair.

"I love you. I love you, Nico Sebastiani." Nico took her hand and walked her back to the couch, where they both sat down. He put his arm around her shoulder and held her close.

"Now tell me everything. I want to know all about what you have been through, and do not leave anything out. I promise I will really listen and try my best to understand."

Aurora took a deep breath, then began her story about all she had been through since meeting Luz, Rosario, and most importantly, La Divina. She also told him how Sofie had been there, through it all with her. Nico listened carefully as he promised. His heart broke when she told him about what had happened to Maddie and the little ones who were trapped in the red brick room. He stood up and paced the room. His heart filled with rage. He wanted to kill the people who did this to them.

"I'm sorry. I just need a minute. I'm enraged at what they did to you." Aurora let him express his feelings. Then he returned and knelt before her, taking her hands in his. There were tears in his eyes. "You, Aurora. They did this to you. God, I just don't understand how anyone could hurt an innocent child like that. I'm so sorry this happened to you." He kissed her hands and sat back down beside her.

"I'm sorry, Nico. I didn't mean to upset you." Nico put his hand up to stop her from apologizing.

"You have absolutely nothing to be sorry about. It's natural for me to be angry about this. Any normal human being would feel outraged at hearing this happened to someone they love, so please don't be sorry. I'm okay, so please go on. I really do want to know."

"I think that's enough for now, Nico. There is so much more I can tell you. We have time, right?"

"Absolutely. We have time. Now come lie down with me. I want to hold you." Aurora lay down on the couch facing Nico, arms and legs entangled, her head resting on his chest. She lay beside Nico, feeling his breath rise and fall. Everyone was quiet inside. She closed her eyes and fell into a dreamless sleep. Then at 4:44 a.m. Aurora bolted up from the couch. The temperature in the room had dropped ten degrees, even though the radiator was on. Still half asleep, she looked around the room, and something caught her eye. Then Nico woke up.

"Aurora, what happened. Are you okay?"

"I'm fine. Do you see anything over by the door?" There was a pale blue cloud of light flickering by the door. She closed her eyes, took a deep breath, then followed her breath down into the eyes of her heart. When she opened her eyes, she could see the spirit of a boy about 7 years old standing in the blue light. He was shivering and had tears in his eyes. He was looking straight at her.

"I see a flickering blue light over there by the door." Nico looked over to the door, squinting his eyes.

"You can see it? Can you see anything else?"

"No, just a faint blue light. Why? Is there something else? What do you see? Tell me."

"I'm not sure, Nico. This is the first time for me. There is a spirit there. Let me talk to him, but I need you to be quiet."

"Okay." Nico nodded, sat quietly, and waited. Aurora walked closer to where the little boy stood.

"Hello. What's your name? Why are you here?" He was wearing a bright yellow T-shirt, with blue and white striped overalls, and blue socks without shoes.

"I'm Carlitos. I'm looking for my mama. I woke up and I was outside in the street. My house burned down. I called for her, but I couldn't find her. Then, I saw La Senora, and she told me you could help me, and the next thing I was just here. Can you help me?" Aurora was confused. She did not understand why this was happening. She thought she was finished with ghosts and spirits.

"What, Senora?"

"La Senora de las Lágrimas, you know, she was crying." Then she understood La Divina had sent the boy to her, but why? How was she supposed to help him?

"How am I supposed to help you, Carlitos?"

"Help me find my mama. Her name is Cloudia." Then, Aurora understood that Carlitos didn't realize that he was dead. His mother had most likely died, as well.

"Carlitos, there is something I need you to understand before I try to help you, and I'm not sure that I can. But I will try. I need to look at something first, okay?"

"Okay." He wiped away the tears on his face and waited for Aurora to do whatever she was going to do to help him find his mama. Aurora softened her gaze and focused on his sacred shawl. Immediately, she could see images of the story that happened to Carlitos and his mama. They were asleep in their third-floor flat. It was an old building. There was an extension cord plugged into the wall that was connected to three other extension cords to the only outlet in the room. The plug overheated, releasing sparks that caught fire to the curtains directly above it. The flames spread quickly to the walls and the ceiling, then to the other rooms where Carlitos and his mother were sleeping. The black smoke filled their lungs and killed them before the fire took them. She saw that they both were jolted out of their bodies before they were burned. She had seen the story on the news. Her heart broke over how they died. Suddenly, she knew what she had to do. She remembered what she had experienced when she found her mother after she had died. Aurora brought her awareness back to Carlitos.

"Carlitos. There was a fire that started while you and your mama were sleeping. The poison from the smoke caused you and your mama to die. Do you understand? This means you died. You're dead." Carlitos started to panic. His hands flew around his neck as he was remembering not being able to breathe.

"It's okay now. You're safe. It's over, and I won't let anything bad happen to you now."

"But I'm dead. I don't want to be dead. What's going to happen to me now? I didn't go to confession or mass on Sunday. Am I going to hell? I want my mama." He sobbed freely, now. As Aurora felt his sorrow, she was filled with a powerful love and compassion for this child. She also felt how precious life is. She had an idea of what to do next. But first, she called for help.

"Mi Divina, please come to me and help Carlitos find his mother." She appeared before Aurora's next breath.

"Hola, Mija. I'm happy that you thought to call me."

"Thank you for coming. What else could I do?"

"You had three choices. You could have simply ignored the child, and he would have continued to bother you or haunt you, as you like to say. You could have sent him away in anger, and he would remain lost until he found someone else who could help him, but you did not choose this. You chose to help him, even though you are not sure of what to do. You followed your heart. It is time for your final initiation."

Aurora had questions arising about the idea of her purpose, but she thought it was best to wait for another time. La Divina moved closer to Carlitos and gently placed her hand on his shoulder.

"Everything is going to be fine, Carlitos. I told you Aurora could help you, and she will. We are going to find your mama and bring her to you." Carlitos sighed and nodded. Then La Divina turned to Aurora.

"What shall we do next, mija?" Aurora gasped aloud, then remembered they were in Nico's flat, and he was watching everything. She looked over to see that he had lain down on the couch and was asleep.

"Forgive me, but I thought once I called you that you would oversee the rest."

"That's not how this works, mija. Now feel into your heart and tell me what the next step is. Remember, do not complicate it." Aurora closed her eyes and breathed into her heart and felt into what Carlitos needed. Then she understood. She opened her eyes and turned her attention to Carlitos.

"Carlitos, I want you to close your eyes and think about your mama. Can you do that for me?" He nodded and did as Aurora instructed.

"Good. Now call her. Show her where you are, so she can find you." Carlitos called his mother aloud.

"Mama! I'm here. Please come, Mama. I need you. I don't want to be dead." Cloudia appeared before he finished his last few words. She wept tears of joy.

"Ay mijo. Mi angelito. I was looking for you everywhere. I was so afraid I wouldn't find you. I'm so happy you called me." Carlitos ran into her embrace and held her tightly.

"Mama, I'm dead. Are you dead too? What's going to happen to us? I don't want to go to hell. I didn't go to confession last week as I told you. I lied. I went to play in the school yard instead."

"I know, Mijo. Don't worry. Everything is going to be alright. Don't be afraid. Death is not the end of life. It's like a door that opens into another place. We're still alive. We just do not have physical bodies anymore. God is not going to punish you for missing confession or for any other reason. Try and understand. Now, let us see how this nice lady can help us." Carlitos quieted and turned his attention back to Aurora and La Divina, who waited to see what Aurora would do next.

"Well, they seem ready. Can you do that thing, where you open the space for them to go through to the other side?"

"Very good. But you need to be sure that they want to go through. Remember your mother and how she resisted until you were able to forgive her? We cannot force them to pass through until we are sure there are no unresolved issues in their lives."

"Carlitos and Cloudia. I want to ask you if you feel ready and willing to go to the other side…um, to heaven." Cloudia nodded and smiled at Aurora for using the word heaven, so Carlitos would not be afraid.

"We're going to go to heaven. Really?"

"Yes, Carlitos. This is La Divina. She is a holy one. She is going to open the door so you can pass through and go to heaven. Are you ready?"

"Heck yes!"

La Divina smiled and lifted her arms above her head. A swirling, golden-white vertical cloud of light appeared in the room. Then, a large, pulsating orb of violet-blue and white light emerged into the room, transforming into a being with immense, white wings. It carried a sword also made of light. La Divina introduced him. Nico woke up suddenly and could see the angel. He had always loved the statues of the angels in the churches, and Archangel Michael was his favorite. He had prayed to him as a child to help his father when he returned from the war, filled with anger and unable to receive the love of his family. He craved only the comfort he found in a bottle of whiskey. Tears streamed down his face as he beheld the angel. Nico could not see anything else that was going on, but he understood that whatever was happening was sacred. La Divina introduced the angel to Carlitos and Cloudia.

"This is Archangel Michael. He will help you to release any last fears, guilt, shame, or sense of unworthiness you may feel, so you are able to pass through the portal into heaven. He will fill you with the light of your new existence." Aurora felt something powerful, sacred, and holy when Archangel Michael appeared in the room. There were no other words to describe it. She bent her head in reverence to the angel. It was an automatic response that felt completely natural. She watched as the angel bathed Carlitos and his mother in a golden-white light and observed the expression on their faces transform into one of peace, filled with the light that emanated around them. They both looked at Aurora and mouthed the words, *Thank you.* Then, Archangel Michael motioned for Carlitos and Cloudia to pass through the portal and followed behind them. In an instant, the portal vanished as if it had never been there. There was a soft blue glow that remained in the room before it dissipated. Aurora's face was pale. She stood there staring at the space where she had just watched two spirits walk through a portal of light. She had seen her mother do this, but she thought that was a one-time occurrence. She did not think it would ever happen again. She felt as if she, too, had been washed in the light of Archangel Michael. Nico had so many questions, but he continued to watch and listen as Aurora spoke aloud to someone he could not see.

"Do you understand now, mija?" La Divina took Aurora's hand.

"Honestly? No. I don't understand. Why did this happen? Why did you want me to help them? Why not have Luz help them?"

"As I said before. This is your initiation. This is who you are. This is the result of all you have gone through, Aurora. You have found your medicine."

"Do you mean that this will happen again?"

"Yes. That is exactly what I mean."

"What if I don't want to do this again?"

"Your mind may not want to do this work, but your soul has already agreed to it. So, you can resist and deal with spirits coming to you, walking through your home, and your workplace, or you can surrender and embrace this as a sacred calling. It is the medicine you have earned. You understand what it is like to be lost and how to find wholeness. It is no different for those who have died. They have a life that they have lived and need healing, so they are able to forgive themselves and pass to the other side."

"I don't understand why I used the word heaven and Archangel Michael. I was not expecting that. Luz never told me about him. I don't know how to feel about it all."

"Luz meant to introduce you to Archangel Michael, as well as the Archangel Sharova, but you were not yet ready to meet them. You will meet Sharova someday soon. You will find that you will use whatever words a person needs to make them feel safe. Sometimes their loved ones will appear along with Archangel Michael to guide them over. You weren't ready to meet Archangel Michael before. He was too close to a belief system you rejected. You see, Archangels, angels, goddesses, and other divine beings don't belong to any religion. Even Jesus existed before Christianity and Judaism existed. We existed before any religions were created. We are here to serve humanity and to help humans evolve to become fully human. Then, they can remember that they are also divine beings."

"I have so much to think about. Thank you for coming to help Carlitos and Cloudia. I could not have done it without you."

"And I could not have done it without you, mija. We all have our parts to play in this beautiful web of human evolution. The spirit world needs humans to help us communicate with other humans."

"I just need time to absorb all of this. How am I going to explain this to Nico?"

"Nico may surprise you. He has been watching, and you promised to tell him the truth. He understands much more than you know. You can trust him. I am happy that you decided to make things right between you. You deserve to experience love, Aurora. Luz and Rosario will always be here to help. Luz still has so much to teach you." La Divina kissed Aurora on her brow, then she was gone.

"Gracias, La Divina," Aurora said. Then she turned to see Nico on the couch staring at her, his face pale and wet with tears.

"Nico, what's wrong?" She went to sit beside him.

"I saw him, Aurora. Archangel Michael—I saw him."

"What? What do you mean? What else did you see?"

"Nothing. I could hear everything you were saying, so I had a sense of what was going on. Then, out of nowhere, there he was. This being with wings of light that filled the room. The funny thing is, when I was a kid, I used to go to church and pray to Archangel Michael to help my dad after he came back from the war and was drinking every night." Aurora put her arm around him and listened.

"I don't know what to say. This is all so amazing. What do you think this means for you? Why were you able to see him, and not anyone else?"

"You're asking me to make sense of all of this? I don't even know all that happened. I could hear you talking to them, but I couldn't see them. I also felt sadness, but I didn't know why."

"We should visit Luz and Rosario later this week. They will be able to help us understand all of this. I mean, this has been so intense. I'm exhausted. Can we get some sleep and talk about this tomorrow?"

"That's a great idea." He lay down on the couch and pulled her gently beside him. Aurora snuggled in close to him, allowing her breathing to relax. Despite all that had happened, she felt peaceful. Nico slept until the sunlight woke him. He left Aurora to sleep and went into the kitchen. Aurora woke to the sound of Nico humming and the smell of freshly brewed coffee. He placed two cups of coffee and two fresh croissants with blackberry jam on a tray. He smiled when he saw she was awake and sitting up.

"Good morning, Cara mía. I thought you might want coffee."

"Oh, it smells wonderful, and croissants. My favorite, yum. I'm so hungry."

"Good. Now you can tell me about everything that happened last night.

"I know that I promised to tell you the truth, but I'm also scared. I don't want you to think I'm losing my grip on reality, and you might want something stronger in your coffee for what I'm about to tell you."

"Don't forget, I saw an angel, and I've never thought that about you. We're artists. We are supposed to have a loose grip on this reality. It's what allows us to dream into our paintings. It's what I love about you as an artist. You're not afraid to follow your vision, even when it's not necessarily where you would consciously choose to go. So, on a certain level, I get it, Aurora. I mean, I don't get everything, obviously. I haven't gone through what you have. But I know that life is full of mystery, and I love the idea of living a life full of mystery with you. It doesn't scare me, so don't worry about that. Just tell me what you can. I'm listening."

Aurora was grateful for this gift of acceptance from Nico. It was not something she was used to feeling from anyone, besides Sofie. She told Nico everything that happened the night before. She decided not to hold anything back. Nico was riveted and listened without interruption. When Aurora was finished, they both sat quietly. Then Nico asked her a question.

"Do you think I will ever be able to see spirits the way you do?" Aurora laughed in surprise.

"I don't know. Do you want to? Let's have our coffee, and I'll call Luz and see when we can visit."

"Great. I mean, I never imagined I would ever see Archangel Michael, and yet I did. I just want to understand more. Besides, c'mon,

I mean it's an amazing thing, right, and suddenly I feel so peaceful, like everything will be okay."

"I do, too. It's something sacred, but when it's happening, I'm terrified."

"I can only imagine." He set down his coffee and touched his hand to her cheek.

"So, this is what our life is going to be like now, huh?"

"Yeah. It looks that way. That is, if you still want it to be," Aurora said.

Nico pulled her close and kissed her.

"I don't want any other life, except with you."

BLESSINGS & GRATITUDE

With my deepest gratitude I would like to acknowledge the beloved writers who have mentored and encouraged me, and who have shared their expertise in writing so generously over the years: Ani Mander, Judy Grahn, Dianne Jenett, Rose Wognum Frances, Joanna Biggar, Kathleen MacGowan, and Luis Alberto Urrea who took time out of his busy book tour to read my manuscript. I would not have been able to complete my book without the ongoing love and support of The Divine Writing community. Thank you, Emily K. Grieves, for encouragement, friendship, and for walking with me on the path of La Guadalupana. To Shiloh Sophia for your friendship and for bringing the gift of The Red Thread Circle to the world. To my dearest Gina Hill for wine and writing dates and heart platicas by the lake. Nancy Hannah, mi buen amiga, Brian Hunter, for allowing me to read chapters to you over the phone in the wee hours of the morning. To Sarah Mackie and Caryl Englehorn, who held candles while I searched the darkness for the courage to tell this story.

I would like to mention that I would not be alive today if not for the loving circle of friends who cared for me while recovering from a nearly fatal accident when I was hit by an SUV while crossing the street in 2023. I was unable to care for myself for months, and unable to read or write very well for over a year. Without the love, emotional, personal, and financial support of my dear friends and community, I would not have survived: Gina Hill, Joanna Biggar, Betsy Schultz, Nancy Hannah, Marisol Nuno, Erika Tinoco, and Brian Hunter. You are dear to my heart, and I love you all. To Alma Perez for being my "Rosario"— our story is not over. I offer special thanks to my attorney, John Fetto, who was relentless on my behalf.

I would like to take a moment to honor and thank my ancestors for the wisdom passed down through generations: my mother, E. Parra Niz, for making me sit at the kitchen table and write stories whenever I complained of boredom, and for the deep initiation we traveled through together in this lifetime. To my grandmother, Eloysa Camacho Munoz, my Tía Aurora Vargas, Francesca Marin, and my father, Jose Vargas, whose stories, wisdom, and knowledge of the indigenous history of Mexico passed through three generations into my heart and hands.

I would not have been able to birth *Keeper of the Sacred Shawl* without the continual editorial support and friendship of my publisher, editor, and book midwife, Jane Astara Ashley at Flower of Life Press. Thank you for always supporting my vision, for your infinite patience, and for your unwavering faith in my story.

Finally, my eternal love and gratitude to my Spirit Team The Celestial Divas of the Rose Light, AKA Sharova, Archangel Michael, Mother Mary, Mi Madrecita Tonantzin Guadalupe, and most of all to La Divina, AKA La Llorona, Goddess of soul healing, who entrusted me with her story, and who has walked with me during my darkest hours to lovingly recover my lost parts. I pray this story will help others to know you and love you as I do.

ABOUT THE AUTHOR

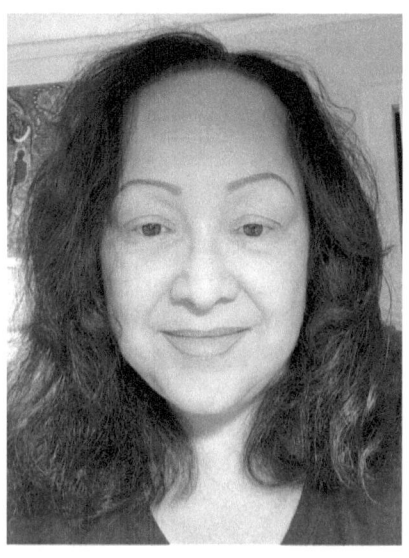

Mari Dreamwalker is a third-generation Mexican-American energy medicine carrier. She holds a BA in Chicana Studies, an MA in Women's Spirituality, and an MFA in Creative Nonfiction Writing from New College of California, where she taught spiritual autobiography and healing. She grew up in the Mission District of San Francisco, immersed in indigenous culture, ritual, and art. She is a Reiki Maestra, artist, writer, singer-songwriter, and an international channel for the divine feminine and the angelic realm. Mari was first visited by the Goddesses Tonanzin-Guadalupe, La Llorona, Mother Mary, and the Archangel Michael and the Crystalline Devas of the Rose Light during times she experienced severe childhood sexual trauma. She has also been a facilitator for restorative justice and an anti-sex trafficking advocate and ally with Oakland Emiliano Zapata Street Academy, Regina's Door, and MISSSEY in Oakland, California.

Mari has been a member of the Healing Clinic Collective in Oakland, CA, for over fifteen years, which brings alternative healing services to low-income communities at no cost. Mari is an initiator and spiritual catalyst who guides women through the darkness of their wounding to bring awareness of the strengths and gifts from within their soul. The Teachings of the Sacred Shawl were given to Mari by the goddesses La Llorona and Tonantzin-Guadalupe. She integrates these indigenous teachings with sacred ceremony, writing, and creativity to help women heal the heart of their trauma and understand their innate empathic and healing gifts.

You can read more of Mari's writing and learn more about her classes and workshops at **www.maridreamwalker.com** to sign up for her blog and receive a special gift. You can find her music at **www. reverbnation.com/maridreamwalker.**

VISIT US AT

www.floweroflifepress.com